The Pickled Dog Caper

Roger Paulding

Panther  **Creek Press**
Spring, Texas

Published by Panther Creek Press
SAN 253-8520
116 Tree Crest
P.O. Box 130233
Panther Creek Station
Spring, Texas 77393-0233

Cover by Adam Murphy
The Woodlands, Texas
Printed and bound by Houston Datum, Inc.
Houston, Texas

1 2 3 4 5 6 7 8 9 10

Library of Congress Cataloguing in Publication Data

Paulding, Roger

   Pickled dog caper, the

   I. Author   11. Title   III. Fiction, historical

ISBN 0-9747839-990000

For the Reader's Information:

While a number of historical characters appear in The Pickled Dog narrative, the author has taken liberties with the timeline to bring them all together in the story. Nevertheless, he worked diligently to remain true to their characters and the spirit of the times. They are:

Olaudah Equiano, whose story of his life as an educated slave was first printed in 1791. This autobiography is still available from a number of sources.

Phillis Wheatley, the slave girl poet who belonged to the Wheatley family of Boston. Phillis was purchased in a slave market when she was around seven years old. The Wheatley family educated her and treated her as a daughter. She read her poetry to General George Washington at Mount Vernon before he became president.

Rev. Allen Bennett, an Anglican priest who was appointed to positions of high stature by Lord Baltimore and has a notorious reputation as a drinker and a womanizer.

Solomon Seney, Sr., 1710-1761, a resident of Church Hill, Queen Anne County, Maryland, and a citizen with a large plantation and a number of slaves. His son John was a member of the Constitutional Convention in 1977. Neville was his youngest son and bears the maiden name of his wife.

All the quotations used to head the chapters are from writers whom the characters could have been familiar with. Special effort has been taken to craft the dialogue only with words in use at that time.

J

The charge was prepared; the lawyers were met
The judges all 'ranged a terrible show.
John Gay
The Beggar's Opera

Queen Anne County, Maryland, 1767

Clad in a plain blue linen shirt and breeches, on his back a red pea jacket stolen from a French sailor, Richard Makepeace sat on a three-legged stool before the bar of justice. Heavy chains circled his chest and looped his wrists and ankles. An iron collar embraced his neck.

"Oyez! Oyez!" the court crier shouted. "The court will please come to order. The Honorable Silas Payne, presiding judge."

When Makepeace turned to look at the judge, the metal choker's rough edge nicked his neck. Blood droplets sprinkled his shirt. An omen, he thought—and not a gracious one.

The judge's countenance was long, withering, and sour as a baboon's. Forlorn hope there, Makepeace figured.

Unmarked by the pox, Makepeace's face seldom failed to inspire confidence in his behavior. Scarcely twenty, he knew he was far too handsome for his own good. Times often were, he thought he could have done better with himself.

"Is the accused this good-looking rascal with the wavy black hair?" Judge Payne inquired.

"That's the ornery thief," the bailiff mumbled. He gave Makepeace's harness a wrench to make sure it was tight enough.

"We'd better move along with it," the judge said. "Swear in the

4

jury, bailiff. Give it your best effort. We have a number of distinguished citizens serving on our panel today."

The judge hammered his gavel on the mahogany bench. Makepeace pondered he could pound a spike nail into the top of the bar with fewer pains.

A kindly appearing aristocrat wearing a brown frockcoat trimmed in gray squirrel was selected to be the jury foreman. Makepeace reckoned the man owned a large plantation, tobacco in all probability. A rich planter would not extend a seed of mercy for him.

The judge spoke to the planter. "Morning, Solomon Seney. I hope you haven't made plans for dinner, because I thought I would take you to the Red Horse Inn for a plate of fish and a glass of wine."

Solomon Seney nodded pleasantly at the judge. The cruel fix was in. Makepeace had no doubt about it, a subtle if paltry bribe. Bring in the guilty plea, Mr. Foreman, and I'll take you to dinner.

"Stand up, prisoner, so you can give your name," the bailiff ordered in an inordinately loud voice.

Makepeace struggled to rise. When he put his hands on the stool to lift himself, it toppled beneath him. He joined it on the floor, his chains clanking like tin church bells. More than a few spectators snickered.

The bailiff strode over to Makepeace, grabbed his harness and yanked him to his feet, giving the chains another miserable rattle.

Judge Payne frowned. "You're a clumsy fool, young man."

"I'm sorry, yer honor," Makepeace said.

The bailiff shoved the chained prisoner back onto his stool and thrust a Bible in his face. "Put your hand on the Good Book and make your plea."

Makepeace placed his hand on the black tome and tried to look righteous, which he did not consider too difficult. By and large, virtue and good-looks were considered betrothed if not wedded. He poured out his oath at the top of his voice, even as he tried to convince himself it was true. "I swear by God that I am innocent of this crime."

Judge Payne rolled his large simian eyes at the ceiling, then turned to the prosecutor. "It's been ten days since this felony took

5

place, Mr. Hammer. Such leniency is an encouragement to the criminal class."

Nor was Makepeace eager to postpone the proceedings, although he felt no encouragement by the delay. He hadn't slept well last night, nor the night before. His basement cell was cold and damp, the air musty and the dirt floor rank with crawling insects of debatable ancestry.

Little chance existed that he would doze off during the trial, the stiff metal collar chafing his neck as it did. At least he weren't hungry. The sheriff's wife was a tolerable good cook. If ye hadn't eaten for a day or two, her giblet pie would be worth getting arrested for.

From the prosecution's table, Elvin Hammer rose, scrawny and tall, his head like death's skull on a mop stick. "I apologize for the delay, Your Honor. The humidity affects my asthma worse than anything God laid on Job."

The judge offered not an ounce of compassion. "Well, be that as it may, Mr. Hammer. God has good reasons for what befalls His creatures."

And He's working overtime on my behalf, Makepeace reflected.

"Jarvis Adams will come forward," the bailiff announced.

The dapper merchant moved toward the witness box. A large man in a scarlet waistcoat embroidered with white stars, Adams looked like a fat red skyrocket set to explode. Makepeace thought he would enjoy lighting the fuse.

Jarvis spoke as soon as he rose from the spectators' section and started for the bench. "Your Honor, this man don't look like no criminal, but he's full of the Old Ned."

Adams wiped his sleeve across his lips. He had a mouth resembling a sparrow. When he spoke, his head opened from ear to ear, like a chick eager for a worm.

"Jarvis, please take the oath before you tell your story," the judge ordered.

"This ain't no story, your honor," Adams whined. "I didn't come here to tell no lies. Bring me the Bible, bailiff."

Adams placed his fat hand on the book and swore to tell the whole truth and the truth only, so help him Almighty God.

Well, they got God in their corner now, Makepeace thought.

"Jarvis, tell the court what the accused did," the prosecutor

6

said.

"That's what I'm trying to do, if you don't mind. Just give me a chance."

"Start at the beginning," Hammer urged.

Adams frowned with obvious vexation. "Your Highness, I'll do just that, only don't interrupt me no more. I ain't used to making public speeches and you ain't no help. Mr. Makepeace took a ladder from me own barn and hoisted it up the side of me house. Him and Mr. Filmore climbed up it to get into me bedroom window. Me and the missus was sleeping peacefully in the arms of God until... there they was! Standing in me bedroom like two bloody actors on the bloody stage. Mr. Makepeace was clutching a lantern and waving his pistol at me."

With his right hand, Adams pointed his index finger at his temple and cocked his thumb. "He threatened to blow me brains away if I don't give him all me money!"

Enrapt, the jury waited for the click of the hammer on Adams' imaginary pistol. The courtroom was as quiet as a church full of Quakers waiting for a moving of the Spirit. Makepeace squirmed on his stool, thinking there wasn't a person in the room who didn't believe it could happen to him as easily as it happened to Adams.

Adams clacked his tongue. A communal gasp rose from the spectators.

"I started praying to God Almighty—oh, how I prayed!" Adams wailed. "I begged dear God for a miracle."

"Oblige the court by telling us what happened next," Mr. Hammer said.

Adams pressed his legs together and bent his knees. "I'm ashamed to tell it, but I wet all over me nightshirt."

Makepeace's lawyer did not join the ensuing laughter. Sitting at the counsel table in his yellow satin suit, his waistcoat aloose to make room for his belly to take breaths without hindrance, he neither smiled nor frowned, although Makepeace heard a small hiccup. But what could he expect from that pettifogger? No help would come from the chap, leastwise not 'til the devil went blind. And Old Nick's eyes probably wasn't even sore.

The judge rapped his gavel handily.

"And pray tell, Mr. Adams, what quandary did your wife find

herself in?" purred the old prosecutor.

"Filmore stuck his hand in the top of Hortense's nightgown and rubbed up against her. Me missus twisted and revolted against him so much, he shoved her to the floor."

"And what else?"

"Tied up me and her with hemp. I still got rope burns on me wrists."

"How much money did the thieves steal?"

"Oh your Lordship, I hadn't counted it for two or three days." Adams scratched at his neck. "More than I could afford to lose, what with the hungry mouths I got to feed—several hundred pounds those rapscallions took."

Makepeace groaned under his breath. Adams was full of lies, no matter what he pledged on the Bible. The man had no more than thirty shillings in his house, coins that purchased him and Filmore a night at an inn and fed them for a couple of days. Then they were bankrupt again.

"Was there anyone else in your house when this cowardly deed occurred?" the prosecutor asked.

"Me five children, Your Honor," Adams said. "The little creatures slept right through it—thank the Lord! No telling what those crooks would have done to those poor innocent babes."

"No one came to your assistance?"

"Me manservant William. He lives in the little house next door."

Little house all right. Makepeace had assumed it was the pump station for the well, that's how small it was.

"And what caused him to get up?" asked the prosecutor.

"Just give me a minute." Adams hitched up his breeches. "William got up to look for his chamber pot. He's a old man what has to get up several times in the night. That's why he heard the noise. He seen these robbers going down me ladder as they was leaving."

"What did William do?"

"He stuck his head out the window and threatened them with the sheriff."

"Did that frighten them?"

Adams snorted. "Mr. Makepeace come back up the ladder and ordered me to shut William up or he'd knock me across the side of me head with his pistol."

Makepeace shook his head sadly—but slowly, so that the collar would not nick him again. He'd done no such thing as Adams claimed. He had behaved like a gentleman robber. He had never behaved in any other manner. Several times in the past, he had apologized for taking valuables from his victims. He didn't suppose, however, that made him any less guilty. He just hoped that if his mother observed his behavior from some cloud in God's heaven, she wouldn't be too ashamed of him.

"Then what happened, Mr. Adams?" Hammer's words were trailed by his labored asthmatic breathing.

Adams continued his story. "Your Honor, William didn't pay those thieves no mind. Straight away went for his trusty musket. Fired out his window at them and loaded up and done it again."

"And pray tell, what—?"

"They fired right back."

Makepeace groaned again. Adams was kicking up his heels and the lies kept spitting out of his mouth. He hadn't a sniff of powder in his pistol. Too poor to afford any. If they'd had any money, they'd have bought victuals at Adams' emporium and not bothered to rob him in the wee hours of the morning, their stomachs grumbling all the time.

"And after that?" the prosecutor coached.

"The robbers run off and William come and unfastened me and Hortense. Then he went and summoned the sheriff."

"And you offered a reward if the robbers were captured?" Mr. Hammer asked.

Adams puffed up like ripe bread dough. "I did that, Your Worship. Five precious pounds. Five pounds they didn't know I had when they robbed me because I hid it real good."

"Was the reward claimed?"

"Mr. Andrew Filmore come forward and claimed it. He said he knew about it because he was a—uh—friend of the accused. That was before he admitted to being his accomplice." Adams' sparrow mouth opened from ear to ear with what Makepeace assumed was a grin. "I didn't have to pay nothing once Filmore confessed to being guilty."

The prosecutor wheezed twice, cleared his throat and sauntered to the jury box. Placing his hands on the railing, he leaned forward. "Members of the jury, I would like to make you aware that Mr. Filmore was brought to trial last Thursday. He was found guilty and sentenced to be hanged. Pending the outcome of these proceedings, he awaits his execution. If it please the Court, I will request his testimony."

It was the first time Makepeace had heard that the lickspittle Filmore had turned state's evidence. He intended to let the son of bitch know he didn't care for his disloyalty.

II

Built God a church and
laughed his word to scorn.
William Cowper
Retirement

𝔄 few blocks from the courthouse, in a back room of Saint Peter's church, the black slave Esakka stood naked before the man who had introduced himself as Friar Redmond. Like thick cane syrup, the friar's beady eyes poured over the slave's well-formed body.

Scratching his scrimpy red beard, the priest puffed like a fireplace bellows. "Magnificent mahogany skin you have there, my young friend. Just magnificent."

Esakka was not sure how he got himself into this predicament. He was extremely distressed. The priest had promised him a guinea if he would help him move some boxes. There were no boxes in this room and there probably would be no guinea. Esakka hoped the trial was not over and that Master Solomon Seney was not searching the courtyard for him.

Redmond's thin lips were dry and he could not help lisping as he spoke. "Your body is a beautiful temple to the Lord. As all bodies should be." The priest's somber black cassock and his black sombrero presented a strange contrast to his delight with Esakka's splendid physique.

Esakka stood tall and responded with dignity. "I am Falashas, honorable Father."

"You are Falashas? You said your name was Esakka. Now you say it is Falashas? Which is it? What are you truly called?"

Esakka eyed his white canvas suit folded on the floor beside black boots, flinching as the priest's stubby finger poked at the firmness of his muscles.

"Falashas is not my name. My name is Esakka. I am Ethiopian. My tribe is Falashas."

Redmond was in Esakka's face again, his breath spirituous, his wedge-shaped finger jabbing at the slave's chest. "What is a Falashas?"

To keep from cowering, Esakka tightened his toes. He was not unused to being naked, nor to having unfamiliar fingers punch and prod him. If this man reached down and cradled his manhood, as sometimes happened on the auction block to estimate a male's success as a breeder, he would strike him a blow on the head. He was not for sale today

"My religion is the same as the Kings of Israel." Esakka's voice projected a strength he did not feel and he prayed silently that God would help him. "My forefathers were the children of Menelik, the son of King Solomon and the Queen of Sheba."

"Is that so? Are you really sure of that?" The priest glanced around the room. Apparently, he did not see what he wanted. He pulled a dull pewter flask from his robe and took a lengthy sip. Without comment, he returned it to its hiding place. Small wonder the priest had such liquored lungs, Esakka thought.

Redmond circled Esakka's body again, touching him at each step, running his fingertips over the slave's silky brown skin. "Your back is very smooth. You have no scars from any whippings that I can see."

"Master Seney is kind to me, and God has protected me through many tribulations."

"You speak quite well."

Esakka sensed the priest meant it as an accusation. He hadn't met a white man who didn't resent the fact that he, a slave, had been educated. "I learned to read on my own, but I have always had goodhearted masters who let me study their books."

Redmond made another circle, his black gown swooshing about his ankles. He widened the distance between himself and the slave. "I see the rite of circumcision has been observed. I've never seen a black man with that done to him."

"My people are a clean people. We bathe everyday and we circumcise. We always wash our hands before eating. We keep the commandments of the Torah and we follow the laws of the Jews."

Redmond's eyes focused on Esakka's loins. He leaned forward for a closer look. A fragment of spittle separated from his lips and ran down his chin.

"The Lord is my shepherd," Esakka said, keeping his eyes straight ahead. The words came out strong and clear and he continued with the Psalm. "I shall not want—"

"I should hope not!"

From the corner of his eye, Esakka spied a grin blooming on the priest's mouth. He resumed the Psalm in a louder voice. "He restoreth my soul. He leadeth me in the paths of righteousness—"

"Enough, enough, enough!" Redmond shouted. "I can see you are a devoted servant of the Lord."

Esakka's patience came to an end. Foregoing any instruction from the clergyman, he reached for his clothes and began putting them on.

"A handsome gift you have there." Redmond swiped drool from his mouth with his black sleeve, his gaze remaining on Esakka until his breeches had been drawn up.

"If I meet a young lass of your station, I will tell your Master about her. In the meantime, do not speak of this to anyone. My plans don't always meet with success, so there's no point in advertising them."

Esakka snatched his vest coat from the floor and thrust his arms into it. He did not think he wanted to tell anyone about the priest's quirky behavior. He doubted he would ever see the guinea he had been promised. He should have known a guinea for moving a few boxes was ridiculous. Next time, he would know better. The temptation had been great because Master Seney had promised him his freedom when he could repay the three hundred pounds of his purchase price.

"Of course, Sirrah," Esakka said meekly as he stepped into his boots.

Esakka left the man talking, bolted out the door and ran for the courthouse lawn. Only when he was nearly there, did he realize that he had left behind the black Kevenhuller hat that Mr. Seney had given him that morning.

13

𝕴𝕴𝕴

. . : death hath ten thousand doors.
John Webster,
The Duchess of Malfi

𝕸akepeace cocked an eye toward his attorney. The pettifogger sat with his arms crossed, his eyes slitted as if daydreaming. He made no objection to the prosecutor's request. Evidently he saw no injustice with the sniveling Filmore's being summoned to drape the noose around his client's neck.

Makepeace wanted to hiss at his lawyer to gain his attention, but when a small *zzzt!* escaped his lips, the bailiff gave him a look of disgust and raised his rod in a threatening manner.

Judge Payne rapped his gavel. "Sheriff, bring Mister Filmore into the courtroom. You're dismissed, Jarvis. But I'll be around a little later in the day to see what kind of material you got for some new breeches."

Still in the jury box, Adams scratched the palm of his left hand. "We have some fine navy blue duvetyn you might like, Your Honor."

"Just don't increase your prices before I get there," the judge warned. "I want to pay the same price the common people pay."

A frown wormed its way across Jarvis' face. "I wouldn't never do that, Your Honor. I know that's against the law."

The heavily chained Filmore was escorted into the courtroom. The sight of his ferret face caused Mrs. Adams to swoon. Judge Payne granted a brief recess while Jarvis revived his wife with smelling salts. Several jurors took the opportunity to stand and stretch their bones.

Makepeace gave Filmore an evil eye as the moth-eaten beggar shuffled across the courtroom. Filmore glanced away as he shambled toward the witness chair. He plopped down and clasped his chained hands as if in church.

In a low voice, Makepeace whispered, "God rot'un, a pox on

14

ye, ye scabby devil."

Filmore's hand twisted the front curve of his thread-bare coat. He shot his accomplice a nervous look, swallowed hard and darted his eyes toward the floor.

The prosecutor's voice boomed against the rafters. "Mister Filmore, you're still under court's oath. Please tell us how you came to the Colonies."

Filmore cleared his throat and crossed his bird-legs. "Mister Makepeace and me was transported from England and put down in Delaware where we was left to fend for ourselfs." Destitute of teeth, Filmore's chin protruded in such a way that when he answered Hammer's questions, his sharp nose closed against it like a nutcracker. "I met Mister Makepeace in Newgate prison, Your Honors. I didn't know why he was there."

"And you were in prison for what reason, Mister Filmore?"

As if it were the first time he had heard anything of this matter, Makepeace listened intently. Filmore's voice took on the churchy-tone that he had used on more than occasion to present himself as a clergyman, after which he produced a basket with which Makepeace collected a few shillings. Some of those sermons Makepeace had heard so often, he could repeat them to the letter.

"I was there because me wife run me into debt and I couldn't get no work to pay me bills. And I don't mind tellin' you, many a day I would have gone hungry if I hadn't been able to catch meself a mouse to eat."

"But when you were turned out in Delaware," the prosecutor continued, "you willingly entered into a life of crime with the accused?"

The witness rubbed his red, sunken eyes with a soiled, blue handkerchief. "Your Grace, we was cold and hungry on the streets. All the time, we thought we would starve or wake up dead from being cold. It's an awful feeling and I don't suppose Your Grace has ever been in that predicament."

Makepeace had a strong desire to say amen but scrapped it, maintaining as stony a face as if Filmore's confession referred to some other person.

Mr. Hammer looked mighty pleased with himself as he turned to the judge. "The prosecution is willing to let the defense cross-examine Mister Filmore."

Makepeace's lawyer rose, his yellow satin suit draping its wrinkles about his rotund body. He started to yawn, caught himself, and gave the judge a toothy smile. He then turned to the witness. "You're a common thief, are you not, Mister Filmore?"

Filmore coughed and covered his mouth with a gnarly hand. "Times, I ain't had little choice but to steal, Your Grace. You knows how the belly demands a little timber now and then. A person has to satisfy it. Once we got caught in Delaware, but we blamed it on some Indians. We got offen that one."

"Your whole life," the pettifogger mumbled, "is nothing but lies and deceit, is it not, Mister Filmore?"

"I gets by as best I can and some days, it ain't none too easy."

"It doesn't look to me like the jury should believe anything that comes out of your mouth. Your Honor, the prosecutor can take back this double-dealing scalawag. It's a travesty that Mister Hammer would attempt to blacken the character of the accused by dragging in the testimony of a felon who's already headed for the gallows."

Mr. Hammer rose from his chair, thundering in the witness' face, "Are you and Makepeace guilty of this crime of robbery?"

Frightened by the prosecutor's tone, Filmore looked at Hammer and then at the jury. Tears ran down his toughened face. "God knows we are. There ain't no use in denying it! Maybe He'll show us a little more mercy than you honorable men has. I understands ain't nobody goes hungry in heaven."

Makepeace noted that Filmore's return of the blame for his predicament had no effect on the guardians of the law. The prosecutor coughed, spit into his white handkerchief and declared, "Let's move on to the subject at hand, Mister Filmore. Who led you into this life of crime?"

"Mister Makepeace, that's who. A man who can read and do sums. He never should ha' let his-self and me fall in the gutter like we done." Filmore stood in the witness stand and pointed his finger at Makepeace. "I thought you was a friend, but you was my tempter."

Filmore sat back down, but not before he had pointed toward hell as Makepeace's final destination, still using that mellifluous tone with which he had scared many a peasant into confessing his sins. After which, he would add an admonition that the more coins he put into the basket, the more certainty he would have a mansion in heaven.

The prosecutor went into a strangling fit like a harlot at a church christening. Makepeace thought Hammer would turn blue and collapse before the court. Nevertheless, the old lawyer gained control, not the least bit dismayed that he had impeached his own witness. "Mister Filmore, did you claim benefit of clergy when you received the sentence of death?"

Filmore muttered his response.

The prosecutor looked quite petulant. "Get the frog out of your throat, Mister Filmore, and speak so the court may understand you!"

Filmore sat up and shouted, "Begging the apology of the Court and Almighty God, I did that very thing!"

The prosecutor's voice dripped acid. "And what other shameful thing did you do, Mister Filmore?"

"I kissed the Holy Book to prove it. I'm sorry, but I did it."

"And how were your calumnies uncovered, Mister Filmore?"

Filmore mumbled his answer and went back to staring at the floor.

"Louder, Mister Filmore," Judge Payne ordered. "I will not have this mealy-mouthed testifying in my courtroom. Speak plainly!"

Filmore looked terrified. Makepeace wondered what Filmore expected the judge to do to him. Hanging were hanging, and in all good faith, it was against the common law to drag out a man's death or exert unnecessary torture in the deliverance of that awful sentence.

When his mouth opened, Filmore stuttered like a child in danger of a beating with this father's horsewhip, his chin thumping against his nose. "I weren't able to r-read f-from the Bible when it were brought to me. Just open it up and read a passage, the j-judge said. I couldn't read the once and I can't r-read now. I plead your forgiveness for that d-dreadful duh-duh-deed."

As if he expected a halo to descend from the beams and alight on his head, Filmore looked toward the ceiling, tears gushing from his eyes. "I'm guilty, as God is my witness! And so is that pickled dog Makepeace! God have mercy on us both!"

Makepeace prayed the bony-faced old prosecutor would have a turbulent attack of asthma. Providence seemed not to understand the urgency of his petition.

The Pickled Dog Caper

The louder Mr. Hammer's voice grew, the less his asthma distressed him. In a high, clear voice he decried the mother country's practice of sending boatloads of convicts to the Colonies. "They might as well send emissaries of the Devil!

"Gentlemen, there is no room for mercy in this case, absolutely none."

The jury deliberated a little short of an hour. It would have taken less time had not the defense objected in closing argument to Mr. Filmore's being put on the stand. He declared it contrary to the laws of England, giving Makepeace a small hope that he might get off, but the judge quickly crushed the bud of that fragile flower.

The bailiff assisted Makepeace in standing so he could face the jury. Makepeace's chains clinked dully as he rose to hear the panel's finding.

"Solomon Seney will deliver the verdict," Judge Payne said sternly.

Mr. Seney peered for several seconds at the paper in his hand, a sad, solemn expression on his face. That a handsome young man like Richard Makepeace should lose his life to the gallows at such an early age distressed Solomon, although he saw no injustice in it. Makepeace seemed about the same age as his eldest son Jonathan, who was in London studying law.

In a deliberate, somber voice, Mr. Seney read the verdict. "The accused is guilty as charged of breaking and entered Jarvis Adams' household in the middle of the night with intent to steal what he could that was of value."

Judge Payne rapped his gavel. "The prisoner may speak his piece, if he be of such a mind."

Makepeace's dark handsome eyes did not twinkle, glazed as they were. His jaunty mouth moved once or twice before the words came out. He desperately needed to scratch his balls, but thought better of it. The iron collar permitted only minuscule movement. In no fashion could he lower his head to appear penitent.

"Your Honor, members of the jury, I want to apologize for the troubles I've caused ye. My mother taught me better. If ye could find it in yer hearts to pray for me immortal soul, she'll appreciate it . . . and so will I."

Makepeace knew no one cared where he spent eternity. He'd been battered, jeered and pissed on by the eternal fates. There would be no charity for him. Not a drop of mercy would fall from the tenderhearted heavens on his head. And a sentence of death in this fancy building was no more glorious than one that might be handed down in a makeshift court met in an ordinary saloon.

Judge Payne struck his gavel three times. "Richard Makepeace, you will be hanged on October fifteenth in the year of our Lord 1767. May God have mercy on you."

In a sad, gritty voice, Makepeace said, "Ma said she hoped someday I would live in the sunshine. I guess there ain't no chance of that now."

IV

I am a woman . . .
When I think, I must speak.
William Shakespeare
As You Like It

"**I** see you've given that slave your Kevenhuller hat," Marianne Seney had said to her husband Solomon before the trial that morning.

Solomon Seney pulled an ivory silk shirt from a drawer in the mahogany press. Slipping his arms into its sleeves, he closed the garment and buttoned it, then tucked it into his gray breeches and bent to fasten the oval-shaped silver buckles on his knees. He joined his wife at the round mahogany table in front of the window of their second story bedroom, seating himself with a sigh.

Marianne wore a soft yellow morning dress that flattered her deep auburn hair. There was no doubt in Solomon's mind, she was the most beautiful woman on the Eastern shore. He constantly forgave her the incisiveness of her tongue. She could be an effecter of hard words.

"My dear, that hat is out of style," Solomon said. "The cock is too high and the brim is much too wide to be worn in fashionable company."

From the table, Solomon took the silver scissors and cut off the tip of a sugar cone, letting a good chunk of it fall into his cup. As the sugar slowly dissolved, Marianne reached across and stirred his tea with her spoon.

"Sooner of later, you'll repent the day you gave that African an opportunity to flaunt himself. Frequently, I've noticed how the women ogle him when he goes to town." She hesitated and gave him the service of a winsome smile. "And not all of them are as dark as he is."

20

Solomon glanced out the window toward the stables. He was pleased to see Esakka had hooked two horses up to the two-wheeled chair and stood waiting for his master. In his mid-twenties, Esakka was one of fourteen slaves belonging to the plantation. Beyond a doubt, he was the handsomest and the most stalwart. One day, Solomon planned to make him an overseer. He had promised Esakka his freedom when he repaid his initial cost. His wife would be very disturbed if she knew that on each anniversary of his purchase, he presented Esakka with a guinea toward his freedom sum.

"Esakka is not all that dark."

Marianne clacked her tongue. She waved her left hand toward the stables and indicated her husband's coal black Arabian, a horse Solomon highly valued for its breeder qualities. "Exactly my point, my dear husband. Pray don't think me vulgar, he would be better off were he as black as Saheeb."

"Esakka cost me a great deal more than Saheeb," he said. "Although I admit his outfits aren't nearly as dear as that horse's tack and saddle."

Satisfied that she'd made her point, Marianne changed the subject. "Will you be wearing a frock or just your waistcoat this morning?"

"I suppose I had better wear my brown frockcoat with the gray squirrel trim. You know what a fuss Judge Payne makes about proper dress in his court. And I never mind being the most elegant person present."

Esakka brought the open two-horse chair around to the front door. Solomon Seney stepped leisurely into it and sat down with a remark about the pleasant weather. It was a fine October day. He would enjoy the five-mile ride into town. He didn't look forward to sitting all day in a stuffy jury room, but it was his civic duty and he enjoyed anything that had to do with politics and the government.

Esakka flicked the whip lightly over the horses in the manner Mr. Seney had taught him.

Esakka looked like an African prince in his white cotton suit. The Kevenhuller hat was very handsome on him. Mr. Seney figured that if it attracted the ladies, that would be Esakka's dilemma.

𝔙

. . . like a moth the simple maid
Still plays about the flames.
John Gay
The Beggar's Opera

"𝔚hat happened to your hat, Mr. Esakka?" the young African girl demanded. "Where'd you go with that corny-faced priest?"

Josie was her name. She was the property of Mr. and Mrs. Adams and was one of their domestic maids. She waited under an oak tree on the courthouse lawn with a number of other slaves.

Hundred year-old oaks spread an acre of shade around the red brick two-story building. A statue of Queen Anne stood in front, the good queen a model of patience and moral virtue for all women.

No more than fifteen, Josie was a pretty girl with chocolate skin and an airy manner. Esakka wondered why she hadn't yet found a husband, as had most girls her age. He had considered asking her himself, but he had a wish that he might find a wife who could read and they could write each other little notes back and forth from time to time.

Perhaps Josie's voice kept her from finding a suitor. Octaves higher than it should be, it was almost, but not quite, whiney. Only a sweet tone saved it from being truly a drone, but Esakka had noticed that the sweetness frequently disappeared.

Still out of breath, Esakka stammered, "Nowhere you need to know about, Little Miss Child."

Josie half curtsied, her eyes soft and flirty. Very comely eyes, thought Esakka. Perhaps he should rethink his feelings about her.

"You be forgetting my name, Mister Esakka! It's Josephine, but everybody calls me Josie."

"A lovely name for a lovely girl." Esakka hoped the praise would distract her from an attempt at acquiring information that wasn't her business.

"How come you forget me, Mister Esakka?" Josie wheedled, gazing at him through her fluttering eyelids.

"I didn't forget you, Josie. You're not a forgettable person."

Josie's face lit up. "Oh thank you, Mister Esakka."

Esakka looked around to see if his owner had missed him. "Have you seen Master Solomon Seney come out of the courthouse?"

"The trial ain't over," said Josie. "So where you say you be?"

"If you must know," said Esakka, "I was looking for some wild flowers to bring you. Alas, I found not a one."

Josie gave him a coy look. "What did that ugly ole priest want with you?"

"Just to help him move some boxes."

"He was certainly 'culiar looking."

"He can't help how God made him look, Josie."

"Yes, but he acts 'culiar." Josie bobbed her head engagingly. "Well, I thanks you for the flowers, Mister Esakka-sir, even if I didn't get 'em. Oooh, there be my sister. I got to say good-by now."

Josie powdered away in the direction of the girl she claimed was her sister. As she ran, she lifted her skirts to ankle length and looked back to see if Esakka observed her. She was not disappointed.

VI

With a tale forsooth, he cometh unto you . . .
Sir Phillip Sidney
The Defense of Poesy

On the day that Solomon Seney served on the jury which found Makepeace guilty, Judge Silas Payne took the gray-haired plantation owner to dinner at the Red Horse Inn on the courthouse square.

A high-class establishment with plaster walls and well-turned tables and chairs, its owner refused to allow billiard tables or shuffle board. He preferred to offer his customers music from a harpsichord with a double row of keys. The musician played Methodist hymns, occasionally lapsing into show tunes composed by John Gay.

Judge Payne smoked a hand-rolled Dutch cigar, its rich aroma mingling with onion and garlic vapors, seeking its way through the fluttering lace curtains at the open windows of the dining room.

In his left hand, Judge Payne held a letter. He waved the paper airily in Solomon's face. "This letter comes all the way from Boston, from Reverend Harrison. His church burned recently. The poor saints up there are eager to rebuild but they are desperate for funds. Reverend Harrison is traveling through the middle Colonies to take up a collection for their new construction and looks forward to meeting us Christians on the Eastern Seaboard. He brings with him a young lady who writes beautiful poetry."

"I suppose I could make a donation," Solomon said. He couldn't figure out why Silas insisted the letter held so much significance.

Judge Payne bent over and sniffed the fish on his dinner plate. At the same time, he placed the letter under its left edge and then put his left hand in his lap. He leaned across the table, his long face

24

practically converging with Solomon's.

"Something other than that is what I have in mind. We are providing an entertainment at my town house in Annapolis for the occasion. I've invited a number of good friends to attend and will take donations at that time."

Solomon leaned back. "Might you be extending an invitation, Silas? We are in the middle of harvesting the Orinoco, you know. It will be the largest and finest crop of tobacco the Seney plantation had ever produced."

If he didn't want to agree to Silas' request, Solomon thought he had established a good excuse to back out.

The judge laid his cigar aside and tested the fish with his fork, then laid his fork aside also. "I thought you might want to have a reception for the poetess with your friends in Queen Anne County."

Mr. Seney tinkered with an oyster fritter on his well-laid platter. He was aggravated with Silas for not handing him the letter and letting him read it with his own eyes. Silas had a secret and it was in that letter. "Aren't the oysters delightsome this season?"

The judge frowned, obviously unhappy with Solomon's attempt to change the subject.

"Not necessarily a big reception," the judge said plaintively. "Although I know you have so many friends—"

Solomon was not in a mood to make any promises. "Well, I don't know about that. What kind of occasion do you have in mind?"

The judge took a small portion of his fish. He lifted it to his mouth and chewed slowly, the white meat showing between his teeth. When he finally swallowed, he said, "Reverend Harrison is traveling with Mrs. John Wheatley, one of his church members. She's the wife of a locally renowned tailor on King Street and brings with her this young lady who writes and reads her own poetry—very remarkable poetry, it's said." With a swig of wine, the judge washed down the last of his fish. "The Reverend declares it to be a splendid entertainment for an afternoon or evening."

Mr. Seney halved a fried oyster with his fork, but left it remaining on his plate. "Please advise me the subjects of the young lady's poetry."

Solomon glanced toward the letter. If the judge was aware of his curiosity, he ignored it.

"She writes in the manner of Alexander Pope and touches on Grecian and Christian themes," Judge Payne said.

That was praiseworthy, Solomon thought, but he gave Silas only a short "Hmm."

"According to Reverend Harrison, she also has something to say about current events and common morality."

Mr. Seney laid the halved oyster on a piece of bread and raised it to his lips. "Is the young lady old enough to impart any wisdom about such things?"

"She's around fifteen or sixteen. There's no record of the actual year she was born."

Intensely suspicious, Solomon chewed his oyster and bread slowly. Then he swallowed and reached for his wine glass. "Is that so? Surely you know a little more about her, my friend."

"She was brought to the Colonies around the age of seven."

Mr. Seney carefully gulped down his wine and returned the glass to the table. He glanced again at the letter. "What else?"

"She was alone," said the judge.

"And?"

"And without any family."

Solomon slapped his hand on the table. "Bless you, you old charlatan, she's a slave girl! You were keeping that back from me, weren't you! That's why you wouldn't let me read the letter for myself."

The judge moved Mr. Seney's wine glass toward him as if suggesting he needed a good mouthful. Mr. Seney gently pushed it back to its original position.

"Yes . . . ," admitted the judge. "She is a young African."

The musician increased the tempo as he pounded out a raucous John Gay song. The innkeeper came to remove their plates. Each gentleman shook his head indicating he had not finished eating.

Then raising his voice to be heard over the music, the judge shouted, "Innkeeper! Tell your piano player to hold it down! We're trying to talk now!"

Payne waved the letter at Solomon again. "I have here a letter written to Reverend Harrison by her owner."

Solomon chuckled heartily. "Go ahead and read it to me, you old reprobate."

Payne grinned with obvious presumption that he had successfully ambushed his friend. Taking out a pair of wire frame glasses, the judge fastened them across his face, then began to read.

"Phillis was brought to America several years ago, being around six or seven years old at the time. Without any schooling and only by what she was taught by other children in the family, she learned English in less than a year."

Solomon pursed his lips and shook his head slowly.

"In a short time, she was able to read the Sacred Writings. All who knew her were most astonished."

Solomon fashioned a purposely cryptic smile. "And what about her poetry?"

Payne returned the letter to his pocket. "The letter says her own curiosity led her to it."

"Well, I have a great deal of curiosity, Silas, but it has never led me to write poetry. Is it your earnest opinion she will be well received?"

The Judge picked up his half-smoked cigar and studied it, but evidently did not want to step over to the fireplace for a coal to relight it. "She is a rarity—a curiosity, if you please, but even more, she appears to be talented. What do you think? Can we be of service to Reverend Harrison?"

Mr. Seney felt composed enough to drink his wine and eat his bread and oysters. He took his time doing so before giving his response. "I don't think so, Silas. I'll make a donation, but a reception is out of the question. We have too much work to do, harvesting the Orinoco."

"You could invite the Pacas, the Hemsleys, the Magruders . . . and oh yes, the Tilghmans," Judge Payne said. "You know so many important people. And your sister-in-law could play your Philadelphia spinet."

"I'm sorry, Silas. That instrument has not been tuned in some time. Besides that, Mrs. Neville is in the increasing way. Has anyone invited Colonel Washington?"

The judge frowned. "In all honesty, Solomon, I must inform you my sister in Baltimore has extended an invitation to George."

"I don't suppose she would change her mind?"

"My sister change her mind?" asked the judge. "Oh, you've

27

never met her, have you? Besides which, she is quite thrilled to have the girl visit her."

"I think it's George your sister is glad to have visit her," Solomon said with a tone of petulance.

The judge ignored Solomon's grumpiness. "Don't you suppose your friends would enjoy the slave girl's writings?"

"They would be more likely to come with Colonel Washington there."

The innkeeper brought a coal in a small pair of tongs and offered the judge a light. Silas puffed noisily on his cigar. Solomon noticed he had barely tasted his dinner. He could not help feeling a bit of pleasure at the judge's plight. It wasn't that he didn't want to do the reception. He was just annoyed with Silas over the manner in which he attempted to manipulate him by not letting him read the letter for himself.

"Who else is the girl performing for?" Solomon asked.

"Mrs. Wheatley and her young escort are stopping in Philadelphia. I suppose the mayor and that old rake Franklin will be her hosts."

"Well, she seems well taken care of. There's no reason for us to tire them out with additional performances." Although to himself, Solomon admitted he wouldn't mind being in the same league as old Ben, or Colonel Washington.

"But you will do it, won't you?" pleaded the judge.

Solomon relented. "Oh, I suppose so."

"Most kind-hearted of you, my friend. I shall put you down for Sunday, October the fifteenth. We'll hang that bastard Makepeace at dawn and then we'll enjoy a lively little respite."

VII

Sir, you shall taste my Anno Domini
George Farquar
The Beau Stratagem

When Friar Redmond arrived to dispense Makepeace his last rites, the trapdoor to his basement cell stood open. Makepeace heard the priest enter the building and inquire of the sheriff's wife if anyone had yet ministered to the prisoner.

"Not a person has showed up to save his soul from eternal damnation," said the sheep-faced old woman. "I was thinking of going for the priest meself, but me husband's took sick and I got to do this here work."

"Counting the tobacco leaves, are you?" asked Redmond. The large leaves were stacked man-high on the floor, held in position by a long steel rod through the stems, fastened to a wood base.

"I ain't just counting 'em, I'm looking 'em over pretty good."

"Is that the way they pay their fines around here?"

"Good as the King's currency in these parts, Father. In fact, better than that stuff they print in London. See that trap door over there? That's where the crook is. Me arthritis won't let me climb down there. Take the keys, if you would. Bring 'em back to me after you've brought the crook to the Lord."

Friar Redmond pulled the trap door open and began the descent to the basement. When he was about half-way, he reached up and pulled the trap door shut. Then he twisted his black silk scarf around his nose to take the edge off the squalid odors of the musty floor and the overflowing chamber pot.

Redmond let himself into the cell occupied by Makepeace, clanged the iron door shut and locked it. He slipped the ring of keys

29

onto the sash of his cassock.

What Makepeace could see of the man's face was covered with red pimples. He imagined the priest must be well-acquainted with the Devil's bonny fires. Strange looking and strange acting. Maybe they were all the same. Makepeace didn't know. He weren't Catholic. Hell, he weren't anything, except maybe a sinner.

"Friar Redmond is my name." The priest spoke through his scarf. He paced the cell back and forth, crunching beetles as he walked, apparently unsure whither he would alight.

"Go ahead, Father." Makepeace did not consider that he had a lot of time left. "I heard ye talking to the sheriff's wife. See if ye can find any salvation for me soul. I don't want to fall into the Devil's clutches."

At the moment though, Makepeace had a more urgent need. He'd best take care of it right away. "Have ye any brandy on ye, Father?"

Redmond lowered the scarf from his face. The bottom half of his countenance was no less blemished than the upper. The priest grinned, displaying without shame a set of yellowed teeth. Clearly pleased to oblige his new friend, he pulled out a dull pewter flask.

Makepeace had a sip, then two. It weren't brandy. It were better. White Coin, clear high proof liquor. Powerful stuff.

The priest sat on the hard bunk next to Makepeace, his thigh pushing against Makepeace's leg. With a sideways look, Redmond's beady eyes brazenly traveled up and down Makepeace's face and then his body. Spittle drooled his lips.

"Richard, you're a handsome man. If Saint Peter lets people through the pearly gates on looks, you'll soon shake hands with God."

Makepeace handed the flask back to the priest. Redmond took a long sip and rested the canteen on his lap. "How old might you be, Richard?"

"Barely twenty, Father. How did I come to stretch the hemp at such a tender age?"

"You tell me," Redmond said.

"A little bulk and file. Me friend jostled 'em and I did the business on 'em—jewelry, money, whatever they had loose in a purse or a pocket."

With the sleeve of his cassock, Redmond wiped the drool from his lips. "Richard, that devil in your eyes tells me you're one who's never well unless he's in mischief. I doubt that there's much tender age in your history."

"Maybe not." Makepeace was in a mood to be polite. "I learnt words and figures when I was young. I never got a chance to use them to earn a living. Always been the chief cock of the walk, surrounded by clowns willing to do whatever I asked. Their willingness to follow me leads me to extremes." His jaunty lips twisted into an embryonic smile. "Sometimes, it's pure scandalous."

"Being handsome can be a curse—a sad commentary on human nature, my son," Redmond said. "We forget beauty is only skin deep. The soul's complexion does not always match that of the face."

Makepeace could not avoid a smirk. Lucky ye, he thought, names don't match faces either. Otherwise, yer's would be Father Nastyface.

Redmond placed his arm around Makepeace. As yet, Makepeace saw nothing untoward in the priest's familiarity. He would have liked another sip of White Coin, but Redmond had taken a drink, a rather long one, and his hospitality seemed at an end. He had secreted the flask on his person.

In a sanctimonious tone that caused Makepeace to look askance at him, the priest said, "You should have used your influence for God."

Redmond's embrace now made Makepeace uncomfortable. He stood and dragged his leg-iron as he paced the dirt floor. A centipede crawled across his path; he squashed it with a quick turn of the boot on his free leg.

"Crimes has got their own reward, Padre. Same as good deeds, although crimes seems to pay quicker. Mostly, I used me talents to keep bread in me belly and a farthing in me pocket. Dirty water under the bridge now.

"When I was seventeen, I fell in with a man several years my senior. I was on the friggin'—excuse me, Father—streets of London, cold and without food. The man appeared to be a gentleman. At least, he had a pretty tongue and a wheelbarrow full of periwig on his head. Offered me to share a room for the night. He was dressed like an officer. I trusted the friggin' son of a bitch."

Something about the priest caused Makepeace to feel there was no need for apology this time. There was a strangeness about the man—there, he knew what it was. The priest kept eyeing him as if he was a pretty girl.

"The inn where the officer took me looked very elegant. Not that I was so wise in them matters. I ain't never lived in the sunshine. Not that I wouldn't like to."

"Lodge probably weren't so fancy." Redmond rocked back and forth on the bunk, his left hand in his lap, an enraptured look on his face.

"It was better than the friggin' cold. He supped me in a hearty manner and tippled me some good brandy. Afterward, we fell into a good feather bed with clean sheets on it."

Redmond's tongue circled his lips and he gawked at Makepeace with a knowing lift of a red eyebrow. Makepeace ignored him. "I slept the sleep of the angels until morning when there came a loud banging on the door. I waited for me officer friend to respond. Finally, I realized he weren't going to. In fact, he weren't in the room. When I got up and went to the door, it was the innkeeper looking for his reckoning."

Makepeace stopped pacing and leaned back against the damp walls of the cell. "I don't suppose ye have any sot weed on you?"

"Sorry, but no." Redmond patted the pockets of the gown in a simulated search. "I've never taken up the filthy habit."

Makepeace sighed. "Filthy friggin' habit it is, but I enjoy it. Anyway, I asked the innkeeper the whereabouts of the officer. Said I should know better than him. That's when I saw the open window in the chamber."

"Your companion escaped?"

"Flat gone and what with me flat broke. The blackguard even took the jewelry and trinkets I'd filched from a few pockets in Haymarket."

Friar Redmond straightened the heavy wood cross hanging around his neck and scowled at Makepeace while he kept his right hand on the cross bar.

Makepeace knew what he was thinking and he grinned. "I don't want yer friggin' cross." He squashed another insect with his foot. "If I had a farthing for ever one of those rascals I've killed, I'd be rich as a gypsy king."

"So there you was in the inn, responsible for the bill?"

"All mine to pay—the night's lodging plus the grand supper. Need I tell ye? Not a penny to me name. Ain't no crime as disgraceful as poverty, is there?"

"No, nor any shame like wearing rags," Redmond said.

"Ye can't get anyone's respect if yer wearing rags."

"What happened then?"

"Straight away to Newgate College for me!"

"Prison, huh?" Redmond pursed his thin lips and shook his head. "There, I'm sure, you learned nothing but bullying and swearing."

"Well, I learned a lot about drinking and whoring. Anyway, I laid by there for three years. Then the friggin' Mr. Raggy buys off the Crown and transports a bunch of us inmates to Jarsy." He gave the Colony the English pronunciation. "New Jarsy, that is. Tried to sell us like we was slaves. I would have gone into indenture—willingly—but no one would pay a guinea for me."

"So Mr. Raggy turned loose those he couldn't sell?"

"Gave us nary a farthing nor a fart." Makepeace returned to sit on the bunk beside the priest. "Are ye sure ye don't have a cigar?"

"I've sworn off the nasty weed," Redmond said. "It's not fit for a priest to be blowing that nasty smoke in and out of God's temple."

Makepeace thought he saw something in Redmond's eyes that conflicted with what came out of his mouth. He yielded to that old feeling he had when he met a fellow sharper on the streets.

"Yer a sly boots." No denying it, a sharper always knows another sharper.

The priest grinned like a rogue caught with his hand in your pocket.

"Go on with ye," Makepeace urged. "Yer passing as a fine minister . . . and yet I have a feeling ye want to come home by weeping cross."

Redmond reached in his cassock and pulled out the pewter flask. He took a long pull on it, and eyed Makepeace hungrily. "My story is somewhat similar to yours, friend." Redmond's eyes shifted for a moment, then he returned the flask to its hiding place.

"Since I'm going to my Maker in the morning," Makepeace said. "Ye needn't worry about me betraying yer trust. Let it be blood for blood."

Redmond gave that invitation a long thought before the confession tripped sadly from his lips. "I came here under a cloud myself."

"Go on with ye."

Redmond beamed and folded his hands in his lap. "My sainted mother taught me at her knee. I was quite religious as a youth— even sang in the choir. But I was orphaned at thirteen. Put out on the streets of London."

"Just like me."

"Forsooth, Richard, I chose the streets. I had no wish to go to the orphanages."

Makepeace snorted in a knowing manner. "Still, ye seem to keep a finger in the friggin' pie. I guess ye found yer way to seminary?"

Redmond chuckled. "I found my way to the steps of Saint Paul's. Curled up asleep there one night, I was rescued by a true Man of the Cloth. Friendly and generous, he was! Took me in and cared for me five years. I slept in the church stables and minded the horses. He would let me follow him around all day long. What he didn't teach me, I learned on my own. I already knew the names of the books of the Bible—learned from my sweet mother."

"Ye got quite an education for one without much real schooling," said Makepeace. "Can ye preach a sermon?"

"After a fashion. When I was alone at night, I played church. Pretended to pray and preach the Good Book to the cows and horses." Redmond swelled up. "I got pretty good, if I do say so."

"There's that old saw, Father. Hangin' and preachin' go by destiny."

Redmond pulled out the flask and swilled the liquor. Makepeace would have liked another swallow himself, but a plan was formulating in his mind. He needed to keep a clear head. He decided he would not ask for another taste.

"Maybe it was destiny."

"Go on," Makepeace urged. "This is yer chance to get it off yer conscience."

"One night, me and the old priest was tippling the applejack pretty good. He got bloody mean—'twasn't the first time. When he got that way, he wouldn't have been sweet to Jesus Christ himself.

34

Up and called me a puddin'-headed bastard. No reason at all."

"The whisky talking," Makepeace suggested.

"Whisky spoke a pretty piece when it was in him. He said I was a scabby-faced gullion, the bastard son of a bastard son. It could've been true. I never knew my father, so I let it go by. He kept tippling the applejack. Got drunk as a wheelbarrow. When he said I was merrily begotten and my dear mother was a common whore, it got to me. My hackles rose up in her defense. I jumped up and struck him on the side of the head with a skillet."

"Devil go with ye, did ye knock him out cold? Ye didn't kill him, did ye?"

Redmond took a long swallow from the flask and sighed deeply. "Friend, I didn't mean to kill him."

"Yer had a forlorn hope to teach him a lesson, I gather?"

"But I smacked him too hard. Bloody hard. He sprawled against the table leg and split his head open. Blood gushed all over the kitchen floor."

"Dead, huh?"

"Turned cold within minutes."

"Yer friggin' skillet killed him?"

"No, it was the table leg. I didn't do it, the table leg did it. He bled to death."

Makepeace restrained his snicker. He sat down again beside the priest, his leg tired from pulling the ball and chain.

"So it were his destiny. What did ye do then?"

"Him and me was very close to being the same size. I went to his closet and got me a set of clothes to replace the rags I wore. I had already noticed no one pays any attention to a Man of the Cloth when he walks down the street. Let me tell you, my friend, it's like magic. They don't see you no more than they see a tree or a park bench. You're just a piece of the scenery."

Redmond took another taste of whisky. A few more swallows, Makepeace thought, and Redmond would have trouble climbing the ladder. This time he offered Makepeace a drink, but Makepeace declined it.

In the glory of the White Coin, Redmond's confessional mood vanished. Makepeace sensed the priest enjoyed telling this story, his mood swinging from penitential to one of high feather.

"That black frock was my salvation," Redmond said. "I found a newly purchased one in his wardrobe and walked out looking like the Archbishop of Canterbury! Took the old bugger's portmanteau and packed it with spare drawers and a Bible. Fifty pounds of silver was stashed in the old man's bureau—I took them, too!"

"Jesus' blood and wounds! You son of a whore!" Makepeace could not restrain the marked amount of admiration in his voice. The man was not a bona fide priest. He was a common thief, nay, even worse, a murderer.

"He filched those coins one at a time from the alms boxes," Redmond said. "Don't you ever doubt it. And I used that money to buy me passage to the New World."

"And now ye're passing yourself off as a papist priest! Pretending to be a real minister, wearing the black dress and that stylish black sombrero."

"It's been my salvation."

Or your damnation, Jack Nastyface, thought Makepeace.

"Wherever I go, the Church takes me in and the fathers feed me well. They provide me a place safe from the thugs on the road. It's not a bad way to play your cards—"

"Still, it depends on how they're dealt."

"Well, sometimes I just happen to have the right card up my sleeve." The priest was so tickled, he slapped his legs with his hands and stomped his feet up and down, dancing a jig without getting up from the bunk. "Sometimes I drop a coin in the alms box. Sometimes I take one out!"

"Yer a real Man of the Cloth." The friar had a smell about him as putrid as horse swot.

"But I'm not here to tell you my story," Redmond went on. "I must prepare you for the afterlife with my blessing."

"So get on with it."

Redmond placed his hand on Makepeace's head. "Anno, anno, anno, glorioso Domingo."

His fingers wandered down Makepeace's cheek. Out of good manners, Makepeace did not wrench away.

The priest fidgeted in his costume for a vial of holy water. "If you would let me anoint what appears to be a bountiful set of secrets . . . ."

36

Redmond licked his drying lips and his tongue slurred slightly. Makepeace could not tell if it was from excitement or from liquor.

"A little holy water here and there—will facilitate your ability to perform in the afterlife. Even after being deprived of the pulsing, throbbing, life-giving sap that flows from the heart."

Redmond flicked his fingers against Makepeace. Makepeace gritted his teeth and restrained himself. Redmond continued, clearly confident that he had bagged his quarry.

"You will become a heavenly rum stallion."

Although he was not in any way nearly as learned in the Holy Book as Redmond claimed, Makepeace figured there was no sex in heaven. It caused too much trouble on earth. In his mind, there was little prospect God would allow it in Paradise.

Makepeace turned to stand before the priest. Redmond extended a hand forward. With a snigger, Makepeace brought up a heartless fist, slamming the man cold. A good right hook to the chin—many a street fight had taught him how to do that and he did it well.

Redmond slithered to the ground. The priest's head knocked hard against the stone floor. Out like a pinched candle.

Makepeace could not help gloating. "No hot macaroni for you this friggin' night, Father Nastyface."

He opened the priest's mouth and forced in the remains of the White Coin, holding up Redmond's head so that the liquor tippled down his throat a drop at a time.

After searching the ring of keys for the one to his leg iron, Makepeace removed the steel band that encircled his ankle. He rubbed his shin to amend the circulation and set about divesting the priest of his magic costume.

Makepeace donned the black frock and added the sombrero. These articles felt so good, he added Redmond's long black scarf, then hung the gold-chained wood cross around his neck. There was no mirror in the cell, but he knew he looked good.

Wrestling with Redmond's body, he dressed the fake priest in his own blue linen shirt and breeches. He hated like ugly hell leaving his red pea jacket behind, but he didn't want to explain it when he passed the old woman upstairs.

He poured the last few drops of White Coin over Redmond's body, grumbling mightily over the sacrifice. The empty flask he poked into an inner pocket of the cassock, then turned the key in the cell door and climbed the ladder.

Still at the front room of the jail counting the tobacco leaves, the sheriff's old woman had stopped long enough to roll one and smoke it. She sat gravy-eyed in a dingy cloud.

The lower part of Makepeace's face was covered by the black scarf. He hoped the red splotches on the priest's face would not prove infectious. He tossed the old woman her keys and saluted with a touch of his hand to Redmond's sombrero that rode so jauntily on his head. The old woman never looked up.

"Mr. Makepeace received the holy rites and is resting peacefully. Yer'll be hearing no more from him tonight."

He was out the door before he thought to call back, "God bless ye, dear lady."

From the deck of the Annapolis ferry, Makepeace watched the shore of Queen Anne county recede into the dawn. He held no feeling of nostalgia for that place, not for its jail nor for the high gallows outside it.

The skirts of the magical black cassock blew around his ankles and the black sombrero was tied securely under his chin. Makepeace knew his airs were as good as those of any sanctimonious cleric.

He didn't care if they hanged Redmond. The posturing priest had murdered an innocent man, a devout man, maybe even a saint, a true member of the Cloth. If anyone deserved the gallows, it were Redmond.

What adventures lay ahead, only God knew. Makepeace decided that he could play the cards just as well, if not better, than that fake priest.

Maybe the sun would shine on him now.

𝔙𝔍𝔍𝔍

> Poetry's a mere drug, sir.
> George Farquar
> *Love and a Bottle*

Across the bay, at the elegant plantation home of Solomon Seney, the entertainment suggested by Judge Payne took place the same day Makepeace was to be hanged.

Following an early morning service at St. Luke's of Church Hill, Mrs. Wheatley, the Reverend Harrison and Phillis were graciously received in the foyer of the Seney home.

Wearing a red taffeta gown, the bodice exquisitely trimmed with brown fur, Mrs. Wheatley carried a matching muff nearly as large as her bosom. Mr. Seney suspected the fur was dyed skunk.

Mrs. Seney was dressed just as fashionably in a turquoise silk dress trimmed with silver lace, her auburn and gray hair topped by a silver butterfly cap edged with pearls. She greeted her guests with a graciousness that made Solomon Seney proud. "Mrs. Wheatley, may I express my pleasure at the fashion of your gown? I find the Turkish influence quite delightsome."

"And may I compliment you on your lovely home?" countered Mrs. Wheatley.

"As beautiful as Mount Vernon," purred the Reverend Harrison. A man of fifty, his three chins were covered with a thick brown beard that extended past the middle button of his plain navy frockcoat.

"Mount Vernon? Bless you!" Solomon knew the compliment was mere puffery. His home could not be nearly as ornamented as Mount Vernon. Nor could his three thousand acres compare to George's estate that overlooked the Potomac and boasted two hundred slaves. But the revelation that the party had already visited George eliminated the possibility that Colonel Washington would be a guest

39

of Judge Payne's sister. Mr. Seney permitted himself a wry smile. "So Phillis read to Colonel Washington several weeks ago?"

"At his own plantation." Harrison chuckled. "Why he calls it Mount Vernon, I don't know. There isn't a mountain near the place— not a real mountain."

After introductions, the party moved to the upstairs drawing room, a room Mr. Seney prized with its Prussian blue walls and alabaster white crown molding. A small fire blazed in the ornate fireplace, just enough to take away the early morning chill. Over the mantel was a gold-framed mirror. It was surrounded by exuberant white plaster garlands of roses, pineapples and pears. Mr. Seney imagined Phillis to be studying the room with an eye to writing a poem about it.

The petite slave girl, thin as a wren, but alert as a hummingbird, sat beside her mistress on the Chippendale sofa that faced her host and hostess. Phillis was demure in a pale pink gown worn with an embroidered French jacket. The style had passed a few years before, indicating it might be handed down, but it was quite attractive on her. A bonnet with pink ruching framed Phillis' lively face and piercing black eyes.

Esakka, who had just entered the drawing room with a tray of cookies and sweets, thought Phillis was the most beautiful girl he had ever seen. She sat quietly with her hands in her lap. If she knew of Esakka's presence, she gave him not so much as a glimpse. He had begged Mr. Seney to let him serve the group when he heard a slave-girl poet was coming to visit.

"We found Phillis in the Boston slave market seven years ago," Mrs. Wheatley said. "The market was extremely crowded that day. It's a wonder we didn't overlook her."

"I fret to think what might have happened if Mrs. Wheatley had not discovered her!" Reverend Harrison focused his eyes on a tray of sweet biscuits on the sideboard.

Mr. Seney caught Harrison's glance and signaled Esakka to pass the tray. After passing the tray, Esakka returned to his post, standing stiff and erect inside the door of the blue drawing room. He listened and observed, but hardly moved an eyelid. Fascinated by Phillis, he never lifted his gaze from her for a moment. If she regarded him as little more than a piece of furniture, she did not give any indication. But he did not consider for a moment that she behaved in any way uppish.

Mrs. Wheatley continued, "Three score little girls came off that ship, but Phillis caught my eye. Just a waif! She clutched a remnant of dirty blue carpet with such a glow in her young face. What a lovely child she was. Her spirit just shown through! I could not resist her!"

The Reverend Harrison's voice rumbled contentedly through his beard. "Phillis was taken from her family at an early age. She has no memory of her mother—"

"But one, Reverend Harrison," Phillis interrupted. "Every morning, my dear mother would pour a pitcher of water on the ground as the sun rose in the East. It was a custom I do not know the reason for, but I recall it as well as my own face in the mirror this morning."

At that revelation, Esakka felt very close to Phillis. Each daybreak, his mother performed the same ritual. If Phillis would only ask him, he could tell her that it was a prayer for rain.

"She has no other memory of her native country," said Mrs. Wheatley. "Ours is the only home she remembers."

"Shortly after the Wheatleys took her in," the Reverend rumbled on, "Phillis exhibited an interest in reading."

Mrs. Wheatley smiled. "With instruction from our older daughter, she learned to read the New Testament."

Esakka recalled his own difficulties learning to read and write and could not help grinning. Phillis observed Esakka's response and positively beamed, although once having caught his eyes, she immediately lowered hers.

"One day, we discovered Phillis using a piece of charcoal to scratch letters on an old brick wall near the barn," Mrs. Wheatley said. "We were astonished to find she had written a poem."

Esakka knew he could never write a poem and gazed on Phillis with renewed admiration. When Reverend Harrison waved his hand for another sweet biscuit, Esakka carried the tray to him. He would employ that as an excuse to hover near Phillis.

"Please tell us, does Phillis perform any household duties?" Mrs. Seney asked.

Esakka detected a slightly shrill tone in his mistress' voice and was certain she thought Phillis should perform a number of duties about the house.

"Phillis enjoys polishing my dining room table until she sees her reflection in it! But other than keeping her own quarters clean, she has no assigned duties. We treat her just as if she were our own daughter."

"And what course is her education taking?" asked Mrs. Seney. Esakka felt sure his mistress did not approve of this educating of slaves.

"The girl is forever reading and studying," Reverend Harrison said. "Her ambition is to translate part of Ovid."

"Ovid?" echoed Mrs. Seney. "The Roman poet?"

Mr. Seney promptly cut his wife off by saying, "Very praiseworthy."

Mrs. Wheatley glanced fondly at her young ward. "Phillis is so delicate, our physician thinks a sea voyage would be beneficial. The salt air is supposed to restore one who is frail."

The Reverend Harrison chuckled as he picked a biscuit crumb from his beard and put it to his mouth. "I do not understand how these doctors reach their decisions. For me, sea travel is terribly enervating. I spend most of the time in my berth and do not eat well at all."

Mrs. Wheatley puckered her brow at Reverend Harrison. "We have an excellent doctor, Reverend. I am sure he knows what is best."

"The Reverend doesn't seem to suffer much from not eating well," Mrs. Seney said with a fulsome smile.

Mrs. Wheatley returned her smile. Esakka thought she had developed a new appreciation for her hostess. However, he wished they would quit the chitchat and let Phillis recite her poems.

"We are thinking of letting Phillis travel to the Mother Country with my son Nathaniel."

"Our oldest son Jonathan is studying law at Inns of Court in London," Solomon Seney said. "He will be home in the spring to conduct his practice."

"He's sending us his portrait done by Sir Joshua Reynolds," Mrs. Seney gushed. "May I inquire, Mrs. Wheatley, what your son will do in England?"

"He plans on setting up an export-import trade between the

Colonies and London," Mrs. Wheatley said. "He will go there himself to make sure he acquires the proper connections."

Mrs. Seney fluttered a small blue fan and spoke with authority. "Please advise him to make sure that he has a cabin porthole for fresh air."

"Oh, he has the very best accommodations on the *Elizabeth*," Mrs. Wheatley assured her.

"Oh yes, I am familiar with that vessel. Your son may want to take along some vinegar to keep his room sanative," Mrs. Seney continued with conviction. "And he will want to carry with him some of his favorite bonbons to relieve the boredom of hoecake."

Reverend Harrison cleared his throat. "Young Mr. Wheatley expects to be dining at the Captain's table."

"Nevertheless," Mrs. Seney said, "a few of his favorite tidbits will keep him from resorting to strong drink."

"Oh, my dear hostess," said Reverend Harrison, "Nathan is a total abstainer."

Esakka thought Mrs. Seney had worn out her fulsome smile, but she came up another one.

"That he may be, but three weeks of pease porridge will drive any man to hard liquor."

Esakka was relieved that Mr. Seney brought the discussion of Nathaniel Wheatley's personal habits to an end. "I'm certain Mr. Wheatley will understand our needs better than those who have never visited the Colonies."

"Not to mention our climate." Reverend Harrison reached for another sweet biscuit.

"This is thrilling news," said Mrs. Seney. "No doubt your son will find us some genuine China. I would like to add a piece or two to my Peacock's Eye pattern."

Esakka thought about suggesting they let Phillis get on with reciting her poem, but he knew Mrs. Seney would banish him from the room. And probably Phillis would be most dismayed of all.

The Reverend lifted his teacup to his lips, then stopped and glanced into it, a dubious expression on his face. "I will be happy if he can find us some decent tea."

"Jonathan sent us some Darjeeling from London," Mrs. Seney said. "It was just marvelous. Everything we buy locally seems to have been tampered with."

Reverend Harrison checked his beard again for crumbs. Finding a raisin, he removed it carefully and laid it on his plate. "Good leaves are adulterated before they make it to the shopkeepers. You no doubt have the same problems we have in the Massachusetts Colony."

Mrs. Seney looked at her own cup with an apologetic expression. "No matter where we buy it, it's corrupted with sassafras leaves."

A murmuring of sympathy went around the circle.

"Well, it would be our pleasure to hear Phillis deliver some of her poems," Mr. Seney announced.

Esakka whispered *Praiseworthy* under his breath.

When Phillis rose to recite, her posture was faultless and her voice soft and clear. "Thank you for inviting me to your lovely home, Mr. and Mrs. Seney. My name is Phillis Wheatley. First, I would like to recite a poem I have written with regard to my origin.

> *" 'Twas mercy brought me from my pagan land,*
> *"Taught my benighted soul to understand,*
> *"That there's a God, that there's a Savior, too.*
> *"Once I redemption neither sought nor knew.*
> *"Some view our sable race with scornful eye:*
> *"Their color, they say, is a diabolic dye.*
> *"Remember Christians, Negroes black as Cain,*
> *"May be refined and join the angelic train."*

When Phillis finished her recitation, the group smiled and applauded. Phillis offered another short poem and the morning progressed rapidly. More guests arrived. Mrs. Seney suggested the ladies repair to the powder rooms to freshen up for the afternoon's entertainment.

Like a daughter, Phillis followed Mrs. Wheatley.

Mr. Seney took the gentlemen outdoors for a tour of his tobacco barns. Esakka was left to clean up the remains of the morning tea, but he did it somewhat absently as he reflected on the young poet's virtues, imagining what lovely poems she might write him if they were betrothed.

On the lawn overlooking the Chester River, Phillis recited more of her poems. Then she curtsied to a round of applause. The program concluded with a brief sermon by Reverend Harrison, including an account of the fire that destroyed the Boston church.

Mrs. Seney's sister Sarah played the Philadelphia spinet. A large woman, she dressed as if going either to church or a ball. Unkind souls had been known to add, "or to hell."

Sarah's headdress was straight out of Gainsborough, a wide brimmed hat pinned to one side, sweeping ostrich feathers on the other. Her rose satin dress gasconaded with gold lace looped across the bodice that bobbled as she sang, "When I Can Read my Title Clear to Mansions in the Skies". As Sarah concluded the hymn, the alms basket was passed and the guests dropped their gifts in.

A lavish table was laid including roast pork, lamb, and fish, accompanied by turnips, yams, corn, and various breads. Dessert consisted of a Huguenot torte made from apples and pecans, piled high with whipped cream. The gentlemen smoked fine Maryland cigars and sampled Mr. Seney's brandy.

The mild afternoon turned chilly as the fog-laden evening air rolled in, but the party ended on a most successful note.

At the idea of Phillis departing after such a brief interlude, Esakka's heart ached in a manner that he had never before experienced. His mind seemed to have no control over his behavior. It kept reminding him he was jeopardizing his freedom sum, but his heart urged him to follow Phillis, and that was what he decided he would do.

IX

Tempt not the stars, young man
John Ford
The Broken Heart

Late that evening, the party from Boston waited for the Broad Creek Ferry to return to Kent and transport them across Chesapeake Bay to Annapolis.

When the party left for the ferry, Esakka excused himself to Mr. Seney, saying he did not feel well. He headed for his quarters, then back-tracked to trail behind the Boston group.

He wanted to keep Phillis in sight as long as he could. He hoped he would find an opportunity to speak with her again, although he had not the courage to approach her. Moreover, he did not want anyone to discover he was abroad without his master's permission.

A large crowd waited for the ferry to dock on the peninsula shore. The fog had increased. The air was extremely damp, but there was a pleasant spirit in the group. Several hummed music from an evening church service.

Esakka went unnoticed except for Josie, the possessor of the high chirping voice, who was traveling to Annapolis with her mistress. She spotted Esakka at once. As soon as she could escape from Mrs. Adams, she sidled over to him.

"Mr. Esakka! Where you be headed for?"

Grateful that Josie had enough sense to modulate her tones, Esakka nevertheless broke out in a cold sweat. His intention was to ride across the Bay, keep his eyes on Miss Phillis a few moments longer, and return home on the next ferry. Now, this silly little flirt had shown up!

Another traveler's busy eyes also observed Esakka. Friar Redmond stayed back, however, until Esakka satisfied Josie's curiosity. As soon as she departed, the priest moved in.

Unaware of the Redmond's incarceration, Esakka did not realize his chirpy disposition was the result of his release from the Anneville jail that very morning.

Redmond had pled the Book, rehearsed the Catechism and preached nearly an hour-long sermon before the sheriff agreed to consult Judge Payne. Although the man reeked of raw whisky, the judge concurred the scragging post would go wanting. The judge hated to disappoint the large crowd of people who had gathered to witness the event, but Redmond looked nothing like the man sentenced to die, and as much as the judge would have liked to accommodate the crowd, hanging the wrong man went against his better nature.

Redmond approached Esakka from the rear. Dryly, he said, "I see you need no help from me in meeting young ladies."

Esakka flinched as he recognized the man's voice.

Attired in a new cassock, courtesy of a local priest, Redmond proudly wore Esakka's black Kevenhuller hat. With its wide brim and high cock, Esakka thought it far too fancy for a clergyman.

Esakka was uncomfortable at being discovered but managed to say, "Good evening, Sirrah."

Facing the red-complected charlatan, Esakka knew he had to be polite. There were too many people waiting for the ferry. Had there been no one around, he would have punched the thieving priest and reclaimed his hat.

"You seem to be pursued by one member of the fair sex while pursuing another," Redmond said.

"That's Miss Phillis Wheatley of Boston. She's traveling with her mistress and the minister of her church. Miss Wheatley read some of her poetry at my master's plantation. They are collecting money for St. Paul's church in Boston which was destroyed by fire."

"Carrying hefty sums, I'll bet?" asked Redmond.

"Perhaps." Esakka had no interest in the money.

"Are you employed as her bodyguard?"

"My master said just to follow along and make sure that no trouble befell her," Esakka lied. The padre had provided him with an excellent reason for his trip. "She doesn't carry the money on her person. I think the Reverend has it."

"Then she ought to be safe from the villains that inhabit these lovely parts," said Redmond.

Esakka wondered if the priest counted himself among those he belittled and hoped the voguish Kevenhuller hat would be the man's undoing.

𝒳

They all fell to playing the game . . .
till the gun powder ran out . . . .
Samuel Foote
Harry and Lucy Concluded

𝔄t that very moment, Makepeace was on the opposite shore, proudly decked out in Redmond's old cassock and sombrero. He had no idea that the fake priest had escaped the noose.

Makepeace thoroughly enjoyed wearing the priestly garb. He had no intention of casting it aside. He had gained enough confidence in his ruse to continue as if he carried a letter from the Roman Catholic Pope.

With Makepeace were two old friends he had chanced upon in the back streets of Annapolis. They were responsible for his delay in heading to Baltimore Town. Those two were Sooty Sam and Juan Pedro, two who cared not what sacrilege, treason or mischief they committed.

Sooty's name derived from the fact that he sometimes engaged in chimney cleaning, generally when it proved favorable for casing a house he intended to pillage. During the epidemic of '58, Sooty suffered a fierce bout with the smallpox. His face resembled a shriveled sponge. Being somewhat allergic to bathing, he was covered with chimney dust and other earthy residue. His hat was so innate with soot that if he deigned to lift it in courtesy, he left the prints of his fingers.

Juan Pedro was from Barcelona and pretended to speak very little English. When it was to his advantage, he understood it quite well. He constantly honed his knife or polished his pistol, only two of an assortment of weapons he carried. Scarcely five feet tall, he sneaked in and out of crowds like a cat and was peerless when it came to cruising for booty.

Makepeace would never turn his back on those two. Neither one could be considered a contributing citizen to the virtue of the Commonwealth. He reckoned the only law Pedro adhered to was the law of gravity, not withstanding Pedro would little understand its principles.

Sooty often claimed that God had given him his gift of cheating, and it seemed at times that Juan Pedro was in a contest with Sooty as to who had received the greater talent.

The city was up to its neck in gossip about the Boston party. Makepeace had forgotten his vow to leave God in charge of his itinerary and could not resist any opportunity to pack his pockets. He and his friends spent the afternoon flinging dust in people's eyes, then taking turns pretending to assist the blinded victim while the other robbed him. The pickings were poor. A new device was required.

"My plan is to rob the church party. We'll pull the friggin' girl aside," Makepeace told his cohorts. "Cause as much fracas as possible. They'll be looking for the stable hands to show up with their horses. We'll fire our guns and stampede the bloody horses. During the hubble-bubble, Sooty, you knock the Jesus reverend out of the picture. Search him for the money. Juan Pedro, you have a bloody go at the young black bitch—"

Juan Pedro gave him a donkey smile.

Makepeace knew what the Spanish joker was thinking. "I don't mean tickle her doodle sack, Juan Pedro. She won't be carrying the money, but I want her out of my way. We might use her for a ransom. I'll take care of the old whore. She's bound to have some money on her and maybe some gold jewelry."

"Aye, aye." On Sooty's withered face, his grin looked more like a leer. The glow of the flares lighting the wharf reflected on his black teeth. "It's our friggin' night, all right. Knocking folks around and collecting coins for it!"

Juan Pedro fidgeted with excitement. "How am I goin' to know which one to grab?"

Makepeace looked patiently at Juan Pedro. "At this hour of the night, Pee-dro, there ain't going to be any other colored lasses about the docks. Whichever one you see, that's going to be her."

XI

Up to Annapolis I went,
To the City situate on a plain
Where scarce a house can keep out the rain.
The buildings framed with cypress rare
Doth much resemble Southwark Fair.

Ebenezer Cook

The Sot Weed Factor

Ebenezer Cook deplored the conditions in Annapolis when he wrote his poem in 1708. But in the intervening years, the flimsy living quarters surrendered to fashionable structures of Georgian and Palladian design, many created by the premier architects of the Colonies.

The city's original inhabitants, the Susquahanock Indians were not only gone, they were forgotten. Also forgotten were those who followed them, the Puritans and the Pilgrims. Their churches had long since been forfeited to decay and demolition, their graveyards ignored while they sank into oblivion. Of those narrow-minded zealots, no modern citizen coveted a single keepsake.

Fashionable.

Worldly.

As avant-garde as that enjoyed by the royalty on the Old Continent.

That was how Annapolitans wanted to be known.

Frequenting the theater, they often saw two different plays in the same week. They spoke constantly of Sarah Hallam's performance in *Cinthia* and looked forward to her return engagement.

Strolling artists could be hired to paint a portrait at the flick of a well-rolled cigar.

51

Magazines from London and Paris arrived with the ink barely dry. Sheet music was imported just as promptly.

Daily, ships from the seven seas swept into the harbor. Soldiers and sailors of all nationalities drank, dined, and danced at Annapolis taverns and inns. Long piers in the Severne River accommodated the heavier ships. Smaller boats docked close to the town shore, only a few steps from the center of the city.

The city boasted its own fire engine, purchased in 1755 from the Newtham and Reagg Company of London. It pumped water one hundred and fifty feet straight up into the air. A year after its purchase, it saved the Court House and jail from a fire caused by a violent whirlwind.

Near the docks, Makepeace had managed to keep the Boston party in his eye. The slave girl Phillis, her mistress, and the portly, bearded Reverend had been easily recognized as they stepped off the ferry.

Makepeace knew he himself made a damned good appearance. He'd grown a beard and a mustache while in jail. Thanks to a razor he had found in Redmond's pocket, it was neat and well trimmed.

A brazen quality had fallen on him. He fancied the cassock's magic was responsible. His previous chicanery was nothing compared to the boldness with which he operated tonight. He congratulated himself for it as he approached the Boston party.

He was not surprised that Reverend Harrison and Mrs. Wheatley nodded at him with cordiality.

"How are ye, Reverend?" Makepeace asked. He spoke slowly, attempting a roundness of tone such as Filmore would have done. He hoped it lent a ministerial quality to his voice. "Some of the parishioners heard of yer calamity in Boston and took up a collection for ye. It's being held at Saint Anne's. If yer'll follow me, I'll see that ye get it."

"We'll be most happy to accept the donation," said the Reverend Harrison. "Let me tell the livery boys to follow with our horses. Then we'll join you."

"Most kind of your people," said Mrs. Wheatley. She gathered up her hooped skirt and took Phillis' hand. "You Christians on the tidewater are exceptionally generous. Reverend Harrison can mind the horses. Phillis and I will go with you. We have seen a lot of water this evening, but none to drink! Is there a well at the church?"

"Of course, Madam," Makepeace said with a quick lie. "We have the best tasting water in the city. Ye ladies can drink to yer heart's desire."

Harrison headed east on Randall Street for the stables. Makepeace led the ladies northwest toward Church Circle.

Sooty Sam had been tailing Makepeace like a runt pig. But he was now confused. Developments were not proceeding according to plan. Unsure whether to follow Makepeace or the Boston Reverend, Sooty decided to start the riot in the middle of the market.

His pistol finger itched for activity. He tamped the powder, raised the firearm into the air and shot it off with a loud cry, "I'll lump your jolly knobs if you don't give me your silver and gold."

A nervous pedlar grabbed Sooty by the collar and asked what the hell he wanted. Then he turned and yelled to the crowd, "This man is trying to rob me!"

Three Turkish seamen grabbed Sooty and beat him to the ground. One wrenched the pistol from Sooty's fist and tossed it into the water. Kicking Sooty in the posterior, the three sailors then marched toward their vessel. Sooty struggled to his feet and skulked away in the darkness, a beaten dog.

Nor was Juan Pedro aware that Makepeace's plans had turned to dust. Across from the docks, sitting in the capacious shadows on the north end of Middleton's tavern, the Spaniard slurped on a bowl of beer, his eyes fixed on Josie.

Makepeace had told him there would be only one dark-skinned lass, and this was the only one he had seen. He was certain she was the one, because Makepeace had mentioned a padre and there was a priest nearby.

Juan watched as Josie parted company with Esakka. He heard Esakka tell the lass she should go in search of her mistress, in case the lady had not been able to find an apothecary and was in distress.

Delicately tiptoeing up the path toward Middleton's, Josie held her skirts high to keep from soiling them. Earlier, Juan had despaired at the thought of fetching her away from the priest. Now he felt jubilant as she pranced softly toward the edge of his web.

Josie made a turn to the right, strolling in the direction of East Street. Juan Pedro wondered why she was headed for the stables, scarcely a place for a pretty young lass late at night. Figuring she was confused, he tested the blade of his knife and waited eagerly.

Josie sang a little tune. Juan Pedro knew she was trying to allay her fear of the dark and rubbed his thighs in anticipation. She was completely unaware that he lurked in the shadows.

As she passed Middleton's second chimney, Juan slipped from his hiding place. He prowled behind her until he was close enough to grab the back of her hair.

"Don't scream, you pretty piece."

Juan grabbed Josie's hair, twisting it as he pointed his knife in her back. "Give me the friggin' gold in your purse."

Through nervousness or because she thought the idea that she might have any gold was funny, Josie giggled.

Juan Pedro resented the giggle. "What's wrong with you, jingle brains?" He thrust his blade through her bodice and felt it tickle her flesh. A red stain appeared, frightening him because he was fairy sure Makepeace did not want him to kill the girl.

Unable to see Juan, Josie kicked backwards, then tried to twist around so that she could face him. Her efforts caused him to push the knife deeper.

A gargled scream erupted from Josie's throat, followed by moans. Finally, she fashioned a few husky words. "Scabby scoundrel . . . ain't got no money . . . God'll deal . . . with y'ur vile soul."

Concerned that someone might hear her, Juan Pedro dug his dirk deeper into Josie's back. "I'm taking what you got, if it's only your secrets. I'll carve out your heart and feed it to the dogs."

Blood gushed through Josie's bodice and Juan jumped back to avoid being splattered. Josie's head teetered. Starting to swoon, she tilted toward Pedro. His blade slid between her ribs into her thin body all the way to its hilt.

Juan Pedro jerked back his knife. He stared at it. A lump came into his throat. He flung the weapon to the ground as if it were burning his hand. Josie sank with a feeble whimper.

Leaning over, Juan Pedro lifted the fallen girl's skirts, looking for money pockets suspended from her waist. *Nada*. His hands brushed against her still warm body. Through her threadbare shift, he could see the girl's legs. Spiked by the temptation before him, wild urges stirred within him.

Cursing Josie's lack of coins, Juan Pedro decided to help himself to a feel. He knelt between the girl's legs and rubbed himself against her for several minutes. Served her right for having no money for him.

Unaware that Josie was no longer breathing, Juan Pedro reached for the worthless locket hanging around her neck. He snatched it off, then rose and hitched up his breeches. Growling like a pleased dog, he ran into the night.

XII

That blessed word Mesopotamia.
David Garrick
Notes and Queries

Makepeace led Mrs. Wheatley and Phillis along Church Street to the back of Queen Anne's Cathedral. At one side of the building, the transept door stood open. He escorted the two women into the candle-lit interior and suggested they have a seat on the front pew while he went for the alms box. Mrs. Wheatley reminded him that she was thirsty. He promised to bring a pitcher of water when he returned.

Realizing that he was now in the brine and his plans were rapidly turning into sour pickles, Makepeace had no choice except to resign his profitless enterprise. It must have been the influence of the cassock on his soul. He had no desire to assault the young black girl or her mistress, or even ask for their money.

He went back out the door and retraced his steps to Market Place where he was to meet Sooty and Juan. All the way, he prayed he would never again cross paths with those ladies.

Before long, he stumbled across Sooty sitting under a bush on the edge of State Circle. Sooty complained about the beating the crowd had given him and the loss of his pistol. He admitted he had failed.

Sooty had a black eye. Makepeace thought about giving him another. "You friggin' ignoramus, you're not worth sheep muck. Look at ye, all bloodied and beat-up. I ought to add a few more knocks to yer blockhead. I'd punch yer dirty face if it wouldn't create a scene."

"Yeah," grumbled Sooty, "you don't want to be seen disgracing your loverly gown."

Makepeace had not thought about that. A priest boxing a street ruffian was bound to bring a crowd, and who knew which side the local muckworms would take? "Where's Pee-dro?"

Sooty shrugged. "Ain't seen him."

"Friggin' shrimp. I'd box his ears for good, damn the outcome." Makepeace glanced up at the darkening sky. "Ye better stick with me. Let's go find a bowl of beer."

"We ain't got no money, has we?" Sooty asked.

"Fortunately, this magic gown turns up a guinea in its pocket every now and then." Makepeace was not sure that wasn't true. He could have sworn the pockets were empty when he first put on the cassock, and later, he'd found the guinea. But as soon as he spoke to his accomplice, he regretted it. Sooty would thenceforth be watching for a chance to disengage the gown from his possession.

Middleton's Tavern thronged with people. Makepeace wondered if it were a holiday. He pointed to a table on the porch and told Sooty to sit down, then went in and came back with two bowls of beer.

"You're a good man, Father Rot," Sooty said.

"Yeah, but I ain't even taken a drink of this healthy brew and I need to take a leak."

"Oh Father, how you talk," Sooty said. "Why don't you just go down there to the water's edge? Unless you got to squat like a woman in that dress you're wearin'. Can I help you in any way?"

Already the scoundrel was plotting to steal the gown from him. Sooty would have no compunctions about leaving him naked in the alley. Makepeace snarled, "I don't need yer help."

He strolled toward the docks and took care of his business. When he returned to the front side of the building to rejoin Sooty Sam, he found Sooty gone. Both bowls of beer sat empty on the table. Well, what did he expect? He'd left the fox in charge of the henhouse.

Thinking it would be wise to put some distance between himself and the Anneville sheriff, Makepeace elected to head for Baltimore town. To facilitate his trip, he uttered a short prayer. His faith was too feeble, his petition too ponderous to soar heavenward through the brooding night. Providence had no interest in his affairs. The prayer traveled no further than the top of a street torch and fell back, lumpish wax on his heart.

Friar Redmond and Esakka left the docks when the French sailor tired of Redmond's overtures and returned to his ship. Esakka had waited patiently, because he thought the pleasure-seeking priest provided him a good cover, but his stomach had begun to ride grub.

Redmond offered to go into Middleton's Tavern and see if any victuals could be procured. He told Esakka to wait at the door and he would bring something out for him.

Returning several moments later, having taken the opportunity to swill down a beer, Redmond handed Esakka a sack of cheese and sausage. Esakka eagerly bit into some cheddar.

Redmond began dancing. "I have to go back in the alley there and do the necessary thing." He headed for the north end of the tavern.

Esakka had scarcely swallowed his cheese before Redmond returned, a nervous expression on his face. "There's a girl lying back there. Looks hurt. In fact, I think she's ready for the holy water. She's the one you're always talking to."

Esakka followed him to investigate.

Josie lay spiritless in the alley behind the store, her skirts in disarray. Esakka knelt beside her. He cradled her head in his left arm and lifted her right wrist to feel her pulse.

"Josie, Jesus bless you," Esakka said softly. "Are you all right?"

"She's the one you know, isn't she?" Redmond asked. "What do you suppose happened to her?"

At the same time, Mrs. Adams's frantic voice echoed through the streets as she searched for her wayward handmaid. "Josie! Josie! Where are you? Show me your face this moment or I shall beat the daylights out of you."

Mrs. Adams came round the building still shouting. "Josie, Josie, when I find you, I'm going to whip you till you're dead."

Esakka laid Josie down and put his ear to her chest to see if he could hear a heart-beat. "I'm afraid she's gone."

He reached under Josie's body to pull out her twisted skirt so she would be covered. Before he did so, he encountered the knife.

He pulled the blade from beneath her. It dripped with blood. To Esakka's surprise, Redmond removed the Kevenhuller hat from his head and placed it over Josie's privates.

"Oh, dear God!" Mrs. Adams wailed. "Oh, God in his Heavens, what have you done to that poor child? I'm going to faint. God help us!" She turned to Redmond. "Do you know what happened here, Father? Were you in on this?"

Mrs. Adams' screams had alerted the customers inside Middleton's and they swarmed out of the tavern. A muster of drunken sailors surrounded Josie's body. One started chanting, "The Negro killed her. The tar-brush killed her!" The others promptly echoed him.

Redmond stood silently, as if contemplating his next move. Mrs. Adams' accusation caused him to cross himself and he declared, "Like you, Madam, I was just passing by this way when I saw this slave—"

"You were talking to him earlier," Mrs. Adams declared. "I saw you! Don't you deny it."

"Peace, dear lady, you are mistaken. I came upon this wretched scene just as you did. This Negro must be an escaped slave—running away with this girl. For some reason, he's killed her."

Oh dear Jesus, Esakka thought, this priest knows I have been with him the entire evening. Why does he not defend me? Can You not, my Shepherd, inspire Your own priest to care for one of Your sheep? Will You let the man turn me, Your faithful servant, into a scapegoat? Does he fear the law that much? Or does he just hate me for the favor I would not do for him?

The ruckus captured the attention of a strolling Constable. He took one look at the situation and blew his whistle for reinforcements.

Esakka thought about running, but he still hoped Redmond would come to his aid. Down deep, he knew the devil would not. And the word of a Negro against a Man of the Cloth would never be believed. Not even when the man wore the slave's purloined hat on his head.

The Constable listened to Mrs. Adams and then to Redmond. Another peace officer arrived and the Constable ordered the sailors back inside the tavern. He turned to Esakka. "Who's your master?"

"Solomon Seney."

With the back of his hand, the Constable struck Esakka across the face. "Show more respect, you renegade."

"Mister Solomon Seney," Esakka said.

"You're a runaway, aren't you?" the Constable asked. "Every time you show a slave a little charity, they take advantage of you."

Redmond leaned over Josie. He flung a dash of holy water over the lifeless girl, sniffing as he did so. "This scoundrel was following the Boston church party with hopes of robbing them so he and this girl could elope. From the looks of things, it was jerry-cum-mumble before he killed her."

"I never did trust her," whined Mrs. Adams. "She was a terrible flirt. I saw her talking to that slave a number of times."

Redmond crossed himself. "The son of a black whore deserves to be hanged."

"No doubt he will be," the Constable said. He took a leather thong from his pocket and tied Esakka's hands behind his back.

"A well-deserved jail cell," Redmond added, "will cool off that hot African blood."

XIII

Oft shifts her passions, like the inconstant wind.
                                                    John Gay
                                                    Epistle to a Lady

Beneath a canopy of oak and sassafras trees, Richard Makepeace sat on the Severne River banks and contemplated his circumstances. Not having a roof over his head was not a problem he deemed worth consideration. But he was sick of the mulligrubs from eating some hay he'd filched from a horse's feedbag, having been as hungry as the night he broke into Jarvis Adams' house.

And not a solitary coin in his possession. Sooty Sam seemed to have picked his pocket of the shillings left after he had purchased that grimy chimneysweep a beer at Middleton's.

Then Makepeace contemplated his good luck. Lucky not to be hanged. Lucky to be rid of that prating blockhead Pedro and Sooty. Lucky to have come into possession of the black cassock and the sombrero. Maybe the cassock would turn up some more coins.

At first, he was quite nervous in public for fear God had written imposter over his head and the faithful would have no problem discovering he was a fraud. But no one looked at him twice. If they did, he pretended to be praying. Strangers seemed to respect his privacy and neither approached nor uttered a word. His only other fear was that the sheriff had sent a bounty hunter after him, but then again, who would contract to insult every holy man on the streets to see if he were a real priest?

Strangely, Makepeace found himself sincere about a couple of prayers. Not that he had never prayed before. Every time he had ever been accosted by a victim of theft, he had uttered a brief prayer for the Almighty Father to save him from jail. Now, each time he prayed, he felt surprisingly pious. He pondered whether or not those feelings were trustworthy.

But lurking in the shadows of that thought was the idea that God might punish him for wearing the holy garment. Perhaps he should not claim that he was a priest—it would be best if he just let the public assume it. Perhaps then, the angels would not blame him for impersonating a holy father.

When Makepeace started for Baltimore Town, the only way to travel was by ankle power. He had no money to hire a horse, much less a chariot. At worst, it would be no more than a three-day journey. With no belongings to carry, it couldn't be too difficult.

The path was well worn. Oak, sycamore and mulberry trees provided plenty of shelter from the sun. The frequent drumming of a woodpecker or the discordant cry of a jay fractured the rustling harmony of tree leaves.

Shortly after he started, Makepeace discovered those with comfortable modes of travel were willing to share them with a frocked father. At times he rode in a coach or on a spare horse. Once a non-believer gave him a ride in his buggy. The man enjoyed harassing Catholics and kept at it during their entire time together. Makepeace suffered the annoyance in silence and felt pious for doing so. The next time he would deny being Catholic. Maybe that would be a star in his favor, telling the truth like that. No doubt, they would immediately assume he was Anglican and he would just smile knowingly, remembering not to present himself as that which he was not.

Then he encountered Drury McCawley, a lad several years younger than himself. While Drury was friendly in his way, and seemed conscientiously honest, Makepeace thought him as little acquainted with the world as a suckling child. He had no fear Drury would see through his disguise.

Drury sat atop a roan, a lean, lank horse as sorry as a worn-out jade, not nearly as prime as the mule that trailed her on a rope. Makepeace looked the animals over. He would be quite happy to be the owner of either one.

"Me employer's sold this mule to the Clankenbell Livery stable in Baltimore Town," Drury said. "This here roan is my own horse

Lucy. I guess the trappings are a little fancy for the old gal—she'll be twenty-two year old come the new grass—so she deserves something."

Makepeace ran his fingers over the roan's blue quilted saddle garnished with a row of gold-headed studs. The gear was probably worth twice the animal's value. Drury talked about the numerous ailments Lucy had recently suffered, and the various tonics he had employed.

"How about a turnout to pasture for the old gal?" If he stole the roan, Makepeace vowed he give the worn animal a handsome retirement, thus easing his guilt.

Drury hooted good-naturedly. "She's about ready for the glue cooker, but I'd sure hate to part with her. "Mule's called Nelly. It'll be all right if you ride her. She ain't got no saddle, but she's better'n shank's mare."

They rode side by side, Makepeace on the mule bareback except for a ragged blanket, his cassock pulled above his knees so that his bare legs hugged the animal's sides.

In spite of her decrepit condition, Lucy managed a prance every now and then, and succeeded in outdistancing the dark gray mule, who was a marked plodder. Eying the blue saddle, Makepeace wondered if it would fit on the mule.

Drury said, "I've got to ride ten more miles today. That's about all I can do, slow as Nelly is. Me employer gave me funds to spend the night at an ordinary and I hope to get there by twilight. I got orders not to let anyone ride that mule, but I'm sure me employer don't expect me to refuse a parson. Tain't seemly for a Man of the Cloth to be seen walking."

"Yer a kind soul," Makepeace said.

Hourly, they stopped to water and rest the animals, seeking shade under the pines and lacy hemlocks. Makepeace ruminated that two animals would be a nuisance, but the mule would make his trip an easy task. God's sun would surely shine on his path.

"Nelly has got to be fresh when I deliver her," Drury said. "If she looks tired, they might turn her down. They've already paid for her so I'd have to walk her back to Annapolis."

Several times, the road passed through farms and the farmer came out to collect his toll. Drury paid with a smile and a salute.

Midday, they stopped on a wooded hillside by a shallow part of the river. Drury removed the worn blanket from the mule and spread it on the ground. Makepeace stretched out on it, the first time he'd lain down since escaping the Anneville jail.

While the animals enjoyed the sweet water and a browse on the grass, Drury sought Makepeace's advice. "Me employer's been good to me and I enjoy life in Annapolis, but something is calling me to Baltimore Town."

Drury pulled several chestnuts from his gunny bag and shared them with Makepeace. "I feel something in me gut. I don't know if it means I'm being drawn to a pretty fortune or to a young lady to marry."

Makepeace clapped Drury on the arm. "Perhaps the young lady will have a pretty fortune. Or vice versa. Then ye wouldn't have to worry with buying and selling mules. Would ye mind taking me flask down to the stream and filling it with cool water?"

He handed Drury the pewter flask he had liberated from Redmond. When Drury brought it back, he said, "I rinsed it out, Father. It smelled of strong liquor."

"For medicinal purposes for my friends," said Makepeace. "I ain't never made use of it meself."

"I been well most of me life and ain't had no need of such medicine." Drury crossed himself. "Finding a man of good senses and a kind nature like yourself was a Godsend. I ain't Catholic meself, but I have no quarrel with those who are." Drury stood and whistled for Lucy and Nelly. "There are a lot of crooks on this road, but I feel safe with a man of God."

"The world is full of scoundrels and jackanapes, Mr. McCawley." Makepeace felt like a snake in the brooder. He had not formulated a plan for stealing the mule but it was incessantly on his mind.

"Have ye a family?"

"Me father deserted me mother for a dairy maid. Soon after that, he went to the Canadas to fight in the Indian wars. We never heard from him again." Drury brushed Lucy's neck and fed her an apple. "When my mother took up with a river pilot, I was left to take care of meself."

"How old was ye?"

64

"Only fourteen, but my Uncle John provided for me the last three years and helped me find work."

"Ye're almost marrying age. I thought of marrying and settling down at yer age. Fell in love with a pretty young lady, but she gave me the jilt."

Makepeace made it up as he went along. He took the brush from Drury and stroked Nelly's back with it. The mule seemed to enjoy the touch of his hand. Perhaps she too was thinking how pleasant a master he would make. Surely, God did not want a Man of the Cloth continuing such a long journey on foot.

Makepeace continued his tale. "A good natured, devoted young lady for whose affection I weren't the only one burning. And not the only one whose fires she enjoyed extinguishing. Me heart was so busted, I didn't know what to do."

"You made a right good choice becoming a Man of the Cloth," said Drury. "You got that air about you."

"As I said before, ye are a kind soul."

As the sun ducked below the clouds on the western horizon, Drury suggested Makepeace spend the night with him at the roadside inn at Dorrs Corner. Having made this trip several times, he said he was acquainted with the innkeeper.

"It's called The Indian Princess and it's a real fancy place. Feather mattresses on all the beds. Looking glasses and pictures on the walls. The food's good and the innkeeper don't allow no card playing or billiards."

Makepeace started to say that was a shame. Then he remembered his new identity. With a straight face, he offered to share the cost with Drury, although he had nothing. He checked the pockets of Redmond's cassock, but no coins had shown up. Maybe a few magic words were required. But a night at the inn could prove quite opportune. When Drury was sound asleep, he would take the mule from the stables and head west. The stable keeper would never question a clergyman about taking the animal.

The Indian Princess Inn was a two story log building with a dormered attic. A long porch stretched across the front of the building. Inside, the primary floor was filled with rough-hewn tables and benches.

The Pickled Dog Caper

Across one end, a large fireplace roared. Two slave women stood at the hearth, tending kettles and pots. The smell of cooking venison and stale beer filled the air.

Completely bald, the innkeeper greeted them like lost leprechauns, himself a troll of a man with salty eyes and a peppery beard. He refused to charge Makepeace a single shilling and in the same breath, advised Drury he need pay no more than half-price for supper and bed, adding, "And I'll waive the fee for stabling the animals."

"Bless yer soul," Makepeace said. "Ye are a true saint." The words fell from his lips with such grace, Makepeace himself was amazed.

The innkeeper instructed his daughter Melicia to escort them to their room. The girl was about Drury's age and Makepeace suspected she was the reason Drury liked the inn. When he saw her wink at Drury with obvious good humor, he was certain.

Melicia was bountifully good-natured. A country beauty she might be, but Makepeace reckoned she was hexed daily by handsome young soldiers, clever traveling men, perhaps moneyed squires. Her raw charms could certainly ignite fires.

Taking a candle, Melicia led them to the second floor, swishing her un-bustled hips as the men followed her up the stairway. Drury looked back at Makepeace to see if he appreciated the display. Makepeace gave him a wry grin.

With its bare wood walls, the room was humble, but as Drury promised, it did indeed have a clouded mirror and a print of the English countryside. Two iron beds, a bench and a table completed the furnishings. Nails on the wall provided a hanging place for garments.

As Melicia's candle crowded out the darkness of the room, Makepeace noticed one bed was occupied by a short fat man. Minus his shoes, but otherwise fully clothed, he lay sleeping atop the blankets.

"That's the pedlar in that bed," said Melicia. "Drury, you and the preacher got the other one. Mr. Pedlar, I brought you some respectable persons to share your room with."

The pedlar opened his eyes and gawked at Makepeace. "If he's the real thing."

66

Makepeace blanched, but pretended not to have heard the man's comment.

"You remember me, Mister Pedlar?" Drury asked. "We stayed together last summer. I bought a iron spike from you."

The pedlar grinned broadly. "So I do, me boy. Pleased to see you again."

"You can trust the reverend," Drury said. "I been traveling a ways with him and he's a good religious man."

"Pleased to share the room with Your Worship. After what happened to me three days ago, I'm glad to have someone trustworthy around me."

"God bless ye," Makepeace offered. He sat on the edge of the bed and took off his shoes, a musty aroma wafting up from his tender toes.

Melicia glanced at his feet. "If you want to wash up, you can take that basin on the table and get some water from the well. I'd do it for you, but I don't wash nobody's feet."

Makepeace nodded absently. He thought he would head for the well and just take the mule. Then again, he recollected how tired he was and decided he could wait until nearer daybreak.

The girl kept talking. "The pedlar's locked his bags in the storeroom for the night. He's holding back a yard of lace for me, so if you look at it in the morning, don't make a mistake and buy it."

"If I bought it, I'd give it you," Drury said. "Though that ain't necessarily a promise—buying it, I mean."

Melicia giggled and jabbed the candle into a wall sconce. She fluffed the feather bed on the side opposite where Makepeace sat, chatting about the weather.

The candle burned brightly a few moments before Makepeace walked over and squeezed the wick between his thumb and forefinger. Taking off his gown, he hung it on a nail between the beds and put the sombrero on top of it. Then he fell into bed and pulled up the blanket.

On the other side of the bed, Melicia helped Drury off with his boots and sat down beside him. Except for the moon shining through a shuttered window, the room was dark.

Suddenly, the pedlar rose and checked the corners of the room. This he followed with a look under both beds and then he knelt beside his. In a loud voice, he stuttered through a long prayer.

The pedlar's prayer included a litany of each article in his wagon. Makepeace wondered if he was trying to sell the stuff to God, until he realized the man sought divine help.

Drury leaned over and equally loud, declared, "God ain't deaf, pedlar friend."

His words were a waste. Ecstatic to be in the presence of his Lord, the more the pedlar prayed, the more excited he became. The more excited he became, the more he stuttered.

"Those six beauteous, embroidered egg-bags I traded those s-sweet nuns for, Lord, so they could have a new pair of s-scissors, you know, Lord, how me heart went out to those s-sweet ladies. I knowed those egg-bags would be hard to get rid of—fancy as they are—but Lord, I have the faith you will send me a farmer's wife who can appreciate them."

Drury and the innkeeper's daughter were whispering and giggling. Were they not so close, Makepeace would not have heard them for the pedlar's loud prayer. Their activities did not abate when the pedlar took them into the presence of God, nor were they hampered by the proximity of a priest.

"And Gracious Lord," continued the pedlar, "bless my friend here, the P-Papist father, and his young friend. And keep us safe for the morrow. And don't let no more robbers find me."

Makepeace said, "Amen."

"Drury," whispered Melicia in a stage voice, "would you help me tie these laces on my bodice?"

"I'm not very good at making knots," Drury said.

"I'll show you how. Put your finger here. No, hold it there. Not your whole hand, Drury! Oh . . . well, reach in there and pull the lace out. Oooh, your fingers are cold."

"They're getting warm fast," Drury stammered. "I got something else here that's mighty hot."

Breathlessly, Melicia piped, "Oooh, so you do! Ooh, Drury . . . oh, oh, oh! That's so nice!"

"Girlie, if you've a mind to drive me wild, you're doing it."

For several minutes Melicia obviously enjoyed herself, but abruptly, she stood up and offered an apology. "Excuse me, Drury. Daddy's going to have a frog if I don't head for the kitchen. Maybe

I'll come back later."

She gave him a noisy kiss and turned to the pedlar. "Do me the pleasure of looking at them egg-bags in the morning."

Drury locked the door behind Melicia, then brought out his iron spike and wedged it between the door and the jamb. "Distresses me some to keep out the good along with the bad, but I got to get me sleep."

Drury removed what clothes the girl had left on him and climbed into bed.

"I do believe these sheets ain't been on this bed before today. Shows what traveling in good company will do for you."

Makepeace awoke three hours later to a violent rocking of his bed. Drury was sound asleep beside him, one leg draped over his groin. Makepeace wanted to move it, but his arm was in the possession of the pedlar, who shook it up and down like a pump handle.

Makepeace fell back in the bed, craving only to return to his slumber, but the pedlar kept pumping his arm. In spite of the man's distress, the pedlar confined his voice to a whisper.

"Father, there's something going on in the next room I want you to s-see. Look there through that knothole. Just look in there! Would you d-do that, now?"

XIII.

... she must have a husband
William Shakespeare
The Taming of the Shrew

𝕸akepeace had no desire to spy on his neighbors. Having walked and ridden an unsaddled mule for a good ten miles, his bones ached. The pedlar continued to yank on his arm. Finally, Makepeace yielded. He trudged over to the knot-hole, the pedlar close behind him.

Through the tiny opening, he could see into the adjoining room. A tallow candle provided the only light. Melicia sat on a wood chair before a tea table. Except for her petticoat and the camisole covering her bosom, the girl had removed all her clothing. Even her feet were bare.

Standing opposite her was a hairy-chested, heavy-set, brown-bearded man. His shirt and boots lay on the floor beside the table. He was at least twice the girl's age. He dangled a pearl necklace in Melicia's face.

Every word could be heard through the wall.

"Do you like this pretty necklace, dearie? It's yours if you take off your camisole."

"It'll take more than that to snatch off me camisole."

Makepeace eyed a pile of trinkets on the table: rings, bracelets, scissors, a thimble. Melicia's proprietary right hand rested on the baubles. Her left hand tugged on the neck of her camisole, pulling it down to reveal the separation of her breasts. Makepeace was certain the girl had played this game before.

The man dropped the necklace onto Melicia's pile and picked a dainty watch from his treasure trove. "How about this timepiece, honey? It's got Swiss works in it."

"Don't need no watch. Can't tell time, you jackass. Anyway, you ain't took nothing off lately."

The man eagerly removed his brown breeches, folded them and laid them on the chair. "I'm down to me drawers. How's that?"

"All right, give me the watch. What else you got?"

The man cradled his privates with his left hand. "I got plenty here you're gonna like."

The pedlar turned to Makepeace. "You see that s-stuff he's got? It's mine." His voice rose above a whisper and Makepeace pulled him back from the knothole. The pedlar shook like an aspen leaf. "That's the s-same pop and galloper what robbed me with a pistol three days ago. The devil's trying to give my stuff to that girl, now."

Makepeace chuckled low. "Looks like he's succeeding. If we don't stay away from the wall, he's going to hear us. Thank God, he ain't already heard ye and come in here with his pops ablaze."

The pedlar went back to his bed, wrapped himself in a blanket and huddled on the side of the mattress. His stuttering grew worse. "D-did you see all that s-stuff he's got? It ain't all mine. I ain't the only one he's robbed!"

Makepeace took another blanket, wrapped it around his shoulders and sat beside the pedlar. "Ye better go back to sleep and pretend ye ain't seen nothing."

The pedlar moaned and doubled up like a child. "Father, that crook is frittering away my profits."

"Methinks yer profit may be in keeping yer life." Makepeace was amazed at the wisdom falling from his lips. There must be genuine magic in that black robe, even when it hung from a nail on the wall.

The pedlar bobbed his head and whimpered.

"Yer life is more dear than those trinkets, ain't it?" Many a time Makepeace had asked himself that same question when about to embark on a corrupt enterprise. By and large, he ignored it.

Makepeace felt a rumble in his abdomen. "Is there a chamber pot in here? All this commotion had stirred up my bowels. Is the porcelain under yer bed, pedlar?"

"That's where I p-put it."

The pedlar reached under his bed and brought out the china

commode. Although it was covered, Makepeace was already grimacing as it was handed to him. Opening it, he cursed mightily.

"By God's rear end, me nose was never entertained by such a foul smell. Did ye do this? Ye ain't even put any salts on it."

"Beggin' your Father's pardon," said the pedlar. "I always do that after my evening prayer. Please, Your Worship, t-toss it out the window and be done with it."

At that moment, an uproar burst forth in the adjacent room. Makepeace slapped the cover on the chamber pot and shoved it back under the bed. He ran for the knothole, followed closely by the pedlar.

The innkeeper had charged into the thief's room. Melicia still sat at the table opposite the highwayman, but now wore only her half-slip, her lovely breasts radiant in the candle-light.

The innkeeper brandished a sword in his right hand. He thrust it against the highwayman's groin. "You bloody child-spoiler! I've got a good mind to cut off your friggin' member!"

The highway man danced back from the sword and scurried toward the window. The innkeeper tossed the sword aside and pulled out a pistol. He tamped the powder and pulled the trigger. An ear-banging flash of fire was followed by a cloud of smoke. The bullet missed the thief and penetrated the wall, whickering past Makepeace's chin.

Makepeace swiped his chin and kept his eye glued to the knot hole. The highwayman jerked the shutters open and struggled through the casement, jumping without hesitation.

Makepeace and the pedlar ran to their window. Just as the robber hit the ground, his right ankle twisted under him. The pedlar grabbed the chamber pot from under the bed and tossed it at the thief. Whacking him in the back, the pot splattered its loathsome contents on his person. Cursing vigorously, the thief hobbled toward the stables.

At last, the commotion awoke Drury. Sitting up in bed, he rubbed sleep from his bleary eyes. "I been having dreams about someone shooting at me."

Another shot resonated as the innkeeper fired again. Drury

jumped out of bed and scuttled beneath it.

"Barking irons! Barking irons!"

The pedlar turned from the window and shook his finger. "You're lucky you ain't the t-target."

From the window, Makepeace watched Melicia's father vault through the adjoining opening and then dash toward the stables.

"Get to your room, daughter," the innkeeper yelled back. "I'll take care of you later!"

The pedlar jumped into his breeches, scurried toward the door and yanked Drury's iron spike from the door jamb. He tossed it aside, barely missing Drury's head, then rushed out to join the pursuit of the thief.

Makepeace turned to Drury. "Back to bed for me. Why don't you take the pedlar's bed? We might as well enjoy a little peace and privacy."

Makepeace crawled back into the clean-sheeted bed and Drury took the pedlar's. The two were soon snoring.

An hour later, Drury's coughing and choking awakened Makepeace. A red glow penetrated the room. At first, he thought the sun was up. Then he noticed the thickening haze. His nostrils smarted from the smoke. He jumped out of bed, trembling in the cold, and shook Drury awake.

"Fire! The inn's on fire!"

Drury bounded from his bed and staggered about the room. When he found his drawers, he jumped into them, and began a search for his breeches. Makepeace ignored the boy and opened the door to check the commotion in the hallway.

In the dark, confusion governed the naked and half-naked guests moaning and clutching their possessions as they milled the passageway.

"I can't find me clothes!" Drury bellowed. "And me poor darling's bound to be in trouble."

"That she is," Makepeace said dryly.

Drury shoved Makepeace out the doorway. Wearing only his drawers, he charged into the corridor. "Melicia!" he yelled.

Makepeace hesitated, considering whether it would not be a

profitable opportunity to loot a few rooms. Something constrained him. He glanced suspiciously at the black frock hanging on its nail. Could it have that kind of influence on him when it hung on the wall?

The room grew warmer and it became obvious he had better get out. Throwing the gown over his head, he clamped on the hat and returned to the hall. At each end of the hallway, he saw a staircase. The one extending back from the highwayman's room was aflame, merrily lighting that end of the building.

The stairway close by Makepeace was dark and a number of guests huddled there. Then someone appeared with a candle and the jittery lodgers streamed downward. Makepeace looked about for the innkeeper. Not in sight. Neither was Drury nor Melicia.

A red-jacketed sergeant scurried back and forth, trying to organize a bucket brigade, knocking down whomever he found in his way. He gaped at Makepeace. "Excuse me, Father, why ain't you down on your knees praying?"

The innkeeper appeared at the top of the stairs, going right up to Makepeace. His breath gave evidence that he was fortified by a courage-giving distillation. "You're in charge up here, Father." He turned and hollered down the stairs, "Man the bucket-brigade! Stay in your places. Pass up the buckets!"

The buckets swept up the stairs, flowing from hand to hand. As soon as Makepeace received a bucket, he slung the water at the fire and swagged the bucket to the man below.

Bucket after bucket, sweating like a roast pig, Makepeace sucked air and swallowed smoke. His eyes burned. His throat was raw. Makepeace did his best to staunch the greedy fire's appetite. Several times, he dipped his hand in the bucket, cupping it to carry water to his parched mouth.

Engaged in this thankless task, he worked so hard, he never gave a thought to prayer. Nor had he time to think about absconding with Drury's mule.

Scampering up and down the stairs, Drury stumbled into the bucket brigade. Once he collided with the red-jacketed sergeant, who knocked him to the floor with a blow to his bare stomach and

demanded, "Where'n your clothes, boy?"

Drury rose without a complaint but turned his back on the sergeant and continued his search. He opened each door and bellowed for his beloved. "Meliciaaaa . . . Meliciaaaa!"

Behind a wood door at the center of the hallway, Drury discovered a steep staircase that seemed to lead to the attic. "Meliciaaaa!"

This time there was an answer. "Drury—come up here!"

Drury sprinted up the narrow steps.

Near a dormer window, Melicia fluttered like a wounded bird. As soon as she saw him, she threw her arms about him, pressing her bare breasts against his naked chest. Her brown eyes pleaded for help and tears oozed down her cheeks. Drury put his arms around her and squeezed her tight, surprised at the ecstasy that surged through his own body.

"Girlie, you're in a fine hole now!"

"Oh, Drury, I come up here to hide from Daddy. I'm so scared I can't move. I lost me camisole and I ain't got nothing to cover me tits." She laid her head against his neck and sobbed. "Drury, I'm in such trouble!"

"Now, now," he said with a tender touch, stroking her back and wondering whither he dare let his fingers wander.

Abruptly, the attic floor creaked and groaned. The fire-weakened rafters gave way. Drury and Melicia plunged to the second floor, deposited on their backs.

For only a minute, that floor held. Then it, too, screeched and broke away, dropping them into the tavern's parlor. They landed prostrate at the innkeeper's feet and lay as if dead.

The innkeeper took one look. His bare-breasted daughter lay on top of the half-naked Drury. The innkeeper's hands flew up, his face reddening like new wine. "Fine kettle of fish, that!" He jerked Melicia off Drury and dragged her outside the inn, his chin chomping against his upper lip, mangling whatever words he produced.

The fire under control, the bucket brigade began dispersing. Makepeace joined the crowd in the yard and surveyed what was left of the Indian Princess. Like the wreck of a great ship, she lay cloaked in a charcoal shroud, a husk of her former self. A lot of work would be required to build her back.

Finally, Drury's moaning attracted Makepeace's attention. He walked over to the boy and observed his calamity. "Shut-up, ye fool," he said without heart. "Don't be calling further attention to yerself and yer affliction."

Makepeace reached down to straighten the boy's twisted leg.

"That hurts!" Drury howled. "Oh God, that hurts!"

"Must be broken." Makepeace placed his hands under Drury's armpits and towed him toward a comfortable spot on the grass. Drury whimpered and pleaded for Melicia. Disgusted, Makepeace dragged him to the girl's side, then walked away.

Melicia sat quietly under a tree, her bounteous bare bosom resplendent in the early morning sun. In a show of modesty, she clutched her breasts with her arms, but as soon as she saw Drury, she abandoned all attempts to disguise her endowment. She leaned over the prostrate young man, the pearly pear-shapes dangling against his thigh as she examined his crooked leg.

Drury's eyes focused on the lush white breasts. They seemed to anesthetize him.

Finishing her examination, Melicia began massaging Drury's chest, her expression softening each time she looked at the suffering young man. Spectators gathered round the couple like pickpockets at a hanging. Entranced with this spectacle, they seemed to have forgotten the loss of their own fortunes in the fire.

An old woman ripped the British flag from the pole at the front of the inn and brought it to Melicia.

"Wrap those beauties in this, duckie."

"I'll salute that!" roared Drury.

Melicia had barely covered herself when the innkeeper returned, carrying one of his shirts. His back was arched and his eyes burned like a cat stalking a three-legged mouse. The innkeeper pulled at Melicia's arms, trying to force the shirt over her head.

She shouldered him aside. "That's all right, Daddy. I'm covered."

"If I hadn't forgot my flintlock, that boy would be dead. But I remember now where I left it."

The innkeeper turned, in as great a ferment as a pot of vinegar filled with crab eyes. He hurried toward the hulking, smoking remains of his inn.

Melicia yelled at her father's vanishing backside. "Don't bring no gun out here, old man. I love Drury and I want to marry him. And leave off the whisky."

Increasingly merry, the spectators seated themselves around the pair. Makepeace reached into a bucket of water and wet his face and eyes. He studied his black frock. It was covered with ashes, but there were no holes or tears. Where his black sombrero might be, he had no idea.

Drury tried to rise, but could not. Melicia's breasts were now covered by the Union Jack and the pain of his broken leg pressed heavily on his thoughts.

"Father, Father, I need your help. The innkeeper's going to kill me! You know I ain't done nothing but follow a man's natural inclinations."

Melicia sat beside Drury and placed his head in her lap. She patted his cheek and cooed, "Poor Drury, poor, poor Drury."

"Rest easy, mister," sympathized the Flag-woman. "We'll find you a doctor. Or at least a barber who can bleed off your pain and rid you of your ill humors."

"Don't be ableeding me! I'm hurting enough."

"Ain't no doctor going to touch you, honey." Melicia patted Drury's head, then leaned over and kissed him on the mouth.

The innkeeper reappeared, striding doggedly toward the pair, his flintlock raised over his head. As he passed, Makepeace breathed a whiff of whisky. If the fire in the rifle equaled the whiskey-fire in the old man's belly, Drury was a goner. Makepeace thought he really should interfere, but he could think of no plan.

The innkeeper placed the bore of his gun against Drury's head as it lay in his daughter's lap. "He won't hurt much longer."

Melicia looked up in astonishment. Makepeace saw that if the innkeeper shot Drury through the head, the bullet would go right through the girl's vital parts.

"God preserve us, old man, you're either drunk or you've got the frenzies," Melicia cried, jumping aside.

Drury's head bounced against a tree root. Without a sideways glance, Melicia leaped on her father's back. The innkeeper's nervous finger triggered a blast. The flintlock sprayed the nearby trees. A covey of raucous mockingbirds vacated its limbs.

Melicia rode her father to the ground. The flintlock flew through the air. Melicia jumped off her father, shoved the innkeeper across Drury's injured leg and ran for the weapon. Drury screamed with anguish.

Moments after Melicia picked up the flintlock, she was able to re-prime it with ammunition supplied by a solicitous guest.

Drury was still moaning. With her foot, Melicia urged her father off Drury's leg and pointed the flintlock into the soft flesh of the old man's neck, her finger steady on the trigger.

"You ain't going to shoot no one. I'm getting married and making you some grandbabies."

Melicia held her position and turned toward Makepeace. "Will you move over here, Father Priest? Find us a Bible. Let's get on with the wedding ceremony."

Makepeace blanched, but no one noticed, since his face was covered with soot. He daren't decline. If he volunteered the information he wasn't a real priest, his life would not be worth a counterfeit guinea.

"Is there going to be a wedding?" Drury asked. "I'm hurting awful bad. Maybe you ought to find me a doctor?"

"Don't worry about a doctor," said Melicia. "You're getting married first."

"Go ahead," moaned Drury. "But don't you think I ought to have me breeches on, if I'm going to be a bridegroom?"

Melicia tossed him the shirt her father had brought her. He struggled into it, back to the front.

Someone thrust a Bible into Makepeace's hands. He stared at it, confused. He took the Book and opened it with no idea where to turn. He was concentrating on the first page when a lad came running toward him.

"Your hat, Father. I've got your hat!"

The hat was on the boy's head, practically covering his eyes. He held the strings tight against his chin. "I found it, Father, I found it!"

The crowd laughed.

"I did! I found it!" The boy jerked it off and handed it to Makepeace, but Makepeace was studying the Bible. He took his eyes away for a moment, then stooped down and let the boy put the sombrero on his head.

"Damn it, Father, do your duty and get on with the marrying," commanded Melicia. "There ain't no time to be wasting. Once the knot is tied, the son of a bitch ain't going to shoot his legal son."

The Flag-woman cackled merrily. "If he does, he'll hang for sure. Bless the Lord, if you need any testifying, honey, I'll be glad to do it. If we can't have a wedding, we can have a hanging. One's about as much fun as the other!"

"Wouldn't be for me," Drury said.

Makepeace's eye fell on a passage he hoped would be satisfactory. He moved to the center of the group. Amazed at the steadiness of his nerves, he began to read:

"And Adam said, This is now bone of my bones and flesh of my flesh. She shall be called woman, because she was taken out of man. Therefore shall a man leave his father and his mother—well, this young man's left his folks back in Annapolis, just like the Book says—and he shall cleave unto his wife and they shall be one flesh."

"Bless the Lord, it's so beautiful!" the Flag-woman cried. "Bless the Lord, I say let the young people cleave."

The spectators applauded. Drury had broken out in a sweat, but otherwise, he lay as if dead. Makepeace decided to omit the next line about the couple being naked and not ashamed, although it was close to the truth.

"Ask who giveth this woman in marriage?" ordered Melicia .

"Who gives this woman in marriage?" Makepeace intoned.

"Tell the preacher you do it, Daddy." Melicia ground her foot so hard in her father's stomach, he belched. "You got to do more than gush, you old fart. Put your hand on the damned Bible and say I do!"

Makepeace saw that the innkeeper had neither the strength nor the courage to argue with his daughter. He thrust forth the Bible to accommodate the old man, who carefully placed his hand on the book. "I would. I do. I am."

"So be it."

Makepeace was too slow for Melicia.

"Father, get on with it. Ask do you take this woman as your wife, Mr. McCawley?"

"Do ye take this woman as yer wife, Mr. McCawley?"

"Oh God, yes." Drury reached up and touched the Bible as Makepeace extended it to him. "I most certainly do."

The innkeeper groaned grievously and tried to move. Makepeace thought he was about to rise up, but Melicia pressed the gun barrel tighter against his Adam's apple.

"Get on with it, Father. Give me the damned Bible so I can swear on it."

Makepeace started the next question only to discover Melicia was talking over him. When he came to the part that went "Do ye, Melicia, take this man as yer husband," she answered twice.

"I do, I do, Father. I take this man! I take my darling Drury!"

Makepeace turned to the congregation and smiled. Now that he was nearly through the ceremony, he was enjoying himself, although he wondered how lawful the marriage might be.

"Are there any objections to this marriage?"

"Hell's bells, what's wrong with you, Father?" Melicia raised the flintlock and pointed it at the crowd while pressing her foot deeper into her father's belly. "Be there any objections?"

None were forthcoming.

Melicia turned back to Makepeace. "Pronounce us man and wife!"

Makepeace held the Bible high in the air, his right hand on the open pages. "I pronounce ye man and wife, Mr. and Mrs. Drury McCawley."

The more enthusiastic in the throng gave a rousing cheer. Makepeace decided he had done a good job. Melicia raised her gun and fired it into the air. Scattered buckshot fell over the applauding congregation.

"That makes it official," she declared. "You can get up now, Daddy. You got work to do." She tossed the gun aside.

Makepeace realized there was no way the groom could stand and kiss the bride, but Melicia bent over her new husband and stroked his hair, then smothered him with a long, wet kiss.

An itinerant doctor arrived on the scene as the ceremony was completed. The man had the look of a country gentleman, but the air of a professor. Seeing Drury's predicament, the doctor stroked his short gray beard and took charge at once. He ordered a table brought from the ruins of the inn. Makepeace and the innkeeper assisted in placing Drury on it.

Gingerly feeling the boy's leg, the doctor mumbled incoherently, seeming in profound consultation with himself. Finally, he spoke in a deep voice. "Young man, it's your good fortune that I am carrying my bone-saw with me, for it appears that I shall oblige you with an amputation."

A ground swell of applause greeted his prognosis. Makepeace considered the winking, leering and impious gestures shameful to observe. The Flag-woman fanned her face vigorously. "Oh dear, I do believe the vapors are about to take me. It's downright sinful having so much fun without paying for it."

"This ain't no bloody playhouse," Melicia shouted. "You vultures!"

Drury groaned and turned white. Makepeace thought the boy would pass out.

Melicia moved to pick up the flintlock. She busied herself priming it with more ammunition furnished by the same solicitous guest. Completing the task, she walked over to the doctor and pointed the rifle into his chest.

"Ain't going to be no amputation, you gory-minded two-bit sawbones."

The doctor coughed and gently moved the flintlock aside. "Excuse me, madam, what is your interest in the matter?"

Melicia preened as she moved the flintlock back into position against the doctor's chest. "I'm that man's wife, Mistress Drury McCawley."

The doctor drew himself up to his full-height and an awe-filled silence fell over the crowd. "Madame McCawley, surely you can see that your husband has suffered a virulent confusion of his tibia. Although his pulse is ebullient, it indicates a need for bleeding. If I draw about six pints of blood, you will see that it is extremely glazed as well as gluteus beyond the maximus."

Keeping the flintlock on the doctor's chest, Melicia turned to Makepeace. "Father, do you know what he's talking about?"

"I can safely say I don't understand a monosyllable."

"Well, I regret that I am dealing with people who are so unlearned in the surgeonic methods," said the doctor. "If you will just permit

81

me to proceed with—"

The doctor carefully placed his left hand on the bore of Melicia's weapon and attempted to move it away from his chest.

"If you put your finger on my gun again, you're a dead man, you old quack," Melicia declared. "Repair my husband's leg and forget about cutting it off."

"Madam, surely you realize an amputation is the finest operation a man of the medical sciences can perform?"

The spectators applauded again. Makepeace was unnerved by their keen blood-lust. He thanked God he'd managed to labor through the wedding ceremony without revealing his lack of credentials.

The innkeeper evidently had a change of heart. "Do as my daughter says, Doctor. She don't want no peg-leg for a husband. If it be within your powers, fix that boy's leg. I got plans for him."

Makepeace thought he detected an eagerness to wish the girl and her cheekiness off on Drury. Or maybe the old man realized that Drury could be a big help in rebuilding the inn.

"He's not a bad looking sort," the innkeeper continued. "Got a horse and a mule—traveling with a priest—that speaks well of him." He turned to Drury, "Young man, I hope it don't distress you none, but I got to inform you, Melicia ain't got no fortune."

"It don't make me no mind," said Drury. "If she owns a bed and some linens, that's all I care about." Drury looked at the doctor. "Fix my leg, sir. Just don't do no sawing."

"If that's the way you want it." The doctor's voice reflected his reluctance. "My fee's the same, either way."

"Fee?" Melicia cried. "Why you money-grubbing old fart, doctors are supposed to work for the good of humanity."

"I do but serve God to his glory, Mrs. McCawley. Doctors has to eat and pay for their lodging, and it would appear that your father the innkeeper ain't in a condition to provide neither. You'll find my fee very reasonable. Only a guinea or two, depending on how long it takes."

From what heavenly hierarchy the doctor drew his sanctimonious expression, Makepeace could not divine, but it would have done any saint proud.

"I got a guinea in my pocket," Drury said, "—if I can find my breeches."

"That will be just fine," the doctor said. "And perhaps we will pass a collection basket for those who feel it sinful to observe the artful proceedings without paying."

Makepeace entertained a wicked thought. Perhaps he should slip away and search for Drury's breeches. A guinea would come in mighty handy while traveling down the road. He decided against it. Probably the coin had melted in the ashes.

The doctor took a bottle of blackberry brandy from his black bag and poured several drops into a glass. Drury downed it with a sour face.

While the doctor waited for the anesthetic to take affect, he set about making a splint. "You'll want to follow my advice, Mr. McCawley. Don't be walking on this leg too soon."

"I don't want to be a limper." Drury grinned at Makepeace. "Looks like I'm stuck here for a while, Father. Would you mind delivering that mule to the Clankenbell Livery in Baltimore?"

XV.

Tell us, pray, what devil this . . . which
can transform men into monsters?
John Ford
The Lady's Trial

Stranded in the Annapolis jail, hungry and depressed, Esakka brooded over his predicament. More than seven years had passed since he and his younger sister Ejoja had fallen into the hands of the slavers. Despite his valiant efforts to live a righteous life, the blessings of God no longer sanctified his existence.

When they were first taken, for a few days, he and Ejoja had been kept together. But early one morning, she had been torn from his side and sold to a chieftain who provided harems for rich princes.

Esakka held hope that he might again encounter his sister, perhaps even rescue her, as the traders moved left of the sun toward the seaport where the slave ships docked. That being the main route from the interior of Africa, it did not seem entirely impossible to Esakka that he might stumble on Ejoja. For this, he prayed constantly to the angels whom he believed watched diligently over him.

And those angels seemed to keep him with owners of kind dispositions. The first, an Arabian prince, had never scourged him, although the prince's fifth and youngest wife, Ktura, provided plenty of reason for him to do so.

Impressed with his clean appearance, the prince assigned Esakka to the kitchen. Being only fifteen, Esakka mostly scoured pots and pans or scrubbed vegetables for the heartless old crone in charge of the scullery.

If the old crone was busy elsewhere, Ktura nosed around the

84

young slave boys. When the prince was absent, she pursued Esakka with spirit. Four years older than Esakka, Ktura had been in the prince's seraglio only a short time. The other wives were jealous of her beauty and constantly ridiculed her, but none of that restrained her quest for pleasure. And the younger they were, the better she liked them.

During Esakka's second week, the old crone told him to watch a kettle of beans while she went to the garden to pluck vegetables.

As if by magic, Ktura showed up in the kitchen. Captivated by her alluring ways, Esakka quickly forgot the old crone's instructions, as Ktura's fingers trolled the fabric of his loin cloth while she rubbed against him with her body.

When Ktura left, Esakka was in a daze. He sat down on the floor, thinking only of her pretty face, her soft slimness, her high young breasts . . . and the strange feelings surging through him.

The water in the bean kettle steamed into oblivion. The dreadful burning odor interrupted Esakka's reverie. He knew he must remove the kettle from the fire, but he could not find the pot hook. The kitchen filled with black smoke. He choked, coughed and cried, worried that he would be beaten with cane switches until blood ran down his legs and filled the gaps between his toes.

Esakka darted out the kitchen door. Across the fields he ran, eyes on the lookout for a hiding place. When he glanced back, he saw long fingers of smoke spilling out the windows. They seemed to point toward him.

The old crone hopped from the garden. One moment she screamed prayers and the next she cursed. When she reached the kitchen and smelled the burning beans, she shrieked, "Esakka, I want your blood!"

The slaves charged in and out of the house creating a great commotion. Finally they gathered to form a posse in pursuit of Esakka, eager to catch him before their master returned.

How incredible, Esakka thought as he watched from the top of a sycamore tree. Such efforts put forth to find an unimportant, harmless child! He shinnied down the tree and sprang into the thicket, diving into the tall grasses, not sure where to run next. Several times, the hunting party came close.

"Esakka, I will break your bones!" the old crone cried, but he treasured his hiding place and did not move.

By the time the sun tired of its efforts to broil his corner of the world, the chase halted. Esakka hiked to an oasis where he and Ktura had gone to fetch water during the dry season.

Somewhere, he lost the blue scarf he wore around his loins, the last souvenir of his mother. Completely naked, thirsty, scared and exhausted, he collapsed under a bush and cried himself to sleep.

***

Near mid-night, Ktura arrived at the desert sanctuary. Sound asleep, Esakka did not hear her approach. Leaning over him, she sang softly into his left ear. Esakka sat up, rubbed his eyes and felt sheepish. There was no point in trying to escape. Anyway, he wasn't afraid of Ktura.

"Poor little baby! You ran so far and only Ktura knows where you hide! But you are so sweaty and dirty! And you smell of smoke! Come with me into the water."

She led him by the hand to the center of the shallow pool and sat him down. Taking a vial of oil from her bosom, she knelt behind him and rubbed the sweet scent into his hair and skin.

Esakka said nothing, surprised that a girl washing his hair could be such a pleasing experience. Then he became further entranced as she pressed herself against his back and reached around to massage his chest. Peculiar feelings stirred within him. Ktura surely knows what she's doing, he thought. She must realize her fingers are tingling my spine.

"Stand up, bambino."

Esakka did as told, his back to her as her hands moved up and down his shoulders. Ktura's nimble fingers drew circles over his hard brown back.

"Turn around, my sweet."

"No!" he cried, embarrassed that she should see him.

"Come now, I'm a married woman and you're only a child. Turn around!"

He did as he was told, but crouched with his knees bent, certain she would be offended.

A small sigh escaped Ktura's lips.

86

"You are a man! I had no idea you were so grownup."

He grinned, still not sure whether he should be embarrassed.

Ktura removed her own clothing and let it float across the water. Esakka stared at her firm young body as she knelt before him, captivated by her lovely brown breasts.

Ktura leaned forward and kissed his belly.

"You are so glorious!"

Esakka folded his arms and dug his toes into the sandy bottom of the pool. Locking his knees, he hopelessly tried to stop shuddering. He did not understand this. It must be wrong. But it was so wonderful that he dared not speak for fear it would end. Ktura sent delicious shivers through his body, leaving him giddy as a bumble bee, a feeling he found ever so delightful.

Finally, Ktura pulled him close, anointing him with wet kisses. He pulled back a moment. "Ktura, am I still a virgin?"

She drew him back down into the pool and laved cold water over him. "You are only an innocent bystander, bambino." She took out her vial and washed her hair with the perfumed oil. "We must go home. It will soon be dawn."

Ktura gave him a cotton shawl when they returned. Esakka curled up on his pallet in the kitchen and slept for an hour. When the old crone awakened him, it was as if the beans had never burned. By the time the master returned from his excursion two days later, Esakka thought the mishap had been forgotten.

Three nights the following week, Ktura came and enticed him back to the springs. They would frolic for hours and then return just before dawn cracked the eastern sky.

Each time, Esakka asked, "Ktura, am I still a virgin?"

The woman would lower her eyes and answer the same. "More or less, my sweet."

Esakka would be exhausted the next day. The old crone kept asking if he was sick, looking at him peculiarly, commenting on the lack of energy in one so young. Sometimes the old crone would sneeze and then comment, "What is that sweetness I keep smelling?" But the way she looked at Esakka caused him to believe she knew what was taking place.

Ten days later, Esakka was put in the slave market. When he

saw Ktura on another auction block, he no longer speculated about the reason he was being sold.

And while in the slave market, Esakka thought he saw his sister Ejoja in a group of young girls being shepherded by a seraglio manager. They were gone before he could call her name. But so sure was he that it had been Ejoja, he wept all afternoon.

Then a kindly blacksmith took an interest in Esakka. After purchasing him, the blacksmith took him farther up the sea coast. His new owner was not cruel but he worked Esakka hard, teaching him the trade, but mostly using him to carry iron and steel back and forth from one vessel to another.

When Esakka tried to work the iron in the forge fire, he continually burned his arms. He despaired that he would ever learn to be a smith.

A few months later, he saw his owner exchange money with a group of bearded white men and he was escorted onto a tall ship in the harbor.

Tall she was with billowing sails, but as soon as Esakka was aboard ship, he noticed every rope of her gear was dirty, tangled and rubbed threadbare. The lines and chains that worked the sails and masts ran as snarled as seaweed. When the ship heaved forward and flopped down on her corpulent tail, she seemed like a brassy old woman, worn-out but still willing. Esakka wondered how long it would be before an ocean storm split her apart.

Hardly had Esakka gained his sea legs before he was tossed in the air by a group of laughing sailors whose language he did not understand. He was certain he had entered a world of bad spirits and that they would kill him.

A multitude of black persons, newly purchased, stood nearby, their expressions filled with dejection and sorrow. Esakka could not look any of them in the face. It was embarrassing to be unfettered, not to mention young and strong, but he knew his liberty would not last. And it was not long before the shipmaster chained him to a mast, his back to that of a young slave who introduced himself as Olaudah.

"The fish in the sea are happier than I am," Esakka said to Olaudah. "How I wish I could join them!"

"Just because you're wet behind the ears doesn't mean you came into the world a swimmer," Olaudah said.

Looking around, he saw a huge copper kettle boiling over a coal fire.

"Those ugly white men with the red faces are going to eat me, aren't they?" Esakka asked. "That's what that pot of boiling oil is for, isn't it?"

"They'll boil their own fish in that pot and won't offer you so much as a fin," Olaudah said. "You'll be put below where the stink and filth will make you eager to jump in the boiling oil and get clean."

Esakka looked stubbornly at his friend. "My people are very clean. We circumcise and we bathe every day. We always wash our hands before eating."

"My people also circumcise," Olaudah said. "We are the sons of Abraham and know all the laws of the Jews."

"We also keep the commandments of the Torah, just as God issued them to Moses before His people reached the promised land."

"I'll tell you right now," Olaudah said, "You can forget God's wonderful promises."

"Don't you think God will take care of me like he always has?"

Olaudah snickered. "These evil men will try your faith like Daniel in the lion's den. The only promise you'll hear is, I promise to beat you until you fall dead at my feet. That's the only promise you can count on."

"Do you really think God will desert me?"

"Before it's over, Esakka, you'll understand that God is not at your beck and call. Your life is about to become more difficult than you ever imagined."

"My skin is more brown than black. Maybe they will not realize I am African."

"You skin will only weigh heavily against you. Those haughty white men don't want to remember that their ancestors were once barbarous and uncivilized. On this hell-ship, there's no sympathy for any other race."

"I wish I could just curl up in a ball and roll over and hide until I can spin down the gangplank like a top."

Olaudah did not restrain the scorn in his voice. "If you get free, wild dogs will eat you. If the dogs don't find you on their own, the slavers will find you and feed you to them."

The hope died in Esakka's heart. He stared into the gray water. "How do you know so much?"

"I've seen many lands and many masters, Esakka. Seen women with iron contraptions on their head to keep them from speaking or eating or drinking while they prepare meals. Iron girdles on their bodies to prevent them from making love to anyone but their master. Many times, I wanted to escape. When I did, I was free all of three days. Then they found me. Turn your head and look at my back."

Esakka twisted against the mast to look at Olaudah's back, covered with open sores. Some of the wounds were scabbing over, but many festered. Never had he seen such mangled human flesh. It looked like the remnants of a hyena's meal.

"Did you get any medicine at all?"

"Only if you count pouring on salt."

Esakka retched and threw up on the deck. Then he started crying. He didn't want to. He was ashamed of himself. In spite of being as big as a man, he knew he was still a child.

"You'll regret losing your meager breakfast," Olaudah said. "You're such a baby! How old are you?"

"I was fifteen, three moons past."

Olaudah was more sympathetic when he spoke again. "I was younger than you when two men crawled over the wall of my father's house and carried me away. Since that time, I have seen many people and heard languages I never knew existed. Some treated me good and some whipped and beat me."

"I'm not a coward, but I don't want them to beat me," Esakka said. "I want to stay alive. I have to find my sister and take her home to my mother and father."

"Don't let them touch your perfect shoulders. You will fetch a better price in the market place. The better the price, the better the master. The more he pays for you, the more he values your hide... unless a crazy man buys you."

"How can you tell if you get a crazy man?"

"There is no way to know until it's too late."

It was the last time he saw Olaudah. Soon after, Esakka was taken to the holds far below. Sweat, human excrement, vomit, and decaying flesh combined to make his stomach roil. The horrifying

90

smell crawled into his nostrils and made itself at home

Around him, Esakka saw hundreds of black people chained together on racks, the racks stacked to the ceiling, one atop the other. Olaudah had told him that once a week, sea water would be let in to flood the decks and wash away the wastes. If a few bodies drowned in the process, Olaudah said it was of no consequence.

The crew never entered the hold. Trustworthy slaves checked the chained bodies each morning. The dead were unchained and tossed into the deeps. Sometimes the sick pretended to be dead, hoping to join them.

Noticing Esakka's nausea, a slave-master handed him a bottle. "Drink this. It'll settle your stomach and you won't puke on our clean decks."

Esakka sniffed, discovered it was strong liquor and handed it back. "I never drink liquor."

"Drink it or take thirty lashes," the master said.

Esakka grabbed the bottle and consumed it like milk. His throat and stomach burned and his head spun, but he felt relaxed.

When the master saw how young Esakka was, he put him in chains near some other children. Drowsy from the liquor, he soon fell asleep.

Esakka slept through the night, waking only at dawn when he heard a soft voice pealing, "Sakka, Sakka, is that you, my brother, Sakka?"

Esakka shook his head groggily, thinking it a dream. Then he realized the voice came from the girl-child nestled in the curve of his arm. He focused on her small body, covered with rags. He knew he must still be drunk from the liquor because the girl looked exactly like his lost sister.

The girl whispered again. "Sakka, it's me, your sister Ejoja."

Esakka roused himself up to look more closely at the girl. He could not believe what he saw. "Is this a dream?" He looked again, filled with wonder. The light coming through the prisms in the hold shined on the girl's face as if she were not real. "No, no, it can't be."

"It's true, Sakka. It's me."

He saw that it was indeed his lost sister. He clasped her tightly and they both cried until they could cry no more.

When he was able to speak without sobbing, Esakka scrutinized

Ejoja's emaciated body and his heart ached for her. "Little sister, you are so thin, I can count the ribs in your chest. What happened to you?" He stroked her face and head. "Your hair is falling out. You must be very sick, Ejoja."

Ejoja's dark eyes were clouded and her voice raspy. "I haven't eaten for days. The only thing they bring me is what Mother called garbage. Never any fruits or vegetables from the fields."

He saw that his sister's body was covered with boils. Esakka's stomach churned; he shuddered with dry heaves. "How long have you been here, little sister?"

"I don't know. Every day is the same."

"What's going to happen to us?" Esakka asked.

Ejoja's voice was barely a whisper. She curled tightly against Esakka. "We will be carried to white man's lands. If we live, we will be sold and put to work."

Esakka felt a little hope. "Work does not sound too bad. I have worked for some masters. It wasn't too bad."

"It has not been good for me, Esakka." Ejoja's voice broke. "I was never treated with kindness. When I was first taken, I was still pretty. Many masters wanted me . . . for their harems."

Esakka cradled her in his arms. "Don't talk now . . . just get some sleep."

But Ejoja could not rest. "I must tell you what happened to me." In a wispy voice, she continued, "Sakka, I was too young for the harems. The men hurt me so much. They tried to do terrible things to me. Always . . . terrible things."

"What things, little sister? What did they do to you?" Esakka's jaw tightened with fear, because he was beginning to suspect what they had done.

"Things to this part of my body," said Ejoja. Her chains rattled as she moved her frail hands to her pubis. She looked at Esakka with tired eyes, black as ebony but far softer. "They did things they said would make me a woman . . . but it was so painful, I screamed and screamed. You remember how good I scream, Sakka?"

Esakka spared her a half-smile although he felt no joy. "You can scream pretty good, little sister."

"But the men became angry. They beat me because I was too small for their enjoyment."

Esakka was aghast. Sobs came from his throat, deep within his body. His cries filled an enormity that seemed to have been created especially for them, cries tore the air apart, like a thousand angry lions, rebounding from ear to ear of the black bodies imprisoned there.

But no one raised his head. Esakka's cries disappeared from consciousness as quickly as thunder in a storm.

Ejoja's voice quivered and her body trembled. "They were like animals. The women said it was my fault. I was too young."

Sadness.

Despair.

"How could it be my fault I am so young?"

"I will kill them!" Esakka cried. "Tell me who they are and I will kill them."

"Sakka, you can never find them."

"I swear I will kill them. I will hunt them down like wild dogs."

"I do not know their names. I do not even know where I was." Ejoja snuggled against him, her body cold and in need of warmth. Her breathing became hollow and haggard; her voice grew weaker.

"Please hold me, Sakka. I wish father were here. I will never see him again. I'm glad you found me. I can die now that someone who loves me is near."

"I love you, little sister."

There was no response. He held her close and put his mouth next to her ear.

"Can you hear me?"

"Yes . . . I hear you . . . can I go home now. . . ?"

"Don't go, Ejoja! I just found you. Ejoja, do you see God?"

"No, Sakka, there's no one."

Desperate, he begged again. "Don't you see God? Ask God to let you stay a while longer."

"No . . . ."

Her voice was so weak, he put his ear to her lips.

"Sakka . . . ?"

Frantic, he pleaded. "Tell me, do you see the Light?"

"I see . . . darkness."

"You must see the angels, Ejoja! Please tell me you see God! Tell me you see the angels! Tell me you see the light!"

"No, Sakka . . . I don't see . . . ."

Forlorn now, he shouted, "I know God is waiting for you, Ejoja. Don't you see Him?"

A shallow sigh slipped from Ejoja's lips and her small body folded into Esakka's arms. He watched her chains slither away and with them, her life.

Esakka realized he could remove his own slim wrists from the chains. He rose and picked up Ejoja's body. Weeping silently, he carried her up five flights of stairs to the main deck of the ship.

The winds blew furiously. The sails belled like huge kites. The winds so fought with each other for domination of the old ship that she sat absolutely motionless while sea water gushed over her, fore and aft, rocking and shaking. Esakka struggled against the storm, keeping a tight hold on Ejoja.

A slave master rushed to stop Esakka, but the pelting rain caused the man to lose his footing and he fell. Esakka kicked the master aside. The crew moved away, struck dumb by the sight of the tall youth marching through the driving rains with Ejoja's limp body.

The sea boiled, tossing the old ship, picking up her tail and slamming it back in the water. Thunder broke the skies apart and lightning jagged its way across the heavens.

Blindly, holding his sister closely, Esakka stumbled toward the railing. Propping his knees against the bar, he locked his legs together and stood erect. His voice poured forth with strength.

"My Lord, my Creator, why have You forgotten me? Why are You so far from me? This innocent one cried and cried for You. Now, she can cry no more. Though I am a worm and a child, I seek Your help. Take this little one to Your breast and hold her there forever."

Esakka lifted Ejoja high over his head and cast her frail body into the gray swirling water. He would have followed her into its depths, but he had sworn to avenge her.

Avenge her, he could not, and he knew it, but for that moment, he hoped for a miracle.

XVI

The feeble God has stabbed me to the heart.
John Gay
Acis and Galatea

𝔄 month later, Esakka was transferred to an English ship, where he was befriended by Rusty Tremont, the son of the ship's Captain and a boy his own age. Rusty obliged him out of his own loneliness. A close friendship ensued.

Rusty's father, a great teaser, frequently told Esakka stories that sent him running to a fly vessel to hide, where he shook with fear until Rusty found him. His friend would explain the Captain was joking when he said he was going to roast and carve him up for dinner. Or when he claimed it was necessary to feed young boys to boisterous grampus fishes, in order to keep them from knocking the ship out of the water.

The Captain made a real sailor out of Esakka. Rusty taught him other things. Three years they were together, before the Captain died of a fever and Rusty went to Plymouth to live with his aunt.

Esakka first saw Captain Tremont reading a book, and then later, Rusty. It was the first book he had ever seen. What an exciting occupation that was!

They told him wonderful things the book had to say.

When he found an opportunity to be alone with a book, he spoke to it. For a considerable number of minutes, he carried on a conversation with the book, expecting an answer. Nothing happened. Frustrated, he beat the book and commanded it to speak. That's when Rusty walked in. It was the only time Rusty ever snickered at him.

Soon after they reached the land of the English, Esakka developed a great respect for the people. They did not buy and sell each other as did the Afrikaans. Rusty said their religion prohibited it.

When they were in port, Rusty frequently took Esakka to the House of God. He had never seen anything comparable to the singing, praying and rejoicing in those little white buildings. He was immediately attracted to it and caught up in it.

After Rusty's departure, Esakka was purchased by an unusually kind master who let him continue his reading quest and gave him books of his own. That master ran a catch of sloops between the islands of the West Indies, providing passage for travelers and business people. Eventually, Esakka came to captain one of them because he was the only one who could keep the sailors from drinking all night and coming to work the next morning so sick they were useless.

However, his sinecure did not last. Bankrupt, wiped out by a hurricane, the owner was forced to put him on the auction block.

Solomon Seney found him on the block. Intrigued with his learning and experience, he paid three hundred guineas for him. Master Seney quickly discerned Esakka's unusual talents and intended to make him an overseer on his tobacco plantation. He had even promised him his freedom when he could repay his purchase sum. But Esakka knew that would never happen now.

He sat in the Annapolis jail, accused of murder. Despite valiant efforts to live a righteous life, the blessings of God no longer sanctified his days. How could anyone believe he had killed Josie? How could that priest not have come to his assistance?

When a young slave was placed in his cell, he became even more depressed. Arrested after escaping from an evil master in Virginia, thirteen-year-old Jacob Mouse looked up at Esakka with big, dark eyes. "I ain't supposed to talk to you. You done killed a girl."

Esakka groaned and tears ran down his cheek. Mouse looked into his face. "I know you ain't done it. I can tell—you is a good man, Master Esakka. Why is life so hard for us?"

Esakka knew why life was hard for Mouse. It was obvious he couldn't command respect. Thin and ugly, the boy was like a toadying pup that everyone disdains. Yet, Esakka saw that Mouse had a good soul and he was drawn to him.

"What happened to you, Mouse?"

"I run off. Master Beuthed was too mean. He done slay my twin brother. I had to git out before he slay me. Master Esakka, why is some masters so mean?"

"I think they're possessed of the Devil, Mouse."

"Master Beuthed sure had de Devil in him. He bought me and my brother, we was ten year old. I been under de cat o'nine a hundred times at once. He say me and Efrim deserve fifty lash a piece, but he act confuse and one of us get both of 'em. He say he make a mistake and look for de other, gave him de same. Keep it even, he say. He laugh, say all Negras look de same to him and us being twins jus' too much."

Esakka put his arm around Mouse and held him closely.

"I didn't ever have no daddy, Master Esakka."

"I was taken from my parents—no older than you, Mouse, but I knew my father. He taught me about God's Laws, and later I learned to read the Bible myself."

"I can't do reading. Efrim neither. We work hard, though. Efrim run back and forth all day long gittin' stuff for Miz Beuthed. She never happy. Git me drinking water, she say. Carry those plants to de field. Carry more, Efrim, she say. She beat him to carry more. De more he hurt, de more she make him carry. He stumble and Master Beuthed kick at him. He couldn't git no more, so they carry him to quarters. Next day they beat him more 'cause he couldn't git."

"God knows I've seen such evil many times."

"Efrim almost die. Auntie Effie come and nurse over him and pray on him and he get better. Soon as Miz Beuthed hear it, she send for him to bring her some spring water. Auntie Effie send back he too sick to work. Mizzie hear none of it. She say she languish de weather and need a drink of cold water from de spring.

"Efrim git off his bed and make it to de well. He git a bucket, but he only carry half. Auntie Effie try to help him, but she old and scared she git beating.

"Efrim gits to de house. Mizzie throw a fit 'cause it only half a bucket. Throw it on de ground and cuss Efrim. She slap him and slap him more. When he fall over, she call for Master Beuthed. He take Efrim, tie him to de clothes line pole."

As Esakka listened, he moved to the window. A thunderstorm was blowing up, the wind howling robustly, rain falling like sticks on a drum, nearly shutting out Mouse's soft voice.

"He take off Efrim's clothes and tie his feet to de bottom of de clothes line pole, tie his arms to de top piece, all de time he singing 'bout Jesus.

"Mizzie she come, beat Efrim with a corn stalk. She go back in house and rest, come back and beat him more. Go on all day. Just go on and on. Morning come, he dead."

Streaks of lightning penetrated the darkness of the jail. Esakka could see Mouse's face set in resolve to avoid sobbing as he told his story, hands twisting his fingers like taffy.

"Neighbors came 'round. See Efrim. Don't say nothing to Master Beuthed. He dig grave for Efrim, say he bury that shiftless boy 'cause he too lazy to get off de cross. Laugh and say he leave him up there three days. See if he do like Jesus an' come down. Mebbe he won't have to dig up his fine black soil to cover Efrim's body so it don't stink up his fine country air."

"And that's when you ran away?"

"Neighbors send for de Law before Efrim get buried. Took Beuthed to jail and give him a trial. That's when I run."

"I hope they hanged him until he was dead," said Esakka.

"Old doctor take one look at Efrim and say he ain't going near him, he have disease, mought be catching. Weren't nothing but beggarman's maunds on him, made from paint and rust."

"And Buethed wasn't punished?"

"Fine him fifteen pence. Say he let Efrim mess around with women of disease and he git it and die. Tell him watch his Negras better, make'em do church all de time."

With the next bolt of lightning, Esakka saw Mouse had bent his head down, arms wrapped tightly about his knees, his eyes closed. His voice was muffled. "I knows I's wrong to run away, Master Esakka, but I scared. I been caught now an' I's more scared."

Driving rains battered the jail as the storm intensified. Water sloshed through the cell window, flooding the floor. Esakka wished he had a candle to lessen the darkness.

"Are you a Godly person, Mouse?"

"Ain't never had no use for religion, Master Esakka."

"God loves you, Mouse. He watches over the sparrows in the field and He watches over you, too."

"Ain't never show it. I been receiving white man's hate a long time and iffen God's white, Master Esakka, I prolly be no better off."

"Mouse, the Holy Book says God made Adam in his own image, out of the dirt of the earth, and dirt is black."

"Even if he be black, it don't look like he doing much for you."

Esakka recalled the words of the Bible: *Out of the mouths of babes comes truth.* Mouse's words troubled him, but then again, the boy had no wisdom or experience in these things and what he might say was not necessarily true.

Esakka went to the narrow window of the cell and looked out. "Just when it is darkest, Mouse, God gives us a lantern for our feet and a light for our path."

Neither moon nor stars was visible. Esakka wondered if the darkness were an omen of his own future. He continued with the Psalm, but his voice did not ring with conviction and the words provided small comfort.

"He holdeth our soul to live and suffereth not our feet to slip."

Mouse sighed loudly. "You talks pretty, Massa Esakka, but pretty talk ain't kept you out of trouble. They tol' me not to get friendly with you, 'cause you was going to hang high in the sky for killing that girl."

"I did wrong, Mouse. It was the dumbest thing I ever did. I left my master's plantation without permission and followed Miss Phillis across the Bay."

"Why did you kill Miss Phillis?"

"I didn't kill Miss Phillis. I didn't kill anybody. Miss Josie was the one who was killed. I found her body. I should not have been there, but I did not kill her. The woman who accused me was wrong. And that priest that was there, he could tell what happened, but he seems to have disappeared."

"Ain't no one believes you?"

"Not yet. Perhaps my master, Mr. Seney, will. I don't think he knows I am here. But I can only wait and hope for God to rectify matters."

Mouse joined Esakka at the cell window. "I hope dey don't leave you here a long time. Some people lay in jail and dey people don't know where dey be." Mouse stared out the window. "Awful black out dare."

"About as black as my by-and-by," Esakka mumbled.

"We needs to get out'n here."

Esakka went back to the bench and sat down. "It's no good talking that way, Mouse."

"We could live in de woods."

"Let's get down on our knees, Mouse, and ask God for his direction. But I'm afraid if we're here, He has a reason for it."

Esakka knew he could not leave. That would be truly running away, and Mr. Seney had told him that if he ran away, he would forfeit his freedom sum for sure.

Mouse followed Esakka's direction, kneeling beside him, his face up-cast as he listened to Esakka's low voice. Once, he interrupted to say, "Talk louder. That storm making a lot of noise and God ain't going to hear you."

Esakka shortly brought his prayer to an end. Mouse gave it a determined "Amen."

At that moment, the silence of the night was broken by a noise like the roaring of a great water fall. The building shook. Rattling echoed through the jail. Stones crumbled from the walls. Rumblings increased. Shudders jagged up and down their bodies. Planks in the floor split and came apart. Esakka was reminded of a time in the Indies when his ship had been cast upon the rocks by a hurricane.

A roaring like falling waters increased. Esakka thought all his sins were staring him in the face and he would be carried away in unremitting fury. The roof flew away, its debris falling on Esakka's and Mouse's heads. Rain pelted down on them.

Running to the window, Mouse was thrown to the floor. He lay there as if struck by an invisible hand. Esakka was certain that God had chastised the boy for his usurpation of the faith.

When Mouse finally moved, he grabbed Esakka's ankles and buried his face in his feet. "Oh, Massa Esakka, de Lord sure answer your prayers fast."

The cell door creaked open.

"It's a miracle!" cried Mouse.

"Get up, Mouse. It's just a tornado. Once, this place burned down because of one. If we walk out, we'll be in real trouble."

"I'se going. God made us this chance."

"I'm not going, so you can just forget it."

Mouse grabbed the cell door and urged it further open. "De door open, Massa Esakka. De Lord, he telling us to git."

"Mouse, I'll end up in a heap of trouble if I leave."

"You couldn't be in no mo' trouble. You going to hang by your neck. You ain't done nothing wrong, but de Law don't believe you. De Lord, he's making de way."

Esakka sat on the bunk while Mouse kept pushing on the open cell door. "De Lord done gave us a sign." Mouse went over to Esakka and tried to push him up. "Let's git out of here!"

Esakka sighed. "It was just a bad storm. God didn't do this, Mouse."

"Yes, he did! I know he did!"

A glimmering yellow light broke through the gloom. Gradually, the brightness moved closer.

Mouse shivered and hung tightly to Esakka's arm. "It's de Lord his self!"

Esakka wondered if the Holy Ghost were about to make an appearance. But even if He did, if He didn't promise him his freedom, he wouldn't heed anything He said.

Then Esakka realized the light came from a flickering candle.

A deep voice penetrated the darkness. "Come along, you two Negras."

"I think it must be a angel!" Mouse cried.

"I don't know." Esakka did not believe God had sent an angel to rescue him, as he had done for the Apostle Peter when King Herod jailed him. He, Esakka, was not worthy of such redemption. Not he, a mere slave and not an apostle. How could such a thing be possible? Within his breast was tumult, madness and delirium.

But he would test the Lord. He shoved Mouse aside, standing with crossed arms as an old woman shuffled into the cell, carrying a fluttering flame before her. She wore a black dress and a black turban. Under her turban, her face was as wrinkled as a dried apricot and about the same color. If she had moved back a step, she would have been hidden from view again.

101

"I tell you, it's an angel!" Mouse declared.

"You've never seen an angel," Esakka said, again resentful of Mouse's claim to religion when he had never been instructed in it.

The vision spoke. "Ah ain't no angel. Ah's just an ole 'gyptian woman. Come on, we going to get out of here. The Constab'lary done left everybody to fend for hisself. Come along, now! I knows the way out of here. Watch out doan nothing fall on you."

The wings within Esakka's breast subsided their flailing. A perfectly normal reason for what had happened. It had not been God and he had better stay right where he was, or his freedom sum would be forfeited for sure.

"Massa Esakka, we's saved! We's saved! Where you think we's headed for?"

"Trouble, Mouse, trouble."

"Naw, Massa Esakka, you's free now. You's really free now! Come on!"

"You Negras follow me," the old woman said.

Could God be bestowing his freedom on him in this manner?

XVII

An open foe may prove a curse,
But a pretended friend is even worse.
John Gay
Fables

Richard Makepeace rode the gray mule Nelly with aplomb. She was a sure-footed animal, gentle and easily managed. Traffic on the road to Baltimore Town was heavy. Opportunities for traveling companions abounded.

While it would have been pleasant to have company, Makepeace trusted nary a soul. He stayed to the middle of the road so that those who inhabited the tree-fringed edges would not have access to him. God knew how often he attracted the wrong sort.

Makepeace smoothed each sleeve of the magical black cassock. He felt like he was living in the sunshine now. He straightened the large wood cross on his chest and said a small prayer for his journey.

Several times, he was tendered a shilling in exchange for a ride on the mule. He turned down all offers. He was too afraid, however, to deny the company of a young priest. There was no point in tempting God; that would be foolish. Besides, the man offered to share his lunch with him.

Sitting under a massive sycamore tree, the tow-haired priest beckoned to Makepeace and held out an apple for his consideration. The man's yellow hair was cropped at ear length, but a dapper lock fell across his forehead. He wore a long brown tunic and scapular with a white cape and capuche.

All morning, Makepeace had ridden without sustenance, having left the hulk of the old inn at Dorrs Corner before dawn. He gladly accepted the apple and presented himself as Reverend Richard Hill.

Jeremiah Smith introduced himself and pulled a hunk of bread and some cheese from a gunny on the grass beside him. After splitting

103

it, he handed Makepeace half. It was a tasty and filling lunch and Makepeace was grateful for it.

Noticing that Jeremiah had several days of food in his gunny, Makepeace decided it would be profitable to ask him if he wanted to travel with him, letting the mule carry his burden. At the same time, he realized he was putting himself in jeopardy of being discovered as a fraud.

Jeremiah looked to be about his own age. He said he belonged to the order of Carmelite; that explained his garb. Having recently left the seminary in New England, Jeremiah was headed for an Indian mission at Sainte Genevieve, near Saint Louis. He planned to travel west to Virginia, take a vessel at Parkersburg and sail down the Spaylaywitheepi until it ran into the Messessebbi River. Makepeace sensed that Jeremiah was somewhat naive and was further pleased to learn the young priest had little interest in theology.

"Padre Hill, who cares how many angels can dance on the head of a pin?" Jeremiah asked. "That's what most theological arguments come down to."

Makepeace filed that for future use. The strange aura of the black gown surrounded him. The feeling that he was blessed by the Almighty overwhelmed him. At times, he even considered abandoning his lowborn thoughts and habits for a higher road.

After an hour of walking, the two men stopped at a tree-fringed stream to let Nelly drink and rest. They sat on the bank under a basswood tree. Jeremiah produced another apple from his saddle bag as well as some pemmican, dried deer meat pounded together with suet and wild berries.

"I'm sorry to hear the Pope shut you down," Jeremiah said.

It was news to Makepeace. He was drinking from his flask at the time. He gulped. Water dribbled down his beard.

Jeremiah continued, "I understand they disbanded the Jesuit mission at St. Mary's."

Makepeace nodded. He quickly stuffed more apple into his mouth so that he would not be expected to reply at once.

"I guess that's why you're wearing the black cassock instead of your usual robes, padre."

After a moment's thought, Makepeace decided it would be best to correct Jeremiah's assumption. "I ain't a Jesuit. I'm Church of

England. But I did hear the Jesuits was turned out to fare for themselves."

Makepeace went back to gnawing on the apple.

Jeremiah pushed his blonde lock off his forehead and focused his brown eyes on Makepeace. For a moment, Makepeace thought he was undone, but Jeremiah spoke in a friendly manner. "I thought you were British. I was born in the Colonies. Second generation. My grandfather came from Germany. His name was Schmidt. I Englished it because I got tired of spelling it. I hope I'm not prying if I ask why you joined the church?"

Makepeace started to tell him the same story he had told Drury, but decided it would not put him in such a good light with a man of God. "I felt the call."

Jeremiah seemed to accept that.

"I stopped at Wilmington City," said Jeremiah. "The citizens who took me in said that their Scottish clergyman had disappeared. Apparently it was no great loss. He was soused so much of the time, he couldn't give church on a regular basis."

Makepeace stroked his beard. "His pulpit was over his cellar, eh?" Feeling confident, Makepeace continued in detail, embroidering where necessary to protect himself. "When I was in Philadelphia, the pastor of a church was in jail for murdering one of his slaves."

As he spoke, Makepeace warned himself to be careful how he told the story, because at that time he was in jail with Filmore for attempted robbery, the one they blamed on the Indians. He figured he'd been in more jails than Jeremiah had churches.

Stretched out on the mule's blanket they had spread on the grass, Jeremiah cradled the back of his head with his hands. "The Delawareans hadn't had a divine service for over a month. They were Moravian, so they appreciated the mass. I was sorely tempted to stay and serve them."

"Ye are truly more interested in helping your neighbors than in preaching the dainties," Makepeace said. "It's encouraging to meet someone like ye. I seen lots of unsavory men pointing the finger to heaven and claiming they had the inside with the Lord."

Jeremiah smiled. "The freedom of the frontier permits all kinds of mischief, padre."

"I heard a man's confession in the Anneville jail. A priest, in fact," Makepeace said, "he was arrested for breaking and entering a merchant's house. Stole a lot of money and was about to stretch the hemp. Called himself Friar Redmond. He unloaded a bundle of sins on me. Even confessed to killing a clergyman in London and robbing the man of his frock. He came to the Colonies posing as a priest."

Makepeace shifted uneasily, unsure that Jeremiah's brown eyes could not penetrate his own masquerade, but the young priest spoke softly. "A sorry devil. I believe there is a special punishment in Hell for those who pretend to be servants of God."

Makepeace swallowed and continued. "He was to be hanged the next morning. Barring any sort of miracle, he's gone to his eternal punishment."

"Many a crook has gotten off by pleading the Book," Jeremiah said. "An old sort of business, but one that frequently works."

"I heard about a smoky devil who claimed to be a Man of the Cloth. When they brought the Book to him, nothing came out of his mouth but hubble-bubble. Couldn't read a word."

They started out again, traveling under a canopy of sycamore and oaks until they emerged into the village of Glen Bournie, a clearing with a dozen log cabins. Chickens and cows overran the road. Several youths came out to throw eggs and tomatoes at them and taunt them for being Papists.

Jeremiah remarked that he thought Catholics in general were much better persons morally than the Protestants. "You should give some thought to becoming Catholic, padre."

Makepeace breathed easily, deciding his own guilt was the main reason for his nervousness, not any gift Jeremiah had for seeing through him. "I been giving it serious consideration, but I ain't had much chance to learn about it."

Several hours had passed since they had rested the mule. Jeremiah pointed to a farm house. "Let's stop and see if we can get some water for the mule. She looks a little dry."

Makepeace was ashamed he hadn't thought of that. After all, it was his animal. That's the way he was thinking of Old Nelly. He no longer had any intention of turning her over to the Clankenbell Livery in Baltimore. He was fairly certain God did not expect him to travel without the assistance of a beast of burden.

106

Jeremiah's uncle was pastor of a small church at Hagerstown. A German settlement that was mostly Lutheran, it nevertheless tolerated Catholics. Jeremiah suggested that if Makepeace continued traveling west with him, he was sure that his uncle's hospitality would be extended to them.

This surely will be a test, Makepeace thought, eager to see if Jeremiah's uncle would accept him. Yet it caused him no small amount of torment. He wondered if God would not be concerned that he was attempting a dabble in the black arts.

Next evening, they made camp on the far side of Frederick under an arch of mulberry trees. Finding two quail in a coppice, they killed and dressed them, roasting the fowl over a fire along with potatoes and corn given them by a farmer in Mount Airy. Jeremiah had blessed the farmer's fields and Makepeace listened closely so that he could perform the same rite if called on to do so.

The farmer had wrapped the potatoes in an old copy of *The Maryland Gazette*. After they ate, Jeremiah read a poem from it called "The Difference between Today and Tomorrow."

"Today man is dressed in gold and silver bright, But wrapped in a shroud before tomorrow be night.

"Today he dines on delicious food. Tomorrow dead, unable to do any good.

"Today he is choosy, scorns to eat crumbs. Tomorrow, he himself is a dish for worms.

"Today he rises from a velvet bed. Tomorrow he lies in one made of lead.

"Today, perfumed as sweet as any rose

"Tomorrow, a stink in everybody's nose."

They laughed over the part about lying in a velvet bed. It had been several days since either one had slept on anything other than the cold hard ground.

Makepeace and Jeremiah reached Hagerstown two days later.

Albert Schmidt came out the door to greet them. "It's good to see family."

Albert's brown hair was cropped in a circle, bald in the middle.

His beard encompassed his chin like a helmet strap. Shorter than Jeremiah, Albert pushed back the sleeves of his black cassock and reached up to give his nephew a hug.

"Tie your mule to the hitching post and come in. I was just visiting with another member of the ministry." He pointed toward a black-gowned man who was rising from a cane-bottomed rocker.

"I want you to meet my new friend, Friar Redmond. He's stopping over on his way to New Orleans."

XVIII

We only part to meet again.
John Gay
Rural Sports

Of a simple manufacture, the furniture in Albert's parlor centered around a fireplace that served the parlor on one side and the kitchen on the other. Through the hearth, Makepeace could see a plump, gray-haired woman tending kettles.

A short, high-backed pew abutted the fireplace. Next to that, a desk and a cane-bottomed chair. Around a trestle dining table, six ladder-back chairs were arranged, one on each end, two on each side. The gentle air of religious devotion was symbolized by a bookcase filled with venerable tomes. The walls seeped the odor of fresh whitewash.

Opposite the fireplace, Redmond sat in a rocker.

Astonished at seeing the imposter priest he had left cold-cocked in the Anneville jail, Makepeace nevertheless pretended Redmond was a stranger and extended his hand in greeting.

Redmond responded in like manner. After shaking hands, each man quickly made the sign of the cross. Makepeace was pleased that such things came easier for him each time.

The ensuing silence might have been overwhelming, but Albert and Jeremiah filled the space with eager and animated conversation. Makepeace exchanged a glance with Redmond, then each warily looked away. When their eyes locked again, an unspoken covenant passed between them. For the moment, each would allow the other his masquerade.

Redmond coughed and finally spit out a few words. "Where might you be traveling from, brother?"

"Anneville." Makepeace smiled, enjoying the man's discomfort. "The name's Hill. What about yerself?"

"Delaware," said Redmond. "Wilmington. Mr. Hill, you're lucky to run into someone like the Friar with a mule to carry some of the burden."

Makepeace did not reply, willing to let Redmond continue with his assumption about the ownership of the mule. But overhearing Redmond's remark, Jeremiah broke off his conversation with Albert to say, "Not my mule, Brother Redmond. It belongs to Padre Hill."

Redmond's expression could be interpreted only as one of admiration. When the woman who had been working in the kitchen made an appearance, Makepeace was delighted to be saved from further explanation.

Wearing a white pinafore apron over her blue sack dress, the woman stuffed her loose gray hair under the starched white cap on the back of her head. In a thick Irish brogue, she asked, "Would you be needing me to set some extra places, Father?"

Albert glanced from stomach to stomach and chuckled. "I thought I heard a few wails of cupboard love there! These men are ready for some home-cooked victuals, Mrs. O'Brien. You've already met Friar Redmond. That's Padre Hill. The ugly one in the brown and white garb is my nephew Jeremiah. Gentlemen, this is my housekeeper, Mrs. O'Brien. She takes good care of me and I'm sure you'll benefit from her praiseworthy efforts."

"God bless ye, Father. If you don't mind me saying so, the one you're calling ugly looks right handsome to me. I'll be fixing some colcannon for the all of you, and if it's all right with Your Honor, I'll be getting out the pewter dishes."

Father Schmidt nodded and Mrs. O'Brien bustled back to the kitchen, humming as she went.

Jeremiah took the chair from the desk. Albert pulled a ladder-back from the dining table and offered it to Makepeace, but remained standing by the fireplace. Redmond returned to the rocker.

"Uncle Albert, you look quite comfortable here," said Jeremiah. "How many rooms do you have?"

"Besides the parlor, there's the kitchen, and a bedroom with a sleeping loft over it. It's commodious enough. Mrs. O. stays with a neighbor down the road. She comes early in the morning and goes home after supper." Albert leaned forward, and spoke in a confidential voice. "Her only fault is she has a languishing eye—

110

but despite that, she reads romance novels till her candle runs out."

Redmond treadled the rocking chair. "You're very lucky to have the woman."

"Yes, I agree, Father. She's a faithful member of my church and volunteers her services here," Albert said. "I hope you gentlemen will excuse the smell of whitewash. We just finished covering the walls. It's necessary to do it every few months because of the smoke from the fireplace."

"All I can smell is fresh bread baking," Redmond said.

"Nice pictures ye have on yer wall," Makepeace said.

"The stations of the cross." Albert pulled a corncob pipe from his pocket and filled it with tobacco. "Done by a traveling artist who passed through last year."

"We noticed you have a winter garden," Jeremiah said. "You must spend a lot of time working that."

"I find it relaxing. My parishioners help with the seeding and weeding. We raise turnips, peas and corn and Mrs. O. has to have her potatoes. Easy to grow and they store well in our root cellar."

Albert bent over and used tongs to pull a coal from the fireplace. He carefully applied it to the bowl of his pipe. "Our fare is plain, but Mrs. O'Brien is inventive and her meals are never dull. She makes fresh bread every day, and she's been pounding cabbage and potatoes to make colcannon."

"Have you a good number of parishioners, Uncle Albert?"

"Not as many as I would like." Albert sucked air through his corncob pipe. The sweet odor of cured tobacco mixed with violet oil joined the aroma of newly baked bread and cooked cabbage. "It's not too popular to be Catholic. The county officials doubled the taxation on Catholics. Some members have seen fit to convert to Presbyterian. I couldn't say as I blame them."

Redmond put his hand to his chin and assumed a musing posture. "You ought to ex-communicate them. That's what the Pope tells us to do."

Makepeace wondered if Redmond knew what he was talking about or was just making it up. He also was surprised that Redmond had suddenly come under the domination of the Pope, having previously bragged about being Anglican.

"I know, I know," said Albert. "I just can't be that hard-hearted.

The Pickled Dog Caper

Josiah Swift used to come in from Sharpsburg—a good twenty miles. Traveled in an ox-cart—every Sunday, without fail, bringing his wife and eight children to Mass. Each one of those children just as clean and dressed-up like young royals."

Redmond clicked his tongue with disapproval and the rocker echoed his clicking. "Cleanliness may be next to Godliness, but you have to participate in the Holy Sacraments and obey the Scriptures."

Makepeace was repelled by Redmond's self-righteousness. He lowered his eyes in disbelief at the man's brazen religiosity. At the same time, Makepeace had to admit a guarded admiration for the faker's cleverness.

Albert ignored the remarks. "Several weeks ago, on his way home, Josiah was attacked by Senecas. His wife and the three youngest were carried off. Josiah and the older boys fought as best they could, but they were outnumbered. A sad day. He became a Presbyterian so he could go to church closer to home. How could I discipline a man who suffered so much misery?"

Mrs. O'Brien carried the tureen of steaming colcannon from the kitchen. The four men sat down at the table and she joined them. When Albert asked Redmond to say grace, Makepeace was delighted. Still, he was hungry and when the prayer turned into a sermonette, he became annoyed. Yet again, his annoyance turned to respect for the man's friendly colloquy with God. In fact, he envied Redmond and hoped he could court the holy water as well if the time came.

Sitting at the head of the table, Father Albert ladled the cabbage and potato mixture onto shiny pewter plates, before passing them around. Earlier, Mrs. O. had placed three loaves of bread and dishes of butter on the table, along with a pot of strong hot coffee. Albert sliced the bread while she poured coffee into mugs whose pewter she must have spent just as much time shining as she had the plates.

Makepeace started to say it was the first time he had had home-cooked food since leaving the Anneville jail, but harnessed his tongue just in time.

"I don't know what I would do without Mrs. O'Brien to keep house for me," said Albert. "She was widowed last year, so I get most all her attention."

"Was your mate lost to the Indian wars, Mrs. O'Brien?" asked Jeremiah.

"Me husband Jack was abducted by a bunch of criminous sailors. British they was. Three years ago, it be now."

"Admiral Copperthorne landed at Philadelphia looking for men to indenture as sailors," said Albert, cutting some more of Mrs. O.'s homemade bread for his guests. "He had a letter from King George permitting him to claim any Irishman he found. The letter empowered him to induct them into the Navy on the spot. Not strictly legal, but after you've been jolly-rogered and put out to sea, what are you going to do?"

"The Admiral took me husband." Mrs. O'Brien forked bites of colcannon into her pudgy face. "Jack told 'em a' right. He told 'em if he dreamed there was a speck of Irish blood in him, he'd cut off his member and let his blood run out like a faucet." She was taken with a spasm of chuckles. "Can ye imagine? Proud as he was of that thing!" Suddenly, she caught herself, looked around with flashing black eyes, and said, "Begging Your Honors' pardons!"

"Jack was as Irish as Mrs. O.," said Albert. "Tongue thick with the blarney."

Between bites, Mrs. O. continued. "No way could he be foolin' them British. They pressed him into the service of His Majesty's Royal Navy." She saluted herself with her fork.

"I thought the poor woman would grieve herself to death," Albert said.

Mrs. O.'s round face went soft like yeast dough that has been punched.

"Jack was a good man, but you'd 'ave swore he'd been dipped in the River Shannon and lost his born bashfulness. Weren't nary a one who was a stranger to him. Always greetin' newcomers like they was long lost friends."

"Confidentially," Albert said, "the dear lady thought Jack had run off with a young bar maid."

Mrs. O. looked truly penitent. "God knows, how wrong I was to jedge me sweet Jack that way."

"But he got away from the Brits?" Makepeace asked.

"Showed up a year later, wearing a set of Jack Tars. I was overjoyed to see him. We burned his uney-form in the yard and danced a jig around the fire. We had another good two years before he went."

"Jack came down with the fever and died last year," Albert said.

"Thank God I weren't left with any mouths to feed, although it'd be nice to have a small remembrance of the good man. May his sweet soul rest in peace. I burn a candle for him every morning."

Redmond leaned back and spoke piously. "The Lord giveth and the Lord taketh away."

Mrs. O. wiped her eyes with her apron. Jeremiah made the sign of the cross and the others followed suit. Makepeace felt quite at home and was impressed by the company he was keeping. But just as he flattered himself, he realized they had also accepted the faker Redmond as coin of the realm.

Finishing his meal, Albert laid his knife and fork across his plate and returned to his pipe. "Jack wasn't a believer. We were never able to convert the chap."

"A real skeptic he was," added Mrs. O., her voice rising. "Always saying how the whole world was fooled by that dreamer and a stray pigeon. I've wept many a night, knowing he's in purgatory—if no worse place!—till the Good Lord knows when."

Redmond reached over and patted Mrs. O. on her arm. "Maybe Jack saw the Light when he was dying."

Makepeace admired Redmond's behavior. The man had a good hold on the religious gammon and patter. Redmond did a lot of things Makepeace planned to emulate later.

"I was there are his dying breath," Mrs. O. said. "If Jack saw the Light, he never said anything. I do give him credit, he never made fun of me for going to church. He never tried to persuade me from my way of believing."

"We all join you in your prayers, Mrs. O'Brien," said Redmond.

"Thank you, Father. You're a kind man. If it wasn't for Father Albert, I do believe I'd like you to be my pastor."

Redmond beamed with such pleasure that Makepeace had to resist a strong urge to stand and denounce the man as a murderous charlatan.

After the mule was fed and stabled for the night, Albert brought out his harmonica. Mrs. O. had a lovely Irish soprano and before going home, she stayed for an hour to sing. Redmond possessed a satisfactory tenor. He and Mrs. O. harmonized over Irish folk songs and Makepeace found it took him back to his childhood when his mother and uncle engaged in similar pleasantries.

After Mrs. O"Brien left, the conversation died with the fire. Sleeping assignments were made. Redmond offered to sleep in the barn with the mule. Makepeace knew neither the faker nor the mule would be there in the morning. Probably, the cow would be gone, too. Thankfully, Albert suggested that Redmond sleep in the loft on a straw pallet.

Makepeace was given a feather-bed placed on the dining table. When everyone retired for the night, Makepeace pushed the table against the door. That made it impossible for Redmond to exit the quarters.

There was only a tiny window in the bedroom where Albert and Jeremiah slept, and they pushed the iron bed against it. Knowing Old Nelly would be safe, Makepeace slept well.

Morning brought a fine autumn day. Albert said it was most likely the last of Indian summer and winter would roll in soon. Redmond said he would be on his way. It was obvious his gut was in turmoil. Makepeace thought it due to the possibility of being declaimed by himself, otherwise known as the Reverend Hill.

Redmond offered Makepeace three guineas for the mule. Makepeace declined politely, wondering how the man had come by so much gold. Was it possible he had found another gown that turned up a coin in its pocket from time to time?

***

Mrs. O. fixed Redmond a parcel of jerky, fruit and vegetables, and included the biscuits left from breakfast. Redmond set out at mid-morning. The others lingered at the breakfast table. As soon as Redmond was out the door, Jeremiah turned to Makepeace and said, "That's the man who's posing as a priest, isn't it?"

Makepeace raised his eyebrows, truly surprised at Jeremiah's comment.

"It's not that I'm all that perceptive," Jeremiah said. "You told me his name was Redmond. I don't suppose there's two of them."

Makepeace chuckled heartily. "If there be two, I never met the other one. It was him."

"Well, it was none of my business." Jeremiah crossed himself. "I saw nothing to be gained by exposing him, so I let it go."

Albert cut off the tip of a sugar cone and dropped it into his tea cup, stirring it gently. "God will deal with him. Jeremiah whispered the story to me last night as soon as Redmond's snoring assured us that he was asleep. We're lucky to be rid of the rascal without any trouble, but he is an interesting counterfeit."

"You know, in spite of what he's done in the past," Jeremiah said, "I think there could be some sincerity in him."

Having poured his tea in his saucer to let it cool, Makepeace lifted the dish to his lips and said nothing, although he could not prevent a wry grin from forming on his face. Albert gave Jeremiah a sideways look.

"Seriously," said Jeremiah, "it's my thought that if he carries the divine doctrine in his mind, eventually it may influence his behavior."

Perhaps, Makepeace thought, but he said nothing and noted that Albert did not endorse Jeremiah's statement.

"On the other hand," Jeremiah continued, "some sincerely believe their sins are of no consequence and they will be redeemed no matter what they do."

"I fear that far too many believe that," Albert said.

"God preserve us all," Makepeace intoned, but praying he, most of all, would be preserved by the Creator, and not a target of Almighty retaliation.

Makepeace and Jeremiah remained one more day before continuing their journey. Winter was on the horizon.

Albert pointed out that it would be a good idea to get over the mountains before the snows came. He insisted they engage the services of a Shawnee Indian guide named White Claws, who could make sure their camps were in providential locations and that there was no danger from wild animals.

"And sometimes, blizzards come suddenly, and drifts obscure the roads," Albert added.

"I guess what you're saying," Jeremiah said, "is that those who have not lived in the woods are ill-equipped to recognize whether the relics we stumble upon are harbingers of good or evil."

"And there's always the possibility of taking a false path," Albert said. He looked at Makepeace so intently when he said that, that Makepeace thought his words carried a hidden meaning.

A faithful member of the church, White Claws spoke fair English as well as several Indian dialects. Albert said he was a bear-dreamer, adding they would discover for themselves what that sobriquet meant.

White Claws showed up at sunrise the following morning. Makepeace was surprised that he was no bigger than his former cohort Juan Pedro. Makepeace had expected a fierce warrior would lead them across the wilds. and was put off by the Indian's fancy dress, a fringed leather tunic ornamented with yellow tassels. The scout's limbs were sheathed in deerskin leggings, laced at the sides with deer sinew. Filled with gear, his pack was carried by a Paint named *Otetiani*.

"Reliable horse," White Claws told them. "Name means always ready."

"And White Claws is just as ready," Albert assured them.

Makepeace was certain Albert was just being kind to the Redskin.

After Mrs. O'Brien prepared a breakfast of venison sausage, eggs and biscuits, the three struck out for the road still known as Braddock's Folly in honor of the old English general.

White Claws walked ahead to check the lay of the land. *Otetiani* followed dutifully. Old Nelly trailed behind on a rope held by Makepeace. The first day went easily enough and Makepeace wondered if they really needed White Claws.

Makepeace applauded himself for being rid of Friar Redmond, but was surprised early the next morning. Six miles west of Hagerstown, the faker sat by the side of a mountain road, a forlorn expression on his patchy, pink face.

XIX

Thou art not what thou wast before.
What reason I should be the same?
Sir Robert Aytoun
To An Inconstant Mistress

Esakka and Mouse followed the Egyptian woman from the jail into the starless black night. The rumbling of the storm had ceased. Not so Esakka's misgivings about escaping the law.

"You can call me Queen Esther," the woman said. "I is named after the lady in the Bible."

"I call you Miss Queen Esther," Mouse said.

The city of Annapolis was deserted, the streets lifeless and quiet. Damage from the storm could be seen everywhere. The rains still fell, albeit gently, as the three picked their way through the wet debris and desolation.

Queen Esther led them along an Indian trail across the rolling swells north of the city. The trees dripped from night rains and laurel's sweet odor hung heavy on the air. A screeching owl punctuated the night calm.

After five hours walking, during which time Esakka and Mouse barely kept up with Queen Esther, they reached a tent village on the Severne River where a canopy of oak trees sheltered a fizzling campfire. Esakka breathed a sigh of relief. Tired he was, and sore of foot and limb.

Eyeing the people gathered there, Esakka made a point of counting them. Seven women of child-bearing age industrious, but tired-looking. Eight men, mostly young and stalwart. Five children, none over ten or twelve, and four horses. A brown dog bossed two small goats.

Surprised at the arrival of Queen Esther, the group gave her a

118

loving greeting, full of respect, with much kissing and hugging. From that, Esakka figured her to be the matriarch of the clan.

"We's got to be heading out," Queen Esther announced. Then she turned to Esakka and Mouse. "This is my family. That handsome one is my son Romano and the younger one is his brother Carlo."

Esakka looked closely at the old woman. Her eyes were blue and in the daylight, her apricot skin shone like sand. She did not appear to be African. Her sons' skin was the same as hers, and their features reminded him of Mediterranean men.

"Master Esakka, they sure got a big family," Mouse said. "Do you think they's brothers and sisters?"

"Mouse, some may be related, but some may be like you and me—added to the family over a period of time. I think we've fallen in with a troop of Gypsies. I've come upon them in parts of the old world."

"I ain't knowing about Gypsies."

"So far, we're being treated like equals. Let's just be happy. But don't get too friendly with those women. They look like the loose sort. If they pay you any attention, they will probably expect you to give them some money."

***

"Where you been, Momma?" Romano asked.

"In jail! But there ain't no jail can keep me. Not if the Lord's got his eye on me. God throw open the door and told us to walk and we walked." She pointed toward Esakka and Mouse. "These two was in there. One of them's got a good strong back we can be using." She glanced toward Mouse. "I don't know about the scrawny one, but he's bound to be good for something."

"Jacob Mouse, at your service." Mouse bowed to Queen Esther. "I'se willing to do anything for you I can."

"Now, I respect that," Queen Esther said. "Supposen you men want to eat something?"

"I thanks you for that," Mouse said.

Romano led them to the campfire, handing Esakka and Mouse bowls of stew and cornbread. "Eat up. Help yourself to more if you want. The rest of us are packing. Soon as you eat, you can lend us a hand. We need to travel as far as possible tonight. We'll sleep during the early part of the day and then see about some work. Later, Momma will read the Tarot cards. If she likes what she sees, she may invite you to join us."

Esakka and Mouse were left alone to eat by the campfire while the family packed tents and belongings into carts, the ponies already standing in the traces.

Queen Esther said it was important for Esakka and Mouse not to look like slaves. She outfitted them with hats and tied bandannas around their necks, making them resemble the rest of the clan. Romano selected several tarnished rings from a bag and placed them on the men's fingers.

Queen Esther never asked why they were in jail, but they were warned that if they ran away with the jewelry, they would be found and their fingers cut off. Her eyes sparkled when she said it, making Esakka think it was a joke. He had seen better looking rings in the Islands for a shilling or two. In fact, several times, he had bought Island jewelry and traded it for a small profit when he returned home.

Soon after that, the rain stopped. The caravan moved north along the river road, the two goats tied to a rope fastened to the last cart. The brown dog named Rat trailed behind, nipping at the goat's heels if they tarried.

As the carts rolled, the troop sang, high spirits ruling the clan. Esakka and Mouse were permitted to ride in one of the wagons. Despite the rocky ride, they promptly fell asleep.

Here and there, the group encountered remnants of campfires. If they passed a farmer's field, the Gypsies helped themselves to corn or other vegetables. Once or twice a dog barked in the night, but not a solitary farmer fired a flintlock at them or came out to see who they were. At mid-morning they made camp, having bypassed B-town and turned east, staying close to the rim of Chesapeake Bay. Esakka noticed Queen Esther studied the coastal horizon from time to time as if she was searching for a ship.

Romano introduced them to the rest of the clan. His other brothers were Cain, Isaac, and Yerks. An old man called The General was Queen Esther's husband. An apparent marriage bond existed between Romano and his wife, Medea. Carlo's woman was Ladora, but her wandering eye told Esakka they were not wed.

When Carlo caught Ladora's gaze on Esakka, he glared sternly at him and turned to Queen Esther. "That's a good-looking African. Just make sure he stays away from my woman."

Romano whispered to Esakka, "That union wasn't made in Heaven. And Carlo's got himself an itch that just won't quit, but he's jealous as a jaybird. Stay clear of his woman."

"He needn't worry about me," Esakka said. "I have other things to think about than rutting with a woman. I am a virgin and intend to remain so until I find the right wife."

Romano gave him a curious look. "Never mind. But I want you and Mouse to think about becoming part of the family. And you will have to pick new names. That's our custom."

While they were making camp that night, Mouse told Esakka that he did not think Queen Esther liked him and thought she would not accept him. He expressed a fear of being rejected by the family or caught again by the law. Esakka told him to relax and enjoy his freedom and the fact that no one stood over him with the cat-o'-nine.

A week later, Queen Esther advised that God had told her to let them join the family. Romano promised a big celebration in their honor and asked what names they intended to choose to signify their adoption. Esakka was not certain how long he wished to remain with the troop, but he complied with the renaming and chose the name of Ibrahim. Mouse selected Jericho.

"That's the name of a city, not a person," Esakka said.

"Maybe the city be named after a person," Mouse said. "I likes the name. I thought of taking your old name but it confuse everyone."

"Rightly so," said Esakka. "I'm glad to see you are thinking, Mister Jericho."

Carlo pulled out his blade and surveyed its edge, flashing it in the sun before returning it to its scabbard. He narrowed his eyes at Esakka and said, "No matter what your name, you'd better not forget you're a slave."

Esakka was annoyed by Carlo's threat, but maintained his peace. He had not looked twice at any of the women and was not sure he

121

could identify Carlo's woman Ladora if he encountered her away from the family. Except for Ladora, the women were not particularly fastidious and did not bathe daily. They looked worn and hard. Esakka did notice, however, that Ladora seemed to keep track of his going and coming with an interested eye.

One afternoon, the men returned from their foray carrying a good sized pig. As if aware of its fate, it squealed loudly when anyone came near it.

The women prepared corn and potatoes. Romano and Cain built a fire for roasting the pig while Carlo did the butchering. He set up his operation in a prominent area, making sure Esakka and Mouse witnessed his agility with his blade.

The initiation into the group began with a speech by Romano. Esakka and Mouse repeated an oath after him and promised to be faithful members of the family, to obey all orders from those in command, and never to reveal any of the family's secrets. Then the three of them slit their thumbs and mingled blood.

"That makes us all brothers," Romano said.

"And brothers never take advantage of each other or lay with each other's woman," Carlo added with an ominous note.

While the pig roasted on the spit, Queen Esther brought out wine. The troop drank heartily and the savory odor of pork caused their mouths to water with anticipation. The ceremony awed Mouse. He had never taken part in, nor witnessed such a party.

"Massa, Massa Ibrahim, I ain't nebber had a family," he told Esakka. "Now, I got a big one. I think I died and gone to heaven. And that Miss Ladora, she must be a angel."

"She's a whore just like the rest," Esakka said darkly.

After dinner, Queen Esther brought out her Tarot cards. "Who wants to hear his fortune?"

Esakka looked away, but Queen Esther had no intention of letting him off. She studied the cards she had laid down, then added another. "God tell me a new life beckons to Ibrahim. His life is long and filled with both tears and happiness. Love come his way, but I sees a dark cloud over his woman, followed by thundering and lightning."

Carlo coughed but Queen Esther gave him an evil look and he pursed his lips as she turned another card. "Then I sees the sun rising over calm waters. Many men surround Ibrahim, some good and some bad and he be confused about which is which. Finally, I sees a man come to his rescue. First, the man has a long beard and then he has none." Queen Esther looked closely at the card in her hand. "He could be a judge or he could be Father Death."

"Maybe he's a jealous husband," Carlo muttered.

"Shut up," Queen Esther said. "Ibrahim, you has to come to me again for another reading. Perhaps the cards will speak more clearly another time."

"Momma has never told a fortune that didn't come true," Romano added. "You can count on what she says."

Queen Esther shuffled the cards and turned to Mouse. "God tell me for little Jericho, there is only happiness. He carries a heavy burden, but it is lifted from him. Dancing girls and children be all around him. Many good things be in store for him."

The celebration continued with singing. Romano and Cain pulled out a flute and played lively tunes. Ladora danced, her skirts swirling, her shapely legs and ankles flashing seductively.

Thoroughly enjoying the show, Mouse said, "The dancing-women part of my fortune already come true!"

Finding no pleasure in the troop's merry-making, Esakka stayed at the edge of the campfire. The Bible did not condone witches and the telling of the future was a forbidden thing. He vowed never to consult Queen Esther again.

It was well into the night before the drinking ceased and everyone settled down to sleep.

*****

Before they retired, Ladora spoke to Mouse. "My name is Ladora, Mister Jericho. I welcome you to our family. I myself have been here for two years. Are you and your friend brothers?"

"No, ma'am," Mouse answered. "My brother was Efrim. He dead. I guess now, Mister Ibrahim's my brother."

"He is a very handsome man," Ladora said. "Do you know how old he is?"

"He told me he be one or two 'yond twenty. He not sure."

Ladora did some calculation on her fingers and nodded her head. "Yes, I think that is about right. Thank you, Mr. Jericho."

123

She pinched him affectionately on his arm. Carlo came and pulled her away, chastising her for talking to Mouse. She stuck out her tongue.

Mouse giggled. Ladora was the prettiest woman who had ever talked to him and she turned and winked at him as Carlo yanked her by the arm. When he saw the wink, Carlo promptly slapped Ladora hard on the behind. "Get along, you bitch."

Ladora smacked Carlo on the side of his head with the heel of her hand.

Queen Esther had ordered Mouse to stand watch for the remainder of the night, being the only one, other than Esakka, who was not drunk. Mouse wanted desperately to tell his friend about Ladora winking at him, but he had promised not to leave his post. It was morning before he could speak to Esakka.

"Good morning, Mister Ibrahim."

"Mouse," Esakka said, "I'm not going to use our new names anymore."

"Why's that, Mister Ibrahim?"

"Things around here are not what they seem. You need to know about women, too, Mouse. They are not easily figured out. What they say and do does not always mean what you think it does."

"But Massa Ibrahim, Miss Ladora sure want to know about you. I know she ain't interested in me, but she curious about you."

"I don't even want to know about it, Mouse. These women are not clean and do not carry the spirit of the Lord with them."

As November passed, the days grew shorter and the nights cold and damp. Early one morning, the men rose from sleeping and left the camp. Not asked to accompany them, Esakka and Mouse spent the afternoon grooming the animals. The women busied themselves performing their various tasks.

At dusk, the men returned, bringing a calf, as well as blankets and winter clothing. Esakka suspected they had not paid for any of their plunder.

A conference was called by Queen Esther. Esakka and Mouse were not invited, but just before the evening meal, Queen Esther announced that they were going to Philadelphia. She added that the calf would be kept to make milk, but they would make dinner with a turkey that God had sent wandering across their path.

A campfire was built with more firewood than they had ever used. Romano brought out his flute and played wild Gypsy music. Ladora, Medea and Lividia cavorted around the circle of flames. Ladora swirled her skirts, dancing closer and closer to Esakka, flaunting her knees and thighs as she waved her satins.

Astonished that the flirting, sexy swaying, and alluring glances were directed at him, Esakka broke out in a cold sweat. The more he stared at Ladora, the more familiar she seemed. And her real name was not Ladora; it had to be a Gypsy name she had taken.

As if aware of Esakka's embarrassed state, Ladora intensified her dancing. She kicked her legs higher and higher and flashed the ruffled fabrics against his face. A familiar odor of sweet oil jolted his memory.

Queen Esther coughed several times. She seemed displeased with Ladora's dancing.

There was nothing angelic about Ladora. Each time she pranced closer, Esakka looked more intently. Burning beans seared his nose and he relived the flight to the oasis when he was but fifteen. A vision of Ktura completely naked, dancing on the sands of Arabia tantalized him.

Carlo sat by the campfire, honing a knife against a whetstone. He pointed the knife at Ladora and gave her an ominous leer. "You better behave yourself, bitch. My knife is hungry for that calf, but it ain't particular."

Ladora would not be stopped. She reached to undo her hair, tossing her head furiously as if it was wet and needed drying. Esakka's brain flamed with memories of Ktura washing her hair in the oasis pool.

No longer able to tolerate Ladora's taunting dance, Esakka cried out, "You're Ktura! I know you must be Ktura!"

Carlo was so startled, he dropped his knife in the fire. The singing and the music stopped. Quick, jittery whispers ran through the group like wind sizzling through the sycamores.

Ladora giggled, ended her dance with a pirouette and ran for her tent. The Gypsy troop sat as quiet as starfish.

The first person to speak was Queen Esther. "Someone has

something to tell."

But Ladora was gone and Esakka had no desire to talk.

A few minutes later, Ladora returned. Now graced with a merry tongue, glancing frequently at Carlo, she told a long story about how she and Esakka served the same master in Africa. She ended with the words, "We were lovers."

Carlo chucked a rock at her head, barely missing her eye.

Esakka kept waiting for Ladora to mention that she was married to the master. He didn't expect her to add that she was the one who seduced him or that he was barely fifteen years old. Nor that their lover status consisted of a few stolen nights at a desert waterhole where she bathed and caressed him. And not much else.

Esakka frowned at Ladora and grumbled, "That was a long time ago."

Carlo scowled at them both, uttering strange Gypsy words that Esakka did not understand.

Romano gave a horse laugh. "We do not hear the entire story."

Esakka kept his eyes to the ground. "I am not the same person. Then I was Esakka. Now I am Ibrahim."

XX

So was the huntsman by the bear oppressed
Edmund Waller
Battle of the Summer Islands

Makepeace was disappointed to see Redmond sitting by the side of the road. Would he never be rid of the faker? Redmond, however, seemed thrilled that they had found him. He jumped up and offered a handshake.

"I know God is with me, but I would like mortal company traveling through the mountains."

"He's already eaten all the victuals Mrs. O'Brien gave him," Makepeace said. "It's not our company he wants, it's our bounty."

"Two shaman wear black dress," White Claws muttered. "New one a fool."

Only Makepeace heard him. He wondered what the Indian saw in Redmond that revealed his true nature. Then he wondered if the Indian's clever scrutiny extended to himself.

Redmond flashed a tentative smile. Obviously, the one person who could unmask Makepeace was Redmond, but the faker seemed willing to forgive Makepeace for decking him in the Anneville jail. Perhaps Redmond had a certain respect for his skillful escape. Makepeace was curious how the impostor avoided his rendezvous with the gallows but figured he had pled the Book.

"Friar Redmond's the kind who'll forgive ye anything if it's to his advantage," Makepeace told Jeremiah when they had a moment alone. "We need to be aware he's thinking to turn things to his benefit. We don't want to be his victims."

"We know Friar Redmond's a renegade," Jeremiah said. "This way we can keep an eye on him. Better a known quantity than an unknown one. Besides, there is some safety in numbers when traveling."

127

"A show of numbers can be helpful if we bump into anyone intending to cause us trouble," Makepeace agreed. "But we may be carrying our own calamity with us. I ain't any confidence in him."

"We will place our confidence in the Lord," Jeremiah said.

Well, perhaps that was a solution—provided the Lord came through. Redmond was the fly in the cream. Of course, if Jeremiah found out what an unknown quantity Makepeace was, the cream would sour and the fly wouldn't matter. Makepeace could find no serenity in this state of affairs. He wished he knew the rosary so he could recite it and get his mind off his circumstances.

The brisk November morning warmed toward noon. Leaves from sassafras and aspen trees had long since fallen, the woodland floor littered with gold and orange relics.

Makepeace was disappointed in the road. While it had been satisfactory for wagons and ox-carts when it was built ten years before, it had fallen into disrepair. Those who owned contrivances with wheels tended to choose the new road to the North created by the Pennsylvanians. Traffic on this road consisted of a solitary pedlar now and then, or several families in oxcarts who traveled together. Makepeace thought he would not want to travel this road alone.

Flocks of chimney swifts and yellow long-billed cuckoos chirped and cawed overhead. White Claws pointed out a bevy of trumpeter swans feasting on the remnants of a corn field. Occasionally, the Indian spotted a deer peering at them from deep fringes of foliage.

Past Frederick, White Claws remarked that a wet spring and summer had increased the vegetation as well as the animal population. Turkeys and guineas scurried for the brambles at their approach. From branches high over their heads, jays and mockingbirds fussed at their intrusion into their sanctuary.

Beyond Sharpstown, in a meadow below, Makepeace counted forty elk grazing. At Turner's Gap, a yellow mountain cat sat on a high branch in a live oak tree, glowering at them. Then it yawned, evidently too lazy to move.

"Nighttime, keep good fire," White Claws said. "Much bear."

"Bear?" Makepeace had heard that bears could stand eight feet tall, weigh as much as a horse, and have a ferocious temper. He had no desire to see one up close. "I hope there ain't many bears."

"Much bear and cat in woods," White Claws emphasized. "Much

128

deer too. Me store packets of food along way on last trip. Each time, take one, put one back in place."

"In these woods," Jeremiah said, "men are the trespassers and may easily be preyed upon."

"Good you travel with White Claws," their guide added. "Me look out for your welfare."

"God's not going to let any bear attack us," Redmond boasted.

Leading them to a hickory tree marked with a crude glyph, White Claws climbed up to the second row of branches. From a hole in the crotch, he pulled out a package of pemmican and tossed it to Makepeace.

Once or twice, White Claws claimed a bear or a cat had found his cache. Scratchings on the trunk indicated which was the thief. If the tree was stripped of its bark, White Claws said a bear had eaten the inner layer. "Bark his bread. Some oak meat not bitter. God give us all our daily bread, no?"

"Bless the Lord," Redmond said. "Bless His Holy Name."

Makepeace thought he would vomit at the man's religiosity and wondered if he himself would ever be able to maintain his new identity if it required such mewling and puking.

Late in the afternoon, White Claws began singing a little tune.

"Little doe, little doe

"Everywhere we see your tracks.

"Little doe, I'm looking for you."

Redmond giggled, his beady eyes full of scorn. "Sure, that deer is just waiting for you, Injun Joe!"

Jeremiah frowned at Redmond. "Be a little kinder, padre. It may save you some embarrassment later on."

Minutes later, Makepeace spotted a small deer bleating from an entangling thicket. White Claws appeared startled to see it. Makepeace was surprised at the ease with which the Indian captured it, but the abundance of game was phenomenal and Jeremiah pointed out the entire country was like the Garden of Eden.

"Red man take good care of land. White man not do so," White Claws declared. "White man kill much game. Much waste."

"God provideth for white man. He made the white man in his own image," Redmond said in a strident tone. He turned his face toward heaven. "Thank Thee, Our Heavenly Father. We thank Thee for your bounteous gifts."

White Claws looked at Redmond with a puzzled expression. "White Claws sing to deer spirit. *Sartain*, doe wait because White Claws sing."

Redmond bubbled with glee. Again, he snorted his dirty giggle. "You're a pagan, Injun Joe."

"White Claws baptized," the Indian said. "Not pagan. You pagan fool all the way to bone."

"That's enough of that," Jeremiah said.

Makepeace considered he was developing a real hatred for the pock-faced faker. For more than one reason, he wished they had left Redmond at the roadside.

Stretching the slain deer out on the ground, White Claws deftly ran his knife from the animal's chin to its tail. He split open the lungs and guts and removed the visceral parts. Those he laid by the stream for the crows to eat, the black birds already cawing in anticipation in the branches overhead.

In a very short while, White Claws had the doe roasting over the camp fire. Jeremiah took the ears of white corn given them by Albert and laid them in their husks among the outer coals.

As the savory odors wafted upward, Makepeace's mouth watered in anticipation. When the meal was devoured, Makepeace regarded their guide with new appreciation. "May ye evermore continue singing to the deer."

"Much thanks," White Claws said.

Redmond mocked them. "Oh, you're having such a wonderful little tea party."

After dinner, White Claws buried the unusable parts of the carcass and made a fire in a pit to smoke the remainder of the venison.

In what Makepeace considered a rare moment of gratitude on the part of Redmond, the faker said, "Let us give thanks to God for our guide. Maybe later I'll tell you a good story."

Redmond looked straight at Makepeace when he spoke, making him wonder if the faker intended to reveal his jail time. Although the promise of a good story was evidently forgotten as the evening wore on, Makepeace felt the venison flip-flopping in his stomach and knew he would not sleep well.

At night, Jeremiah, Makepeace and White Claws shared the

watch, absolving Redmond of duty since he had walked so much while they rode. Redmond did not seem disappointed.

Awakening at dawn, Makepeace did not see White Claws. The coffee had been set aboiling on the campfire and *Otetiani* patiently grazed beside the mule Nelly.

Then Makepeace spotted White Claws standing naked on the crest of a nearby hill, his arms lifted to the sky. He watched the Indian bend to the ground and rise with a bear mask on his head. White Claws then began a fast, rhythmic dance accompanied by a strange lament as he banged a short stick against a hand drum. A big silver cross flapped against his bare chest.

White Claws completed his ritual by sitting cross-legged on the dirt and smoking a short calumet for a considerable number of minutes. Between drags on his pipe, he wailed a mournful song.

When White Claws returned, he was fully clothed. Makepeace could tell Redmond was dying to comment on the Indian's activity. He was thankful the man held back, but sooner or later, he was sure the faker would not be able to control his tongue.

During the course of the day, they cached additional jerky. More frequently, they found the hiding places empty. Huge claw marks on the tree indicated bears were stealing the meat. White Claws measured one set and declared the bear to be seven feet tall.

"Weigh much as two fat men. Make fine blanket. White Claws kill with bow and arrow." The Indian did a little dance. "Wear bear claws around neck! Show White Claws mighty warrior!"

Redmond patted his sides with his hands, shook his hips, then gurgled and snickered as he stomped a circle in imitation of an Indian dance. Makepeace did not resented White Claws' bravado, but he longed to put down the faker Redmond.

Even Jeremiah questioned their guide's judgment. "That bow and arrow will not be worth much against a charging bear. I saw a few of those monsters in New England. It takes several good flintlock balls to stop them."

"Great Spirit give me strength to kill bear," White Claws said. "My arrows strong. Have iron points. Much sharp." Under his breath, the Indian grumbled, "Paleface too much book. All the time, much book. Little know woodlands."

"I saw you up there this morning, Injun Joe," Redmond said.

"Naked as a jackdaw, doing your little dance. I don't know who you were praying to, but it wasn't anyone going to help you."

White Claws moped the rest of the day. He spoke only when necessary until they had settled into camp. Then he again offered more bear tales. Obviously, Makepeace thought, the Indian relished his position as royal story-teller and had no intention of abdicating his throne.

As a child, White Claws told them, he had lived in New England. His mother urged him to become a visionary and he took the Bear Spirit as his mantra. Once on a hunting trip with his father, when White Claws was no more than seven years old, his father had killed a stag deer.

Hauling the deer home on a toboggan, they stopped to rest a bit and were suddenly confronted by a gargantuan black grizzly. Caught between the bear and the toboggan hauling the fresh-killed meat, they froze in their tracks. The grizzly reared up on its giant hams and growled ferociously.

"Some people say bear think like man," White Claws explained. "Those people wrong. Bear think like bear. Not fear anything. Let nothing stand in way of dinner. Nose go crazy with smell of fresh kill."

White Claws jumped up and demonstrated, tossing his head around, sniffing at the wind, searching for its secrets, then growling and exposing his teeth.

"Bear show big fangs. He roar. Scared little boy like me think bear able to reach up and grab thunder from clouds. Start crying. Father throw me under bush and fall on top of me."

"Clearly, the bear did not eat you," Makepeace said. "What happened?"

"No more story," White Claws said. "Maybe tell later."

"He made it up. Now, he needs time to think up the rest of it," Redmond said. "The bear ate both of them."

White Claws gave Redmond a dirty look, then went about checking the firewood. He tossed more logs on the campfire and stirred the coals until they blazed.

The temperature was dropping rapidly. Makepeace thought the fur blankets would feel good tonight, but he knew he would lie awake half the night wondering about the end of White Claws story.

White Claws headed for the bog to relieve himself.

"He's a masterful storyteller," said Jeremiah, "even if he has a tendency to embroider."

"Just stringing together a bunch of lies," Redmond said. "I think there's a commandment against that."

"That may be," Makepeace said, "but telling stories is a gift from God."

When White Claws returned, Jeremiah said, "Would you please finish your story?"

Makepeace and Redmond seconded the request.

White Claws sat close to the fire, obviously delighting in his importance. "Bear grab deer and run. Not eat me, not eat father. We go back to camp without meat. Everyone hungry. Very sad. We get posse up, look for bear. No bear. That night I dream about Bear Spirits. Much protect and guide me all my days."

"I don't think those crazy Bear Spirits will protect you from grizzlies again," Redmond said. "You were lucky you had a dead stag for him to eat."

"Here not worry about grizzlies," White Claws declared. "Bad bears live in North."

"You silly little man," Redmond said. "All bears are bad."

By the end of the third day, White Claws exuded confidence that he was under the protection of the Bear Spirit. "Two more days! No sign of bears!"

"That Indian would not brag so much if he was not sure we would see no bears," Redmond said.

"He's traveled this path enough times to know there ain't no bears in these mountains," Makepeace added, hoping it was true.

"Nevertheless," Jeremiah said, "Our guide appears trustworthy. I have a lot of faith in him and you gentlemen should thank him for his services."

That night, camp was made by the side of a stream. Sheltered under a grove of oak trees with great horizontal limbs nearly as long as the trees were high, Makepeace felt secure. He eyed each tree, studying it for accessibility in case he had to climb it to escape a ferocious animal.

Following the evening meal, White Claws spun a most outrageous story about a warrior who married a bear woman. Unable to give up the special delights of this creature, the warrior moved into her cave. Over the years, she bore him fourteen children.

Although they possessed the wisdom of Indian warriors, all the children looked like bears. White Claws explained, "Bear medicine more strong than human medicine."

"That's tittle-tattle," Redmond said. "God's medicine is the best."

Jeremiah looked at the man with obvious frustration. "Let White Claws get on with his story."

White Claws rose and moved around the campfire like a bear in search of food. "Young bears come down in valley. Eat chickens. Eat turkeys. Bear children grow up. Make more bear children. Year after year, bears come and come."

"How did they manage to feed all the bears?" Jeremiah asked. "Where did they get enough meat?"

"Bears raid farms in valley. People mad at bears. People want to make bears dead. Others say kill bears, make Bear Spirits angry."

"More with the infidel spirits," Redmond declared. "That Indian had better ask God for forgiveness for believing that pagan nonsense."

"For goodness sake, try to be kind," Jeremiah said.

"Let White Claws tell his story," Makepeace added. He was still trying to picture a bear that a man would want to bed.

Redmond looked crossly at Makepeace. "We've all got our stories, haven't we?"

White Claws continued. "Time pass. Hungry bear eat child. War start. Every day, bear kill person, people kill bear. Bears multiply. Always hungry. One day they come marching down mountains like army. Many, many bears. Too many bears to count."

Makepeace was impressed that White Claws was so caught up in his story, nobody could stop him.

Redmond rocked back and forth on his haunches. "Now you're going to tell me they took over the village and held elections for Lord Mayor."

"Many bear come. Scent ride on air. Villagers smell bears. Villagers hide, make big ambush."

"That must have been some massacre," Jeremiah said.

"Villagers kill one hundred bears. Lay bears out so they can bury next day. When morning come, dead bears have human faces."

"Well, that has to be the finish," Redmond said.

Makepeace gave Redmond a disgusted look. He wanted to hear the rest of the story, and as usual, the faker was causing trouble. He thought seriously about decking the man again.

"You want to hear end of story?" White Claws looked very superior. "Maybe you wait until tomorrow night."

"Oh go ahead," Redmond said grudgingly.

"Please tell us the rest," Jeremiah added.

White Claws continued. "One bear still left in hills. That bear a she-bear. Same gift as grandmother. Villagers want to kill her but they feared warrior succumb to her charms. Finally, they choose strongest brave in clan. Send him into mountains. Next night, he shoots she-bear, two cubs. Bear spirits much filled with anger. Same night, all Indian babies die."

"Humbug," Redmond said. "If they all died, it was because God sent a plague."

"*Sartain*, Bear Spirits make revenge," White Claws declared. "Warrior not use sacred bow and arrow to kill bears. Bear Spirits gnashing teeth, much angry."

"And what happened to the warrior?" Jeremiah asked.

"Villagers exile warrior to mountains to make peace with Bear Spirits. Then he wish he marry she-bear. He die, never know the delights of a woman. So help me, God!"

Even White Claws joined their laughter.

For a strange reason, Makepeace had a feeling they were about to enter the kingdom of the bears. *Sartain!*

Makepeace slept peacefully, undisturbed by the distant cries of owls and wolves. After rising the next morning, he made tea, and doled out the pemmican. Then he brushed Old Nelly while Redmond brushed *Otetiani*. Jeremiah packed gear at White Claw's direction.

Before Makepeace could tie on Nelly's pack, the mule pawed the ground and brayed nervously. Nose and ears aquiver, she reared, knocking him to the ground, then galloped through the remnants of the camp fire, bolting for the stream. *Otetiani* was fast behind her.

Makepeace, his elbows bruised, his face in the dirt, raised up on his arms and knees to stare into the black snout and bleary red eyes of an enormous brown bear.

Jeremiah and Redmond grabbed the remnants of the burning logs from the campfire and hurled them at the bear. Struck in the nose by one, the animal stopped in his tracks and looked around, eyes bulging evil intent. Jeremiah reached into White Claws' gunny for a stick of pemmican and tossed it toward the bear. The bear looked at it and sniffed in disdain. In the moment the animal was distracted, Makepeace rolled away from him.

White Claws yanked his bow and arrow from his sling and aimed for the bear. His arrow penetrated the bear's neck several inches. The beast was infuriated and used his massive paws to brush at the arrow. He roared angrily and slammed his teeth together like a steel trap.

Makepeace rolled further away.

Redmond jerked an ugly little flintlock pistol from inside his cassock. Pointing it, he pulled the trigger. It clicked noisily, but failed to fire.

"Climb tree!" White Claws ordered.

Jeremiah scrambled up the nearest oak tree. Makepeace hunkered beside a bramble bush, not moving a muscle. White Claws inserted another arrow into his bow and took aim.

Still pointing his useless pistol, Redmond retreated, vainly clicking the trigger. The bear lumbered toward him. He threw the gun at the animal, hitting its brow, which further infuriated the brute. Stepping backward, Redmond stumbled over a rock. His cassock caught under his heel and he fell on his spine.

With a ferocious roar, the bear forged astride the fallen priest, straddling him, sniffing, bellowing its way toward the priest's head. Redmond flailed his arms helplessly against the bear's brawny legs. Makepeace could only watch as the animal opened its cavernous jaws and clamped Redmond's neck between them.

Redmond's feeble cry filtered through the bear's muzzle. "Blessed Jeeee-e-e-us!"

The bear snapped his jaws shut, crunching Redmond's neck bones. Makepeace looked away as a red geyser spurted from the man's craw.

White Claws yelled again, "Catholic medicine man, you climb

tree!"

Eyeing Redmond's pistol lying several feet behind the bear, Makepeace darted for the weapon, then scurried toward the nearest oak, the bark snatching at his gown as he struggled upward.

The brute rose on its hind legs, Redmond's head held tenderly between his jaws. Raising his eyes toward the heavens, the bear bawled victoriously. Redmond's head vaulted, then plunged to the ground. For what seemed like an eternity to Makepeace, the head became a ball while the bear rolled it playfully in the dirt.

Abandoning the head, the animal returned to Redmond's carcass. With his long yellow claws, he raked away the black clerical clothes and ripped into the priest's stomach. Like a beaver gnawing wood, he went after the man's guts. Makepeace cringed as he watched blood and flesh fly through the air.

The indomitable White Claws fired another arrow. It penetrated the side of the animal's chest near the pit of his right front limb. The beast staggered at the impact, blood spewing forth, staining his reddish-brown fur. He snarled and swiped at the arrow, broke it off, snarled again and went back to what was left of Redmond's black-garbed body.

Sitting in the crotch of the tree, Makepeace studied the pistol, hoping to discover why it had misfired. The flint looked good. The lead was in the chamber. He tamped the powder with his finger and shook his head in bewilderment.

White Claws scrambled up the tree that Jeremiah had climbed, urging him higher. Jeremiah's robe caught on a brushy limb. He could go no further. White Claws was stuck below him in the second elbow.

On a rampage, the bear circled the camp, nosing his long snout through their blankets and gear. Unhappy with what he found, he barked and headed for the tree where Jeremiah and White Claws clung to the lowest level of its branches.

The brute stood on his hind legs and encircled the trunk with his paws as if he intended to climb. The bear snapped at White Claws' right foot, almost scoring a toe before the Indian yanked it away.

Suddenly, the bear backed down, snarling and spitting blood.

"Arrow go deep!" White Claws exclaimed.

Without doubt, White Claws' second arrow had penetrated the

animal's lung. The animal's black muzzle dripped thick red gore. Makepeace questioned whether it was Redmond's or the bear's blood.

Angry and in grim pain, the bear bellowed. Pieces of white flesh flew from his teeth. Bloody saliva dribbled from his snout. Lumbering toward the tree that held Makepeace, the bear broke into a strong-minded charge.

Makepeace quietly examined Redmond's pistol. Satisfied with the state of its priming, he tested the muzzle. That too seemed in proper order.

Back and forth, back and forth, the brute rammed his shoulder against the trunk, shaking the oak until its branches quivered. Struck by plummeting acorns, the bear looked up, and snarled. He wrapped his great paws around the tree and clambered upward.

The bear drew closer, evil eyes focused on him. Makepeace smelled its vile breath. He pulled a walnut from his pocket and chucked the nut at the bear's head. It struck him on the snout. With dead calm, Makepeace leveled the pistol and aimed straight at the animal's eye.

This time the pistol worked. A stream of fire vomited from the barrel. A smoky cloud enveloped the bear's head. White Claws and Jeremiah cheered as the bear's hold on the tree weakened.

The animal fell backward, his legs crumpling beneath him. Rolling, rolling, rolling down the slope, the beast tumbled into the stream and lay prostrate. From its mutilated eye, Makepeace watched blood gush into the silvery waters.

White Claws gave a loud whoop and scrambled down the tree. Jeremiah jerked his robe free of the branch and followed White Claws.

Makepeace delayed a moment before joining them. For a considerable number of minutes, the three men stood together and stared at the creature.

"Bear dead," White Claws said.

"Yer sure?"

"*Sartain*. Pull bear out of water."

Makepeace stepped into the stream, followed by Jeremiah and White Claws. Makepeace reached for the bear's hind foot. The bear's muscles jerked.

"He's not dead!" Makepeace shrieked. He ran back to the grove, followed by Jeremiah and White Claws.

They hunkered behind a huge oak, watching with alarm. Several moments passed, their eyes locked on the huge, unmoving body.

"Dying spasm," White Claws finally declared. "Bear dead now."

"You go first," Makepeace said, a slight tremor in his voice.

White Claws marched back into the water. He walked over and kicked at the animal's snout. The bear gave no response.

"Him dead." White Claws said. "Lend hand."

Makepeace and Jeremiah helped drag the carcass toward the campfire. Makepeace was surprised at the bear's size. Although the body was emaciated, it was at least six feet in length.

White Claws patted the bear's stomach. "Him very hungry. Look for food before long winter sleep." With a reverent tone, he then spoke to the animal. "I am sorry to kill you, Grandfather Bear. Your spirit is a credit to your people."

The Indian pulled a short reed pipe from his pocket, filled it with tobacco and fired it up. Inhaling and exhaling four times, he blew a puff of smoke to the north, to the south, to the east and to the west. He looked quite pleased with himself and declared, "Now Four Winds will continue to bless us with their secrets."

White Claws jammed the pipe between the animal's bloody lips. "Be at peace, Grandfather Bear. Today I suck the holy breath from your body. But me and my friends thank you for gift to our welfare. Much grateful to you and all Bear Spirits. Rest happy in Far-off Hunting Grounds."

The guide turned to Makepeace and Jeremiah. "Bear continue to feed us with their flesh. Permit us wear their skins. Must always be thankful to animals for gift. *Sartain*, you can expect them to accept arrow of death."

With his long hunting knife, White Claws vigorously ripped into the animal's stomach. He sliced it open as he had the doe and reached inside the cavity to remove the guts. Soon he was covered with bear blood.

Makepeace glanced at Redmond's remains and wondered if it had been himself lying there, would he have been ignored while the bear received all the attention?

As White Claws worked, he chanted low to himself. Frequently, he stopped, looked at the sky, then murmured something that

Makepeace did not understand. When White Claws noticed Makepeace's concern, he turned and spoke.

"Make hole in earth. Bury brother. Search for animals."

Jeremiah and Makepeace looked at each other, but did not challenge their guide's orders. Makepeace set about clearing the rocks from a patch of ground while Jeremiah dug a shallow pit with a shovel White Claws had produced from his gear. Together they placed Redmond's gruesome body and displaced head in the grave. Jeremiah volunteered to fill in the dirt and suggested that Makepeace go in search of the horse and mule.

Half a mile downstream, Makepeace found Nelly grazing. He whistled for her attention. When his shrill blast pierced the air, *Otetiani* appeared. The animals whinnied greetings and he led them back to the campsite.

On the way back, it occurred to Makepeace that the black cassock was responsible for saving his life. The cassock's medicine was definitely stronger than the bear's. Without it, there would have been no magic. And without it, he would be dead. So intent was he on his own good fortune, he did not acknowledge that Redmond's cassock had provided no protection for him.

Later in the morning, the temperature fell drastically. A light snow drifted across the mountains. White Claws looked again at the heavens and nodded. Makepeace decided the Indian had been praying for cold weather so that the bear meat would not spoil.

White Claws continued the butchering of the carcass, warbling a song about having bear steaks for dinner, and wearing bear teeth and bear claws to the next big powwow. He painted visions of a hero's welcome. Once, he stopped, took his shield from his pack and performed a short dance of gratitude to the Great Spirit.

Using fallen limbs he found on the forest floor, Jeremiah made a cross for Redmond's grave and pounded it into the ground. He stabilized it with rocks from the stream. Makepeace nodded his approval.

Along the river's grassy bank, they helped White Claws stretch out the bear's skin, anchor it with rocks, and then watched while he scraped it clean. He examined the bear's mouth but said he would wait until he was home before removing the teeth.

Studying the bear's paws, White Claws discovered three claws missing. He asked Jeremiah to see if they had stuck in the tree's bark when the bear fell. When Jeremiah found them, White Claws removed them gingerly so that the points would not be damaged.

As night came near, White Claws instructed them to build a circle of fire around the camp. He helped Jeremiah and Makepeace pile on limbs and brush to keep it burning high. *Otetiani* and Old Nelly remained inside the circle, along with the bear's remains. Redmond's grave was also within the enclosure.

White Claws slept by the carcass to guard against wolves. More bullets were found in Redmond's gear and White Claws took the pistol from Makepeace and kept it primed.

Several times in the night, they awoke to find themselves surrounded by the eager eyes of predators drawn to the camp by the smell of bear blood. The circle of fire kept the hungry animals at bay, but the following evening, White Claws tied the bear's leg bones to the limb of an oak tree some distance from their camp site. It was too high for the wolves to reach, but it kept them occupied through the night, although their yelping and barking made impossible a good night's sleep.

On the second day, White Claws finished butchering the bear. Makepeace and Jeremiah cut it into smaller sizes. On the third, the meat was smoked and prepared for making pemmican. White Claws then built a travois from tree limbs and strapped it to *Otetiani*.

As they prepared to leave, the Indian turned and looked at Makepeace. "You!" He pointed at Redmond's rock covered grave. "Make funeral for fool-priest!"

XXI

The unpremeditated lay.
Sir Walter Scott
Lay of the Last Minstrel

Makepeace looked at Jeremiah and hoped his friend would say a few farewell words on behalf of Redmond.

Jeremiah exchanged glances. "You knew him better."

Makepeace stalled, having no desire for Jeremiah to find out what a wretched priest he might be, unable to deliver a simple eulogy. "I can't say anything decent about the faker."

White Claws again pointed at Makepeace. "You make funeral."

Makepeace realized White Claws had selected him because the black cassock meant something to the Indian, whereas Jeremiah's brown robe did not. Makepeace stepped to the grave, grasped the edges of the crude cross and raised his eyes heavenward.

"Here we are, God, beneath the mantle of yer heavens. We look to Ye each day for guidance because we don't know what the day will bring." In a blurred voice, he continued, granting to the power of the black gown whatever sense his words had. "We look down that long path before us and we see part of today, but tomorrow is over the hill and we can't see that."

There was a moment of silence. Jeremiah's face was impassive. Makepeace wondered if what he said had any significance. His eyes met Jeremiah's. The priest seemed to recognize his need for help. Makepeace hoped he credited his stumbling speech to misery over Redmond's death and not to a want of piety. He stifled a sigh of relief as Jeremiah picked up the homily.

"Lord, our brother came along with us so he would have

142

company going over the hills. We know where his body was going, but in what direction his heart was traveling, we can not say. Lord, we did not know him well. Perhaps he was traveling in the right way or perhaps he was only pretending. It may be that in time, he would have discovered the right path—as we hope we all will. We ask only that you have mercy on his soul. And protect us for the remainder of our journey. This we ask in the name of our Lord."

As Jeremiah concluded, White Claws said, "Amen," as solemn as could be. Then he glanced at Redmond's grave and said, "No pipe."

It was such a flat statement, Makepeace felt White Claws had rendered a judgment rather than pointed out an oversight.

After the burial ceremony, they headed out. White Claws gave *Otetiani* to Jeremiah to ride while he walked ahead.

As Makepeace mounted Nelly, he felt his face go soft. He glanced at Jeremiah and their eyes met again for a moment. Then Makepeace clenched his teeth and directed his gaze toward the mountain-filled horizon.

The rest of the morning, nothing was said. Makepeace had no desire for conversation as he contemplated whether or not God was more intent on vanquishing him than assuring him a place in the sunshine. Jeremiah seemed to be having equal difficulty coping with Redmond's gory death.

Makepeace considered whether or not it would be best if he separated from the party and went his own way. At least then, he wouldn't be under this constant fear of being defrocked. And if God decided to rain vengeance down on him as he evidently had Redmond, no one else would have to suffer. But as the weather skidded downhill, the idea of traveling alone turned disheartening.

The snow flakes grew larger, although none stuck to the ground. When there was an opening in the trees, White Claws studied the sky, appearing pleased, rather than anxious, with the darkening cloud cover. Makepeace thought the guide relished the cold and exuded a feeling of superiority for not requiring more protection from the elements.

As if to emphasize his hardiness, White Claws pulled a set of long underwear from his backpack and handed it to Makepeace. Grateful, he immediately removed his black cassock and donned the

143

garment. The arms and legs were a wee bit short, but at least he was warmer when he hiked up his gown to ride the mule. He wrapped Redmond's long black scarf around his head and put the sombrero on top of it.

Jeremiah pulled a knee-length fur tunic from his belongings and put it over his long robe, raising the capuche so that it sheltered his ears.

Farther up the road, they stopped at an inn and drank beer. For two hours, they rested and felt civilized. The innkeeper remarked that ordinarily he did not serve Indians, but since White Claws was in company of two Fathers, he would make an exception.

"God bless ye, that'll save ye from excommunication," Makepeace said. Then he advised himself to be wary, for fear he would sound like Redmond.

Oldtown was a village of teepees, wigwams and long houses. There, they left White Claws at his brother's hut. The excitement over the travois loaded with remains of the bear brought a congregation of friends and relatives and a party quickly developed.

Makepeace did not feel like celebrating. He and Jeremiah thanked White Claws for his guidance through the mountains and they headed out. Jeremiah expressed an eagerness to reach Fort Cumberland, near which there was a Catholic settlement. They still had a night or two on the road.

That evening, high in the mountains, at the place they chose to camp, Makepeace tied Nelly to a hollow mulberry tree. When he did, he discovered a youth asleep in the tree. They did not disturb the young man, but set about building a campfire.

Exchanging glances with Jeremiah, Makepeace led the mule to a nearby brook. He shooed away a fish-hawk and while Nelly drank, he pulled up his gown, rolled up his underwear and walked into the stream. A few feet from the bank, he slid his hand in the water. Fish darted between his fingers and legs. Makepeace held his hands still until he felt a nudge. Then he grabbed it. Within minutes, he had four trout.

As the fire blazed higher, the youth awakened, surveyed the situation and came out. His wild black hair was pulled together at the back of his neck with a leather thong, the dried head of a raven tied in it. Makepeace thought he was an ugly sort—the kind he had no trouble in the past enlisting in his villainous schemes.

"Glad to meet two men of the cloth. My name's MacDuff Lawson. I'm heading west. Where mought you be coming from?"

The man spoke to the ground. Makepeace was disturbed that he would not look him in the eye. Every time he tried to make eye contact, MacDuff shifted his gaze away.

Makepeace turned up his palms. "I guess you might say we're here-and-there-ians. That looks like a quality iron yer carrying."

"Ain't none of your business, but I got it in a poker game."

Somewhat sheepish, MacDuff extended the weapon for them to examine. The butt was decorated with crude hex symbols. Makepeace noticed a brown swatch that looked like it could be blood. The same substance rimmed MacDuff's fingernails. If he was recruiting rabble rousers, Makepeace thought, he would pass this one by. For one thing, his odor heralded his arrival long before he made his appearance. The man would never be able to lose himself in a crowd.

After the fish were cleaned, they shared dinner with MacDuff. The boy fluttered his arms in an expansive gesture. "My folks got massacred by a bunch of Indians. Kilt everybody but me and my sister."

"How were ye so lucky?" asked Makepeace.

"If I had a drink of whisky, I'd tell you."

Jeremiah smiled. "Sorry, we're not carrying any."

MacDuff shrugged and continued. "Hid in a old well till the next day when some settlers came along. It still makes me puke to think what them Indians did. Begging Your Honors' pardon, I won't go into the details because you'd have nightmares for sure. A man gets hungry for some whiskey after what I been through."

"If we had any whiskey, we'd share it," Makepeace said curtly. He wished he hadn't said it because of what Jeremiah might think. MacDuff evidently decided they deserved a few nightmares and continued with his story.

"They tortured my old man bad. Stripped him naked. Painted him all over with blood and pulled the hairs from his beard one by one. Told him if he hadn't been such a fool for living so long, he mought not o' fell into their power."

MacDuff's obvious relish at telling his story turned Makepeace's stomach. On the other hand, the story seemed to have no effect on the youth's appetite. Something about the young man troubled Makepeace, but he couldn't put his finger on it. God knew, he'd been around this kind often enough. This one was pure misfortune. He seemed to enjoy dealing in distress.

"You mind if I have another ear of that roasted corn? I ain't et for three days."

"Help yerself, brother, and then ye can help me put some more wood on the fire." Makepeace said.

A half-moon shone down from an otherwise bare sky, windless with a feral calm. The night grew colder, the chill nibbling at their haunches. They huddled close to the fire.

MacDuff talked about Girty's Town. "You ever been there?"

"Can't say I have," said Jeremiah, "but as I understand it, if you see a slatternly woman headed west, that's apt to be her destination."

"From what I heard, they could use lots of good preachin'," MacDuff said. "I'm not sure about this Catholic padre, though. Looks like he might have trouble fighting off the women."

Jeremiah laughed. "I think he can hold true to the faith. Right now, we need to bank the fire and get some rest. We expect to make it to Cumberland in two or three days. Would you take the first shift, MacDuff?"

"You can trust me," said MacDuff. "I wouldn't do no harm to men of the cloth. Anyways, you ain't got nothing I want. That mule of yours, she'd be more trouble than she's worth."

Makepeace glanced at Jeremiah and rolled his eyes. For Makepeace it was nothing new, but pondering MacDuff's demeanor, he wished they had not encountered the man. He would only pretend to sleep, keeping an eye on MacDuff until his watch ended.

The next morning, Makepeace and Jeremiah parted company from MacDuff, a sigh of relief on both their parts.

"A strange lad," said Jeremiah. "Not one I would care to encounter were I traveling alone."

"Why do you suppose he wears that dead bird tied in his hair?"

Makepeace asked.

"Perhaps it's an Indian relic? He may consider the raven his talisman."

Makepeace shuddered. "We're lucky to be rid of him. I pray I never encounter him again. I lay awake most of the night keeping my eye on him."

Jeremiah eyed MacDuff's vanishing backside. "He'll be coming back for your mule."

XXII

I hate all that don't love me
and slight all that do.
George Farquar
The Constant Couple

After several days on the road, Esakka, Mouse and the Gypsy clan arrived at Philadelphia. The sleeping routine reversed itself. Most of the day, the men and some of the women were gone, and did not return until dusk. Neither Esakka nor Mouse were asked to accompany them.

The Gypsy coffers were suddenly filled with jewelry, money, and merchandise that Esakka knew had been stolen. For Esakka and Mouse, there were tents, one for each of them. He was dismayed over profiting by the fruits of Gypsy thievery, but held his peace. The old General helped set up their tents and warned them not to build any fires or burn any candles inside.

Within the week, the troop moved south into New Jersey. Esakka did not feel useful. He had no desire to aid in the clan's dishonest enterprises and was depressed by the lack of meaningful labor, although he and Mouse were kept busy watching children, milking goats and keeping the camp clean.

Mouse did not share Esakka's mood. He was happy to have no one standing over him with a whip.

Ktura kept her distance.

Once, Medea tried to get Esakka into a conversation about the woman, but he merely answered yes or no to her questions and volunteered no information.

Carlo scarcely spoke to him, but seemed to keep an eye on him at all times, especially while honing his knife.

148

Queen Esther looked at Esakka with new respect.

***

Winter vanished and spring teased them with sunny, mild days. Grass and leaves turned green. Fluttering blue jays and industrious wrens enlivened the meadows. Bud by bud, blossom by blossom, flower by flower, the fields overflowed with the colors of summer.

One day late in June, Carlo did not return with the group. That night, Ktura came to Esakka's tent.

Esakka slept on his pallet. As was his custom, he lay on his back, wearing only a loin cloth. Ktura lay down beside him and placed her head on his outstretched arm.

Although he turned and sighed, Esakka did not awaken. For an hour, Ktura lay curled against him, her leg over his side. Still, he did not respond. At last, she rose and dressed. She leaned over to kiss him and left.

The next morning, the Gypsies packed and moved toward the seacoast. There was no word from Carlo. When the Gypsies reached a shore side village on Cape May, Queen Esther and Romano left them camped in a grove near the beach and went into the town.

The troop buzzed with excitement about a great treasure soon to come their way. The clan eagerly anticipated Queen Esther's return.

In excellent spirits, Mouse patronized Esakka and tried to engage him in conversation. Moody, Esakka's mind was focused on a strange dream about Ktura. In it, she was so passionate and the portrayal in his mind was so vivid, he did not want the fantasy to diminish.

All day long, the following day, Ktura made eyes at him, as flirtatious as she had been in Arabia. Each time she came near him, his blood surged through his loins. He tried to concentrate on passages from the Psalms, but pictures of naked Ktura drove them away. Over and over, he reveled in the images, making a souvenir of each one.

The next day, ten men on horseback came into the camp. Three of them spent the morning going over maps with Queen Esther and Romano. Having navigated ships and being acquainted with similar maps, Esakka was certain they were studying sea lanes.

Although the men had white skin, they accepted the family as equals. When they weren't grooming their horses, the strangers pinched and trifled with the women. Cain and Tyler seemed flattered by the attention given the women. The old General proved quite garrulous. Esakka found himself jealous if one of them flirted with Ktura. He was pleased that she did not carry on in her usual wanton manner.

At eventide, Queen Esther broke camp and moved down the coast to an inlet where Esakka saw a ship. The ship looked capable of carrying a hundred or more tons. It was either a snow or a brigantine. Because it had been outfitted with square sails, he could not tell which it was. He had a notion the sail arrangement was intended as a disguise and suspected they were about to be involved in smuggling a large cargo.

At dark, lanterns flashed between the ship and the beach. Within moments, oars sculled the water, and Esakka counted lamps on a dozen fly-boats as they slapped their way toward the beach.

All the Gypsies, plus the sailors, were required for unloading the cargo. Crates, boxes, and barrels were piled on the sand as high as a man's head, forty stacks of them. From the boxes, enough of the contents filtered out to reveal they contained tea and sugar. Forty barrels had sweet sticky residue on the outside that smelled of molasses. Just as many oak casks had Ron de Barbados stenciled on the side, the odor of rum seeping through the wood. One sailor laughed and gnawed hungrily on the side of a barrel.

The men worked quietly until one broke the spigot from a cask and it leaked. Before it was patched, they were each permitted a cup. Their merriment increased and they sang as they moved the cargo off the beach and onto horse-drawn carts. Esakka worked as hard as any sailor and Queen Esther complimented him on his vigorous labor. Mouse was mostly in the way, but no one passed judgment on him.

It took until dawn to move the goods a mile to a vacant warehouse on the plantation's edge. Once, a Constable on horseback encountered them.

They greeted the officer like a compatriot and gave him several packages of tea. He wished them luck in disposing of their merchandise, adding that he had many friends who were eager to buy without paying the heavy English taxes.

The Constable asked about Carlo. Queen Esther replied that he had gone to live with his new wife's people.

Two nights later, Ktura returned to Esakka's tent. He slept soundly. She lay beside him. Sometime in the night, he became conscious of her presence. In a dream state, he put his arm around her and clung, moaning softly. He pressed against her, his body shaking until it seemed the vibrations would never cease. Realizing he was still asleep, Ktura rose, dressed and slinked away from his tent.

When Esakka awakened, he thought it was a dream, but the memory was so strong, he had difficulty accepting it. Still half-asleep, he reached for Ktura, surprised to find she was not there. Then he shook his head in disbelief at his own behavior. Just to be certain he was not dreaming, he whacked the side of his face.

All the next day, that dream occupied his thoughts. Ktura watched him through hooded eyes. If she caught his gaze, she smiled saucily, making him wonder if she knew about his dream. He felt a half-smile slither across his lips. Then he frowned and quickly looked away.

Mouse had seen Ktura enter Esakka's tent. Although Mouse shortly fell asleep, he awoke in time to see her make her exit. Already uneasy with the way Esakka was giving him short shrift, he did not mention what he had seen.

Esakka worried about the group's criminal activities, concerned that they might be arrested. So he intended to leave at the first opportunity and make his way back to the Seney plantation, hoping that his voluntary return would keep his freedom sum intact. He resumed the use of his real name.

As they were folding their tents, Esakka became annoyed with Mouse's clumsy ways. Thinking to divert Esakka from chastising him, Mouse said, "I wonder when I'se going to meet that woman

Queen Esther told me about."

"Mouse, I think you were supposed to get on that vessel with the privateers and sail with them. Your woman is on some other shore and if you don't start looking for her, you'll never find her."

"You sure got a bad humor, Massa Esakka. I 'sposed you be happy after doing it all night."

"What's that supposed to mean, Mouse?"

Mouse bent his head and looked at his feet. "Nothin'."

"But you said it. It must mean something. What made you say it, Mouse?"

"Nothin'. Doan mean nothin'."

Esakka grabbed the boy by the throat. Mouse gagged as the air was squeezed from his lungs. Then Esakka moved his hands to Mouse's shoulders and shook him roughly.

"Mouse, I want to know why you said that!"

Mouse sank to his knees and hugged Esakka's legs, his mind swimming with remembrances of his former master's mistreatment. "Oh, Massa Beuthed, I's sorry, I's sorry. Please don't whip me."

Esakka sighed loudly, then collapsed beside the boy and put his arm around him. "I'm not Beuthed, Mouse. I'm sorry. I don't know why I feel so mean."

Memories of old beatings were obviously grievous in Mouse's mind. "It's all right, Massa Esakka. I shouldn't be smarty."

"What did you mean, Mouse?"

"Nothin', Massa Esakka. I saw Miss Ladora coming out of your tent last night. That's all. I shouldn't mentioned it. Ain't none of my business." Mouse did not add that Queen Esther had sat outside her tent and watched with a bitter expression on her face.

Esakka crossed his arms and exhaled noisily. "Never mind, Mouse. I thought I was having crazy dreams. Now I know why they were so real."

Esakka strengthened his resolve to leave Queen Esther's family. Ktura did not mean anything but trouble. One way or another, she would bring havoc on his head again.

The next day, Carlo returned to the family, bringing with him a woman. He announced that they were married. She belonged to another Gypsy clan, she explained, but Carlo was unhappy staying with her tribe because he had no one to boss. He had talked her into joining Queen Esther's family.

Carlo treated Ktura like a stranger. Whatever she did, he did not appear concerned. In turn, she ignored him and stayed near Esakka. But certain that Carlo still harbored jealous feelings, Esakka worried about the Gypsy sticking a knife in his back.

Although they had disposed of most of the contraband, Queen Esther said they would return to Dover and Wilmington where she intended to sell the rest of it.

A day later, they were on the move again, following Indian paths close to the seashore. Esakka and Mouse had long ago lost the privilege of riding in an ox cart and walked with the rest of the troop. All seemed glad to be traveling, the dog Rat especially eager. He nipped enthusiastically at the goat's heels and Mouse's too, if the boy dawdled.

Coupled with Carlo's return, the success of the smuggling venture was good reason for a celebration. When they reached the edge of the Delaware River, Queen Esther instructed Esakka and Mouse to build a fire on which they could roast several meats. She ordered Carlo to open a cask of rum.

After a heavy meal and much drinking, those who were not too drunk, danced and sang.

Romano kept calling, "Dance for us, Ladora, dance for us! Dance for us, Medea!"

Medea was too big with child for dancing and tossed him a disgusted look. Ktura smiled teasingly, but made no move to get up and perform. Esakka enjoyed a pleasurable feeling because she no longer flaunted herself. But then he rebuked himself, for Ktura should not be his concern.

The rum took its effect on the Gypsy men. When the fire burned low, Esakka stirred the logs for the benefit of the old General. Being the oldest, the General was the one who most needed its warmth. Finally, Esakka repaired to his tent. He had erected it behind a sand dune, far away from the rest, although he was not able to keep Mouse at too great a distance.

By midnight, everyone was asleep. Esakka changed into his nightshirt and settled onto his bed, the sound of yodeling loons gliding

The Pickled Dog Caper

across the waters. Off to the south, a wolf cried for its mate.

While Esakka slept, the scent of the sweet oil Ktura had bathed him with in the oasis wafted through his tent. The aroma caressed his languid body.

Esakka stretched in slumber until he felt a hand touch the hem of his garment. He opened his eyes slightly, a sigh escaping. Ktura loomed over him, naked, all dark curves, moonlit skin, inviting lips. Bending to drag his shirt over his chest, she straddled his body. Holy Gog and Magog! He could not believe this. Was it another dream? One more sigh fluttered his lips, but he was ready for her. The heat of her body melded to his.

"You have seen the wild mustangs when they mate," Ktura whispered. "Go like the wild mustangs!"

He was nervous that he would not do it right. He thrust gently, slowly joining the rhythm of her body. As easy as breathing. Steady rocking. Followed by bucking and pounding. In a stampede-like mayhem, Esakka found himself on top. He was surprised at how long he could maintain his tempo, utter joy surging through his body as if this were the only thing for which he had been put on the earth. And when the moment arrived, he thought a cyclone had flattened him. Thunderbolts rived the top of his head.

He collapsed by Ktura's side. Breathing was difficult, but he felt good, very good. As if he had been enticed to eternity's precipice and shoved over. Left by the gods to float until the end of time.

Ktura leaned across and pierced his lips, her tongue darting in and out like a snake, the taste of her like roasted peppers. When she rolled atop him once more, he was delighted to find himself crazy again for her. She seized his spirit and transported it to a summit far afield the range of divine deliverance.

When she finished, Ktura kissed his neck and purred, "No more a virgin!"

If only it could go on forever. But then she was gone, leaving him to lie there in ecstasy. Thinking.

He debated with himself whether maintaining his virginity had been worth the struggle, it having departed with so much delight. For the denial of this pleasure, he had wrestled with demons and dark angels to remain chaste? Had he been insane?

He could have persuaded himself it was all a dream, if it had

154

not been for the close musty air of the tent and the killing softness of his loins.

But his mood turned when he realized the whore had sneaked up on him. He was but a victim. She had stolen the one thing of value that he owned and left not an ash of tribute. And certain he was that he had already lost his other precious possession: his freedom sum.

At dawn, Esakka awakened with a sledge-hammer headache and dogs barking rowdily. He crawled over to lift the flap of his tent. Four armed men on horseback and a pack of braying hounds surrounded his tent. Carlo seemed to have led them there. They had to be bounty hunters.

"He's a peaceful Negro." Carlo pointed at Esakka. "He won't give you no trouble at all. He's got a woman here you can take and sell if you want, and there's a little slave boy in that other tent you can have."

One of the men strode over to Mouse's tent. He lifted the flap and then called back, "Ain't nobody here."

Carlo laughed and slapped his leg. "Guess that little runt run off. He wasn't worth five shillings. You didn't lose much."

Another of the men looped a chain around Esakka's neck. "Your master's gonna pay a good bounty to get you back."

XXIII

Reason still keeps its throne,
but it nods a little . . . .
George Farquar
Love and a Bottle

After leaving Oldtown, Jeremiah and Makepeace followed the Potomac River on a westerly course. When they reached Fort Cumberland, Jeremiah obtained directions to a Catholic outpost where their petition for lodging and rest would be met with warm response.

The next morning, Makepeace was riding Old Nelly while Jeremiah walked on ahead. Nelly stepped on a rattlesnake. The snake's frantic rattling frightened her and she reared up in panic, tossing Makepeace to the ground.

Landing on his head, Makepeace lost consciousness. He lay utterly still, his eyes wide open. Jeremiah ran to the river and scooped up water to bathe the padre's face.

Eventually, Makepeace came to, but his eyesight was gone. His speech had no meaning. Jeremiah tried to help Makepeace to his feet, wondering if he were speaking in tongues.

Each time he was erect, the padre was thrown to the ground as if seized by invisible forces. Jeremiah decided the angels were wrestling with the devil for possession of Makepeace's soul, but said nothing for fear he would frighten him.

Makepeace shielded his eyes with his hands and cried, "The Light! It blinds me!" Then he put his hand to his ear and exclaimed, "Speak louder, Lord!"

Jeremiah went back to the stream and filled the pewter flask with cool water. When he returned, Makepeace was looking heavenward and talking to the clouds.

156

The previous evening, Jeremiah had read Makepeace the passage about the disciple, Doubting Thomas, who asked to see the Lord's side that had been pierced while He was on the cross. Makepeace now seemed to think he was talking to Jesus. He, too, asked to see Jesus' wounds.

Jeremiah helped him with a drink from the flask, but most of the water dribbled down his beard.

"Oh, Jesus!" the young priest said.

"You called?" Makepeace asked.

Non compos mentis, Jeremiah thought. He sat down, baffled. If he continued along the river path, he wasn't sure the padre would follow. He would like Makepeace to get back on the mule, but Nelly was skittish. And he wasn't sure Makepeace would understand that he was supposed to sit on the mule and let the mule provide the foot work.

Makepeace stumbled around, but stayed within a few feet of Jeremiah and Old Nelly. They made some little progress, coming at last to a place when the river coursed north.

"Can you make it across the water?" Jeremiah asked.

"God bless you," Makepeace said.

"You can't see the river, can you?" Jeremiah asked.

"There ain't nothing that I can see," Makepeace said.

Jeremiah knew he couldn't lead Makepeace across the river on foot. If the padre stepped into a sinkhole, he would drown. He didn't know if the man could swim. And if Makepeace became confused, the water would inevitably claim him.

"Would you like to ride across on the mule?" asked Jeremiah.

"Mule?"

"Do you comprehend mule?" Jeremiah spoke each word plainly and slowly, omitting not a single syllable. "You are going to ride on the mule. Here, let me show you how to get on."

He took Makepeace by the hand and walked him over to the mule's side. Nelly seemed to sense there was something out of the ordinary. She stood patiently, waiting to be mounted. Makepeace might have been thinking Nelly would mount him. He stood by just as patiently.

"Get on the mule," Jeremiah ordered. He took hold of Makepeace's right leg and tried to raise it in such a manner that

Makepeace would get the idea.

"Get on!" Jeremiah begged. "Get on the mule, padre!"

Makepeace pulled up his gown, put his leg up and moved his body astride the mule.

"That's it." Jeremiah thought it fortunate the mule was short. If she had been a horse, Makepeace would never have made it astride.

When Makepeace was on, Nelly moved a step forward. With no saddle horn to hang on to and no stirrups in which to put his feet, Makepeace tilted and swayed like a drunken drummer. Jeremiah thought about tying him to the mule's neck with the lead rope, but when he wrapped it around Makepeace, he became agitated, waved his arms and growled as if possessed.

Jeremiah decided he should give the two time to get accustomed to each other before trying to cross the river. He grasped the rope and guided Nelly along the river path. She moved slowly. Makepeace managed to balance himself with the swing of each step. Gradually, the man and the animal seemed to reach an understanding, but it took them an hour to go a mile.

Farther along, they found a post had been erected by the riverside. A primitive sign was nailed to it.

Ferry
ring bell

On the other side of the river, at least three hundred feet away, Jeremiah could see a raft with a shack on it. He figured the pilot was curled up inside.

"You can't see anything yet, padre?" Jeremiah asked.

"I can't see the sea," Makepeace said.

"I'll ring the bell. Maybe the ferry will come across for us."

Jeremiah plucked up an iron rod that lay against the post. He struck the bell several times. Each time the bell rang, Makepeace shouted, "Hallelujah!"

There was a stirring on the barge. Someone came out of the shack. When the person appeared, Jeremiah saw the pilot was a large woman. She held a battered black hat against her head while the wind tore at her tattered brown dress.

"What do you want?" she shrieked in a gravelly voice.

158

"A ride across the river," Jeremiah howled back. "For me and my friend on the mule."

"A shilling a piece for you and the priest," the woman bellowed. "Two shillings for the mule, just in case I have to clean up any messes."

"We don't have any money."

"A pox on you," the woman hollered. "I ain't out here for me health. You got anything to trade?"

"Nothing except the good Lord's blessing."

"That's nothing all right. Walk on up the river—about two miles to the narrows. It's pretty deep here, but you can cross on foot there. Ain't more'n to your waist. Where the water runs white—you can't miss it."

The woman settled back into her shack.

"For God's sake, woman," Jeremiah cried. "My friend's blind and he hurt his head—"

She stuck her head out of the shack. "God didn't give you no shillings to pay, He didn't intend you to travel in style. All you finger-pointers go around expecting charity. I'm having enough trouble keeping up with me own self." She retreated into her hut.

Since he had taken his vows, Jeremiah had never uttered a curse, but this time he was tempted to the point of asking God to strike the woman dead. He turned to Makepeace to say something, but the padre was bobbing his head and staring at the clouds.

Maybe God was testing him, Jeremiah thought. Maybe God was testing them both. He supposed in God's good time, he would get where he was going, but he thought God had already made things difficult enough for him.

"Well, I guess I should be grateful I wasn't eaten by a bear," he mumbled.

Makepeace started to shake. He screamed, "Bears!" He thrashed around on the mule to such a point that Jeremiah thought Nelly would toss him again. He could tell Makepeace was having a bad vision about bears. The padre kept shouting, "Help me, Jesus! Help me!"

Exasperated, Jeremiah roared, "There aren't any bears here. Calm down, padre, you're upsetting the mule. Just calm down!"

Jeremiah stroked Nelly's head, and murmured, "There, there,

Nelly," in as sweet a voice as he could muster. Makepeace settled back on the mule and Nelly stood meekly.

The two-mile stretch to the wading place was a long, little used path filled with cocklebur and thorny brush. Several times, Jeremiah caught his robe on sharp thistles and had to wrestle it clear, leaving the garment tattered. Finally, he pulled it up and tied it at his knees, figuring it was better to get his legs scratched than destroy his robe. His legs would heal, the cloth would not.

The farther they went, the worse the terrain became. Although it was downhill, the foliage increased. On the other side of the river, the bank rose sharply, slanting up for at least sixty feet toward a timbered plateau.

Jeremiah groaned. The supposedly easy, shallow walk across the river would be compensated for by a difficult climb up that cliff.

When he reached the place that the old woman said was the fording place, Jeremiah was beset with grief. The water was dark and gave no clue about its depth as it ran rapidly, dashing against large rocks in the middle and kicking up white foam. He debated crossing by himself first, testing the bottom and feeling out the difficulties Nelly would encounter. But he didn't think it would be a good idea to leave the padre and the mule at each other's whimsy.

Jeremiah stepped off the earthen bank and put his foot into the water. Satisfied with the firmness of the riverbed, he pulled on Nelly's rope. She looked at the water, but didn't budge, the line taut between them.

"Come on, Nelly," he begged. To Makepeace, he said, "Padre, we're going to cross the river. If you sit quietly, we can make it."

Makepeace grunted.

Jeremiah tugged harder on the rope, drawing it up Nelly's neck and stretching it against her ears. Although irritated, she moved a step forward, then two. Jeremiah kept pulling, hoping Makepeace did not fall off. The mule maneuvered her way down the short embankment into the water.

Once in the stream, Nelly expressed her anxiety. She looked at the swirling white waves and brayed; the cold water patently distressed her.

"Come on, sweet Nell," Jeremiah pleaded. "Come on, gal."

Jeremiah stepped ahead two paces, taking up the slack in the rope. Nelly took a step forward, extending her foot cautiously into the mud.

Another two steps and Jeremiah sank to his thighs. With his foot, he felt his way around. The floor of the river dropped off, but continued smooth and hard. He walked ahead several more steps, shivering with cold. The riverbed remained solid.

He walked back to Nelly, shortening the length of rope between them. "Come along, old girl," he coaxed sweetly.

When they came to the step-down in the river bed, he was exceedingly patient with her. She put her left foot forward until it was flat on the step-down. Her nose kissed the edge of water. She yanked her head back and snorted, spraying Jeremiah with mule snot. She advanced another step until submerged to her belly. The water swirled about her and lapped at Makepeace's calves.

Jeremiah halted a moment to let Nelly get used to the cold water. As his own flesh adjusted, it became less agonizing and he trusted it would be the same for her. He rubbed the back of Nelly's neck.

"Come on gal, you can do it. If I can do it, you can do it."

Makepeace seemed to have left his body. He said nothing intelligent, but looked at the clouds, grunting and speaking gibberish. Jeremiah no longer considered it the language of tongues. He hoped the cold water would startle the padre out of his catalepsy.

Makepeace drew his legs up, so that his knees were against Nelly's withers. He began to sing a little ditty that Jeremiah thought he must have learned in his childhood.

Nelly lifted a hoof and inched forward. She seemed pleased with her progress. She took another two steps. She kept that up until they were nearly half-way across. Then she stopped as if contented with what she had accomplished.

"Come on, Nelly!" Jeremiah shouted. "Come on, Nelly!" He yanked on the rope. Couldn't the stupid animal understand that soon she would be out of the cold swirling water? He trudged to her backside, and slapped her a good one, his hand burning from the contact with her hide. Hesitantly, she moved several steps forward.

"Good girl," Jeremiah exclaimed. He slapped her again. Abruptly, as if she had enough abuse, Nelly scampered through the water and onto the opposite bank.

As soon as Nelly reached the solid ground of the narrow beach, she dumped Makepeace and sprinted up the hill. Makepeace lay in the dirt, doubled up as if dead.

Jeremiah thrashed his way out of the water. He gave Makepeace a single glance and headed up the bluff after Nelly. The padre would be distraught if his trusty animal disappeared. What kind of a steward was he that he couldn't keep up with a mule? Just a fool cleric with his head in the air without the sense to master a simple-minded farm animal.

The plateau was covered with trees. Jeremiah called for Nelly. There was no response. He ran one way and then another, following paths that had been chopped through the trees.

When he decided to give up and head back to the riverbank, he realized he had no idea which trail led back. All around him, it looked the same, canopies of dead leaves above, inert brown relics covering the ground. The shadows were somber and gloomy. Here and there a rosy finger of sunshine teased him and seemed to point the way, but he was too confused to pursue it.

He sat down and mumbled a prayer. In his whole life, he had never felt so abandoned. Wearied beyond measure, he fell asleep against a tree trunk.

Moments later, Jeremiah awakened with a start. He had no idea how long he had slept, but it was too long. What if Makepeace had wandered off?

Maybe the sleep had refreshed his mind. Jeremiah seemed to think he remembered the way. He could smell the water and walked in the direction he thought was east.

Reaching the edge of the clearing, Jeremiah saw the padre lay curled up on the river's shore. A large bird had descended on the scene and hovered over the padre's prone body. Too large a bird, Jeremiah thought. Like a vulture, but too big for a vulture. It flitted in a circle around the helpless padre, making strange bird noises.

Then Jeremiah realized it was a four legged bird. No, not four legs. A bird with two legs and two arms. There wasn't any such thing. It was an apparition. The same one he and Makepeace had encountered in the mulberry tree a few nights before. The distinctive behavior, the flitting, the cawing, could only mean MacDuff. Had that scoundrel been following them for the last two days? But why would he do that? Just as he was about to shout a warning to MacDuff to back away from the padre, MacDuff looked up and saw him.

"Halloo there, Father Smith!"

Even before he came near, Jeremiah realized that the smell he thought was the river must have been MacDuff. A rank, musty odor, an odor stinking of decay emanated from the man. Or maybe it was the cloak MacDuff had fashioned from dead bird feathers that surrounded his gaunt body.

Jeremiah started down the hill, loosening pebbles and stones as he went, sending a shower of debris onto the river frontage. Twice, MacDuff had to leap aside to avoid a flying rock.

Jeremiah tried to figure out what MacDuff was doing to the padre. MacDuff had a staff in his hand. A gunny lay on the beach beside Makepeace. What it contained was anyone's guess. Doubtful if it contained anything that would help an ill person. Of a certainty, the intractable youth possessed no medical talents.

MacDuff leaned on his staff. "I remember you. You and the padre fed me pretty good."

"Have you been trailing us?" Jeremiah asked.

"I was going before you," MacDuff said. "Crossed on the ferry with that old woman. Cost me a shilling. Watched you make your way down the river and wade across."

"So where are you headed for?"

MacDuff drove his staff into the ground as if he were staking a flag. "Where the devil takes me, that's where I'm going!"

"We need to get the padre up the cliff." Jeremiah glanced at the gray sky. "You can never tell about these rivers. This one may swell on us if it rains upstream. We'll be in real trouble if that happens."

"What did you do with the mule?"

"I never found her," Jeremiah said. MacDuff seemed more interested in the mule than he was the padre's welfare.

"You'll never see that jackass again," MacDuff said. "But I'll go look for her in a little bit. How we going to get the padre up the hill?"

Feeling short-tempered, Jeremiah bit off his words. "Same way the jackass got up."

MacDuff fluttered his wings. "I can carry him on my back. I'm used to carrying heavy loads. I used to lift a calf out of the brambles all the time."

163

Jeremiah looked askance at MacDuff. He was thin, but wiry. Maybe he could do what he claimed, but was he trustworthy?

"You bring my stuff," MacDuff said. "Don't forget my gunny."

Jeremiah watched MacDuff as he took off his feathery cloak and hoisted Makepeace onto his back. He started up the cliff like a mountain goat. Or did he flit up it like a bird of prey?

Jeremiah gathered up MacDuff's gunny, surprised at its weight. He glanced in it. The sole object was an ax. He grabbed MacDuff's staff and started up the hill, leaving the smelly cloak in the sand.

After MacDuff carried Makepeace up the hill, Jeremiah went in search of Nelly. Night would come on soon and he wouldn't be able to find his way out of the forest a second time. He didn't trust MacDuff to look for the mule. He might get on her and ride away. Never see either one of them again.

He hated to leave Makepeace at the mercy of the stupid bird-boy. Makepeace was right, the man could not be trusted. Although why he would harm the padre, Jeremiah had no idea. Surely, MacDuff would not do anything cruel to the padre.

Makepeace had a vision as he lay curled up where MacDuff had deposited him. He and Jeremiah were in the Temple in Jerusalem, received by seven devout priests and taken into the Holy of Holies. Inscrolled on the breast of each priest's garment was the name of one of the seven deadly sins. The priests chanted and prayed as they led him and Jeremiah to the altar of Abraham, where they were told to prostrate themselves. Then the priests threw back their cloaks and revealed huge bear-heads and long white teeth dripping with blood.

Makepeace awoke with a start. He was cold and shook uncontrollably. Had God sent the bear to devour Redmond? Or had he sent the bear to devour him, and the bear got confused? Could the dream be a warning that he, like that faker Redmond, was about to become a victim of God's dreadful vengeance?

His mind was alert, but he still could not see. He could feel the warmth of the campfire before him, save his gown was wet and clung to his limbs.

"Hello!" he called. There was no answer. "Jeremiah?"

Still, no reply. He started to get up and then realized he should not. Blind as he was, he might stumble into the fire.

He was damned hungry. And the cold gnawed hungrily at his bones. He wished he was dead. Death could be no more troublesome than this awful thing that had happened to him. Sightless as a newborn cat!

Then he heard the crackling of twigs and leaves. Footsteps came toward him, preceded by an odor of decay. He put his hands out in case the person intended harm.

"Hello," said a strange scratchy voice. "So the padre's up and about."

"Who are ye?"

"MacDuff Lawson. Jeremiah's gone to look for your mule. I carried you up the hill. If you can't see, you want to be careful. You start walking around, you might fall down that cliff."

"Do I know ye? Where did ye come from?"

"Sure you know me. You cooked some fish for me three nights ago."

Makepeace thought a moment. "Ye still got that dead bird around your neck?"

"That's my good luck piece."

"Where did you say Jeremiah went?"

"Your mule took off and he's gone to look for her."

"Could you build that fire a little higher?"

"I'm working on it," MacDuff said.

Makepeace could hear MacDuff as he flitted about, making bird noises each time he picked up a limb or a piece of debris for the fire.

Crunching forest debris as he walked, MacDuff came back to where Makepeace sat. Makepeace fervently wished he could see what was going on. He felt uneasy and in the crazy youth's power.

Makepeace heard Nelly's bray, followed by her loping trot as she cantered out of the grove.

"Where'd you find the mule?" MacDuff called.

By the sound of his voice, Makepeace could tell that the boy had moved away from the campfire.

165

Evidently, Jeremiah trailed behind the mule, for he responded to MacDuff. "She found me. I was lost. If it hadn't been for her, I'd still be going around in circles. How's the padre doing?"

Makepeace raised his right arm in greeting. Jeremiah clasped his hand momentarily.

"Can you see yet?"

"No, but I'm with ye."

"That's a step in the right direction," Jeremiah said.

MacDuff came toward them. First, Makepeace smelled the dead bird, then he heard MacDuff chuck a log on the fire. There was a whoosh as the youth plopped down in the dirt with a grunt.

"Got anything to eat?" MacDuff asked. "My gunny's bare."

"I think we have a few ears of corn," Jeremiah said. "Why don't you see if there's any fish in that stream? I thought I felt one or two swim between my legs when we crossed."

Makepeace could hear MacDuff as he went down the cliff to the river, rocks and pebbles rolling down the hill. The boy cackled like a hungry crow.

Jeremiah leaned over and whispered in Makepeace's ear. "I know we need to keep a watch, tonight, padre, but you can't see, and even if I take one, that leaves the other one to him. No telling what wicked plans he has. Stealing the mule might be the least of them."

"We are at God's mercy," said Makepeace. "And lately, He seems to be a little miserly with that commodity." He crossed himself. "No blasphemy intended."

A few moments later, MacDuff came bounding up the hill. "Got three fish!" he exclaimed. "How's that?" He had donned the feathery cloak again.

***

Old Nelly greeted the morning sun with a loud bray. Jeremiah threw a rock at her and turned over on his side. Nelly responded with a sharp bleat. Jeremiah could hear her stomping and pawing the ground. By the time he got his eyes open, he saw that MacDuff was pulling her by the rope toward the bluff.

"What are you trying to do?" he yelled.

MacDuff looked startled. "Taking her down to the water for a

166

drink!"

And across the river and on your way, thought Jeremiah. Old Nelly was too smart for the youth; outsmarted by a dumb mule.

"Maybe she doesn't want one," said Jeremiah. "Leave her be."

MacDuff had his gunny over his back. In his right hand was Nelly's rope, in his left a sturdy log he could use as a cudgel. He seemed to hesitate a moment, as if debating whether he had any particular use for the log. He looked at Jeremiah, then back at the cudgel. Disgusted, he chucked the wood on the ground.

"Well, I can't do no more good here," he said sourly. "I guess I'll be on my way."

He disappeared down the cliff.

Jeremiah called after him, "God bless you!"

Through his closed eyelids, Makepeace was conscious that the sun had lightened up the sky. Sitting up, he asked, "What's going on?"

Jeremiah grunted. "MacDuff tried to steal the mule. But he's gone now. God has delivered us from his evil intentions."

"How much farther we got to travel?"

"About a day, I reckon. Are you up to it?"

"Much as I'll ever be."

Makepeace stood. As soon as he did, it happened again. He started thrashing his arms as if wrestling with an unseen foe. The invisible enemy overcame him, wrenching him to the ground. Makepeace grappled with his shadowy adversary, screaming and shouting for mercy. This went on for several minutes until, exhausted, he collapsed face down, stretched out as if dead.

With caution, Jeremiah approached the padre, carrying the flask of water with him. He leaned over Makepeace.

"Are you with me, padre?"

Makepeace groaned.

"Would you like a sip of water?"

Jeremiah placed the flask against the padre's lips and Makepeace drank thirstily. Then he sat up. He remained sitting for several minutes, still drinking. Finally, he handed the flask back to Jeremiah.

"What's happening to me, Jeremiah? What's God trying to do to me?"

167

* * *

While Jeremiah walked, Makepeace balanced himself astride Nelly's back. The forces that seemed eager to wrestle for his soul did not manifest themselves further. As the day wore on, Jeremiah attempted to answer Makepeace's question about what had happened to him.

Jeremiah declared Makepeace's event was similar to the Apostle Paul's vision: a Light gushing down from the heavens, a striking down of the proud person who refused to follow God's will, a need for penitence and the new birth of the soul. In short, an epiphany.

At the time, Makepeace thought Jeremiah read more into his accident than could be reality, but gradually, he came to accept the young priest's explanation.

Jeremiah further suggested God was trying to convert him to Catholicism. Makepeace decided he would let Jeremiah hold that thought. He wanted to make a clean breast and wondered if what had happened was God forcing him to tell the truth. But one confession would lead to another, and he seriously debated whether he should make known to Jeremiah that he had stolen the black cassock from Redmond and the mule from Drury, that he was nothing but a common thief and had been most of his life. He valued the priest's respect and did not want to alienate him.

Makepeace considered that if he confessed, his eyesight might return, but he was unable to bring himself to that altar. He would wait to see if God would not sort out things for him.

XXIV

... leaving mercy to heaven
Henry Fielding
Tom Jones

The sight of the Seney plantation loomed before Esakka like a billowing yellow ocean, the freshly cut tobacco fields stretching to the horizon in all directions. Heaven could not be more joyful to behold.

He'd walked a hundred miles in heavy chains, dogs yapping at his heels, Ktura alternately cursing Carlo and then him for what had happened to her. Several times, he wanted to slap her crazy, just to shut her up.

The bounty hunters had scarcely bothered themselves to feed either him or Ktura, tossing them a morsel of pemmican or occasionally a tidbit from the fire if they roasted a turkey or a chicken, mostly a crumb of bread with little thought of water. They treated their animals no better and themselves seemed to thrive on the pounding hooves of their animals.

Nor did they make any attempt to trifle with Ktura, which surprised Esakka. They seemed all business, intent on collecting their bounty. They read their Bible a lot, and Esakka sensed they were Amish or Quaker.

And despite the lack of food, Ktura's belly grew bigger.

They made their way through the treacherous brown stubble left from the harvest. When the tobacco barns came in sight, Esakka could see Mr. Seney's youngest son, twelve-year old Neville, riding his Pinto pony around the horse walks. Suddenly, the boy stopped, waved, and spurred his horse toward the house.

Going for his father, Esakka thought. At long last, he would confront his savior. While he knew he could not expect a grand

169

homecoming, he was thinking at least he might be welcomed back, maybe given his old job, and soon life would settle down into its ordinary routines. No those were foolish thoughts. There was the law to contend with.

Several minutes later, Neville returned, followed by his father on the ebony Arabian horse, and someone Esakka did not know, a man only a few years old than he, perhaps in his mid-twenties. He wondered if Mr. Seney had hired a white overseer.

The horses navigated their way through the reedy stubble, the bounty hunters' hounds braying with excitement. Mr. Seney had taken his flintlock from the wall and wore it slung it over his shoulder.

In a few minutes, they were close enough to be heard.

Esakka called out, "Master Seney, it is I, your slave Esakka."

One of the bounty hunters waved his quirt in the air and said, "Shut up slave until you're spoken to."

"Sir, we don't use whips on this property," Mr. Seney declared. "I am the owner of this plantation and this is my son Jonathan. He's a lawyer and I myself am running for High Sheriff in the next election. What brings you gentlemen here?"

A burly man rode from the back of the group and addressed Mr. Seney. "We're the Fielding brothers and we're returning your runaway. At least, he said he belongs to you. If you want him, there's a hundred pounds bounty on his head. Otherwise, we'll hang him and keep his woman to sell."

Mr. Seney glanced at Ktura, her body poorly concealed by her thin ragged clothing. Esakka looked down at his own clothes, conscious that they were the same garments he had worn when he left the previous fall, now threadbare and shabby.

One of the Fielding men grabbed Ktura's head by the hair and pulled her face back in profile. "She's a right purdy one. We can get a good price for her."

Mr. Seney dismounted his horse.

Esakka stood tall in spite of the heavy chains weighing him down. "Master, I am in great distress. Like Job, I have been deserted by God, but I have returned to face my tribulations and seek your help."

Jonathan intoned coldly, "You didn't return. You were brought."

Neville spoke eagerly, his voice commanding for one so young.

"You deserted God, Esakka. Don't blame God for your wicked ways."

"You shall have all the help the law allows," Mr. Seney said. "Who is this with you?"

Esakka bowed his head in deference to his former master. "Her name is Ktura. "She's a whore. She says she's carrying my child. If it is truly mine, I will marry her. But if it has Gypsy blood—she can look to her Maker for mercy."

Ktura's flat expression did not indicate that she heard or comprehended Esakka. She kept her head lowered, her face in shadow.

"She does not understand English?" Jonathan asked.

"She understands it," Esakka said. "She just does not want to hear what I say."

"You gentlemen come to the house and I will make arrangements to pay you," Mr. Seney said. "I imagine you are hungry. One of my cooks will prepare something for you."

"Leave the chains on them," Jonathan said to the bounty hunters as he turned his horse toward the house. He spoke to Neville. "You can go for the sheriff, little man."

Esakka wanted desperately to ask about his freedom sum, but he lacked the fortitude.

Dorah, the oldest of the cooks, was picking herbs in the small garden just outside the kitchen wing. She spent half her time out there, and Esakka could not remember when she had given him a kind word. The woman always seemed to be in the right place at the right time to know what went on. No one knew for sure how she managed it. Mr. Seney had frequently whispered to him that he thought Dorah had witch's blood.

Dorah was talking to herself in an undertone as the men approached. "Needs to dig up a little angelica root in case anybody gets the gout. 'Sparagus coming along real good. We'll have a mess of that in few days." Then she lifted her head and stared at the people coming her way. At that point, she raised her voice, calling to her husband. "Mercy me, Thummas, the runaway done been brought back!"

Dorah rubbed her hands across her apron. Esakka knew her fingers itched to give him a vigorous slap on the face. He didn't

171

know why she felt such antagonism toward him.

Thummas had come to the door at Dorah's command. Esakka felt the old man's beady eyes on him like he was a useless dog that couldn't trail a scent.

"I see him." Thummas said. "Brought a wife with him, huh? I guess he need someone to wait for him while he in jail."

Dorah sighed showily. "Doan have no trouble finding a woman wherever he go. That man too comely for his own good."

"Look like she carryin' his baby," Thummas said.

"Poor chile gonna be an orphan," Dorah proclaimed. "His daddy be hanging from the oak."

"Never you mind, Dorah," Mr. Seney said. "Can you bring these people something to eat?"

"Not going to be an orphan," Ktura declared. "I'll see to that. No child of mine is going to be no orphan."

Dorah gave Ktura a look of disapproval. "She a sassy one." She turned to Mr. Seney. "Massa, they sit under the tree, I see what I can do."

Not far from the kitchen wing, a wood table where slaves and field hands were served sat under a spreading sycamore tree. The bounty hunters plunked down on wood benches. Esakka squatted on the grass against the tree trunk.

Ktura followed his example, but said with a bitter tone, "Should have known better than to be keen on a slave."

Dorah, Thummas and a younger maid brought cornbread and bowls of corn meal mush with syrup. Esakka took his eagerly. The offered fare may be miserable, but he was home again.

Mr. Seney headed inside to find payment for the bounty hunters.

"How far have you traveled?" Jonathan asked.

"Five days," the chief bounty hunter answered. "Night and day, all the way from New Jesus."

"I hope you understand, Esakka," Jonathan continued, "that we must turn you over to the sheriff. When I return from a trip I have scheduled, I will see what we can do about your trial and will make an effort to present whatever defense you think you have, according to common law."

"Sirrah, you are more than kind," Esakka said.

"I have business that will take about a fortnight," Jonathan said.

172

"But as soon as I return, I will investigate your circumstances and see what plea we can enter."

"I guess you can have my freedom sum in payment," Esakka said.

The following day Jonathan took the ferry to Annapolis to commission the Scottish cabinetmaker John Shaw to construct him a mahogany desk with satinwood inlay. He spent the afternoon at the tailors, adding new suits and furnishings to his wardrobe. He intended to set up his practice in Annapolis and had rented a townhouse on Cornhill Street with a parlor suitable for receiving clients.

When his business was finished, Jonathan took the coach to Philadelphia, where he planned to call on Benjamin Franklin. He had met the old rake in London and was eager to compare notes with him about the women of that fair city. Dr. Franklin could also be beneficial in seeing that he received some very important cases for his practice of law.

He planned to return in a fortnight.

XXV

A barren superfluity of words
Sir Samuel Garth
The Dispensary

𝔄 week after Makepeace and Jeremiah reached the Catholic outpost in western Maryland, Makepeace's sight was restored. It was during Mass and he was so astonished, he shouted, "Hallelujah! I can see again!"

The abbot and Jeremiah immediately set about swinging the incense canisters, lighting candles, and chanting Hosannas in Latin.

Later that day, Makepeace told Jeremiah he thought he would not continue west with him. Not only his masquerade but the theft of the mule and his escape from the gallows weighed heavily on his conscience. Having made many promises to God in exchange for the return of his sight, he considered returning to Queen Anne County without delay. But one blizzard followed the other. The winds howled without mercy and the snows grew deeper. The abbot advised that thawing would not occur for several months.

Jeremiah also postponed his journey. He was caught up in Makepeace's conversion and had no desire to leave. They both decided to spend the winter at the mission.

Makepeace began to read the Bible, starting with Genesis. When he got to the story of Samson and Delilah, he took a vow to cut neither his hair nor his beard. He would let his locks grow as a reminder of sins for which he had yet to atone. Jeremiah said he looked like an Old Testament prophet and suggested that as God had done for Samson, He would endow Makepeace with righteousness and strength through his flowing black hair.

When Jeremiah left in the Spring, Makepeace stayed. He took his studies seriously. By the end of summer, he had memorized the Catechism, the Ten Commandments and the Sermon on the Mount. The abbot baptized him and then ordained him. Makepeace assisted in giving Mass and even took confessions, mostly from children whose chief transgression was feeling proud or using a bad word.

When Fall arrived, Makepeace declared his intention to depart, indicating he would head for Anneville. He wanted to stop in Baltimore Town and return the mule to the Clankenbell Livery. By that time, he had confessed all and the abbot said he had been through enough tribulation, he did not require penitence.

Makepeace gave no thought to giving up the black cassock. He had earned the right to wear it. He intended to enjoy its miraculous powers and made efforts to honor rather than disparage it.

At the end of October, Makepeace took the road back to Queen Anne county. He would have liked to offer a ride to a fellow clergyman in order to strengthen his party, but there was not a Man of the Cloth traveling the lonely path.

Of ordinary travelers, many there were, but he had no wish to invite their company. He knew how often he attracted renegades. He was lonely, but not uneasy. Armed with Redmond's pistol, well-oiled and filled with dry powder, he felt no harm could come to him. Besides, was he not under the protection of God?

The time passed quickly. Makepeace kept repeating the Catechism over and over to himself. As Makepeace put Mount Airy behind him, dusk settled over the mountains. With fast fading daylight, the nights were turning cool, the air heavy with the odor of wet leaves and the musty smell of rot.

The abbot had insisted Makepeace carry a good supply of oats for Old Nelly, since few fields worthy of grazing existed in the climbs. The mule wore a light blanket to cut off the brisk evening air and plodded across the carpet of pine needles with nary a concern.

Outfitted in a fur tunic supplied by one of Elliot's parishioners, Makepeace was quite comfortable. He had even been given a set of fur leggings. Nelly seemed to enjoy their feel against her withers.

No other travelers were in sight when Makepeace spotted three men huddled by a roadside fire. There was no way to avoid them. Except for a small clearing where the men had built their fire, a thick stand of massive sycamores guarded each flank of the path.

The fact that they were not hiding in ambush allayed Makepeace's suspicions. Still, they did not look reputable. Their clothing was ragged and scarves were wrapped about their faces against the cold wind.

As his mule drew near, the tallest of the three men rose and stood in the middle of the trail, his flintlock across his chest. Makepeace looked down at the man with disgust.

"Stand and deliver!" shouted the bescarfed leader.

A furious mood came over Makepeace. The blood rushed to his skull; his heart thumped against his ribs. Who did they think they were? Commanding a priest to step down and give them everything he owned, meager as it was! Did they intend to rob him and steal his worthless mule? How dare they issue such a challenge to a man of God?

Like the prophet of old whom he resembled, Makepeace hopped off the mule, his untrimmed beard and flowing black locks thrashed by the breezes. Clutching his Bible to his chest with his left hand, he swept the air with his right, spewing the vernacular he had sought all summer to lose.

"God's fire and brimstone on yer venal souls! Holy Jesus' blood and wounds! Yer nothing but the damnèd sons of whores. Have ye no respect for the cloth?"

Two of the men looked at each another and started laughing. They punched each other's ribs and laughed some more, finally collapsing and rolling in the dirt, carrying on like two playful dogs.

"It's not!" one said.

"Yeah, it sure is!" said the other.

Dressed in deerskin, war paint on his face, the third man— what?—an Indian?—looked on, as bewildered as Makepeace.

Finally, the leader rose from the road. He pulled the scarf from his face and revealed his familiar countenance covered with ugly pockmarks.

"It's me, Sooty Sam! Me and Juan Pedro! Friggin' wrath of God on you, too, Makepeace!"

Sooty clapped his hands gleefully and roared with laughter. Still on the ground, Juan Pedro rolled in the dirt and howled like a wolf. "Awooorh-ooorh-ooorh!"

"Yeah, it's downright hilarity, ye friggin' idiots. My God!" Makepeace declared. "About to be robbed by the very two I taught the business! Ye didn't know it was me. Ain't ye feared of robbing a man of God? Ain't ye got no fear of God's wrath?"

Sooty Sam chortled. "It's God's wrath, all right. Handing it back to the guy who taught you how! That's what I call the bloody revenge of God."

"I have a mind to ram yer heads against each other so hard ye don't remember how to rob nobody."

"Aw, we ain't even got no ammunition," Sooty said.

Makepeace had not the least fear of those two. The third one, the Indian in the war paint, did not look any smarter. Juan Pedro became so excited, he sprang a leak and had to run to the bushes. When the Spaniard returned, Makepeace said to him, "Take my friggin' mule and tie it to a tree."

Juan Pedro readily did as he was told.

"Put some more wood on the fire, whoever ye be," Makepeace said to the Indian. "I've got some smoked rabbits in my bag and some ears of corn. Ye can roast them for supper."

The Indian mumbled something, but it sounded like a curse and Makepeace ignored it. As he took charge, all three fell under his command. It was the way he'd always done. It never failed.

"I've taken a vow of poverty and got no money on me," Makepeace went on. "If ye've a mind to rob me, ye can forget about it. The mule ain't mine. If ye want it, ye can have it, but God will deal with ye."

"Aw, Makepeace, we didn't mean nothing," Sooty Sam said. "We knowed it was you all the time. Well—Henry, there—he didn't."

"Henry?" asked Makepeace, realizing that the Indian's mumbling had been an attempt to divulge his name.

"We call him Henry," said Sooty. "It don't make no difference what you call him. He's just a Indian."

"*¡Caramba!*" snarled Juan Pedro. "His name's too damn long. We can't say it."

"He can't write it no-ways," said Sooty. "It was sort of a game on him, too."

"My mother called me Teantontalogo," the Indian said, standing erect. "But it's no matter. You can call me Henry. You got food, eh?

177

Juan Pedro killed a turkey last week with his sling, but we ain't seen a squirrel since then. We eat walnuts and wild onions for two days now."

"I've got plenty of food," Makepeace said.

Juan Pedro saluted. "I thought you was a real Senor El Padre, Makepeace. *¡Madre de Dios!* I really did. Afore Sooty said it was you."

Makepeace doubted that either one recognized him before he stepped down from the mule, but he was in charge again and he'd go along pretending to believe them. Juan Pedro was too dumb to lie with conviction.

"I'm warning ye, I take my religion seriously." Makepeace wanted them to get that straight right away. "I'm not wearing this robe for its magical powers. I've been ordained into the Catholic Church. If it strikes me pleasure, I have the power to consign yer friggin' souls to Hell."

Makepeace could see that Sooty Sam and Juan Pedro did not know how to take that. Maybe he was just pulling their leg again. He frowned at them to show how serious he was and neither of them said a word. To emphasize matters, he added, "I'm not playing the pickled dog. Those days are over."

It was several minutes before the Indian broke the silence. "Once I feared your God. When I was a boy, my father got a present of clothes from your Mother Queen Anne. He was grateful for the articles, but he hated the preachers she sent across the waters. The only thing her holy men taught my people was to drink and quarrel."

Juan Pedro gave the Indian a dirty look. "¡Sangre de Dios! You dumb Indian, don't talk like that to Padre Makepeace. I'm in need of confession real bad, *muy malo*. I hurt that girl back in 'nnapolis." Juan grabbed the sleeve of Makepeace's gown. "Can you get me out of trouble with El Papa?"

"I'll take yer confession after we eat, Pedro. But if ye're just wasting my time and ain't got no intention of performing the penance I give ye, I'll turn yer soul over to the Devil. Forever. Might save us both a lot of trouble, anyway." Makepeace gave Pedro a small smile. Or maybe the smile was for himself. He was delighted with the way things were going. He would invent a really difficult penance for the sneaky bastard.

"I know about the Trinity," Henry said. Makepeace looked at him askance, but Sooty and Pedro seemed to be interested in his explanation. "It's like a piece of pork. You got the lean meat, the fat and the bone, but it's still one piece. Ain't that right?"

It was a curious analogy, but one frequently used by missionaries. Makepeace did not reply and Henry went on. "I just ain't figured out which is God and which is Jesus."

"Or the Holy Ghost?" asked Makepeace.

"He's got to be what's left," Henry said smartly.

***

Fiddling nervously with his sling, Juan Pedro told Makepeace the story of what had happened to Josie, although he did not know her name.

"I didn't mean to kill her," Juan Pedro said. "She was such a flighty little thing. I just meant to tap her with my dirk, but she wiggled and squirmed, and first thing I knew, she fell on my blade and she was on the ground."

Even if that were true, Makepeace thought, doing business with Juan Pedro or Sooty Sam meant getting blood on your own hands, no matter how you tried to keep them clean.

"I only meant to scare the girl out of her coins, but the knife slipped between her skinny ribs. I hid in the bushes afterward and watched the priest and this big man-slave—"

"A priest?" Makepeace asked. "What did he look like?"

"He had a big red face. Sores all over it."

Redmond, Makepeace thought.

"The law come and the priest acted like he didn't know the slave. I was scared they would find me, but I stayed quiet and they didn't."

"And the girl?"

"She didn't do nothing. She was dead, I guess. The slave pulled out my knife and there was blood all over it. Then they took him off to jail."

"And what did you do?"

"I pulled this necklace off her." Juan Pedro jiggled the tarnished chain that hung around his neck. "Then I went looking for Sooty.

So what do I have to do to get in good with El Papa? Are you going to be give me a hard penance, Señor Makepeace?"

"Yeah, give him a hard penance, Makepeace," Sooty said. "Make him sweat real good."

Makepeace looked at the pathetic Juan Pedro. The Spaniard's big brown eyes gazed expectantly at him, waiting for a penance that would save him from hell's deadly fires. Makepeace had not a smidgen of an idea what that penance should be.

"Pedro, if it had been Sooty who killed that girl, what do you think his penance should be?"

"Sooty been there, I wouldn't have made that mistake," Juan Pedro said. "But she was a purdy girl. He do it, I say he should walk the rest of the way to Baltimore on his hands and knees."

"Ayaiyeee!" Sooty laughed. "That's three, four days on the old prayer bones!"

"Then that is what yer penance will be," Makepeace said. "What ye selected for Sooty is suitable. Ye can start on your way in the morning. Do you have a rosary?"

Makepeace slept with his right hand in his fur vest, clutching the butt of Redmond's pistol. The firearm was primed and ready to discharge at the movement of his finger. White Claws had insisted that he and Jeremiah take the pistol. Jeremiah wanted nothing to do with it, so it had fallen into Makepeace's care.

And he had given the weapon ardent care, cleaning and oiling it, keeping it in good order in case he needed it. Now, it provided additional confidence in his ability to handle Sooty and Pedro.

His confidence was ill placed. Shortly after midnight, he awakened with a pounding headache and cold feet.

Makepeace was alone. The campfire had dwindled to a few coals. The mule was nowhere to be seen. Sooty and Pedro were missing. Even the Indian had disappeared.

Makepeace sat up and felt his head. There was a good sized knot on his temple. Whacked by a rock from Pedro's sling while he slept, he guessed. He had a faint recollection of Pedro saying, "*¡Chengo!* You give me penance to walk on my knees to B-Town, now I ride your mule."

Makepeace looked heavenward. "Great God in His Heavens, preserve me!" The stars burned brightly and the moon floated among wispy clouds. A serene vista. Not a sign that anyone up there heard his prayer or knew anything about his predicament.

Neither was there anyone in the vicinity to hear his petition. Not another traveler on the road. Not a flicker of a campfire in either direction. Makepeace sat on the ground, shivering and cursing those three renegades and himself for trusting them. Then he realized for the first time that he was naked.

His black gown was gone. So was the sombrero. Once too often, he'd bragged about that gown's magic. Now one of those ruffians wore it, hoping to benefit from its wondrous powers. His fur vest, the scarf—the wood cross were also gone. His pistol was gone. God's justice again! Not that he didn't deserve it, but somehow, he had hoped that returning the mule to the livery and going back for his hanging would guarantee him a little bit of time in God's sunshine.

In the process of collecting more logs and sticks for the fire, Makepeace spied the mule's blanket lying against a tree. It must have fallen off Old Nelly. The scabby rascals had overlooked it. There was not enough kindness in their evil hearts to leave a token for his well being. That was God's own truth.

The blanket wasn't the cleanest piece of fabric in the commonwealth. It smelled like mule sweat. Well, what did he expect? At least there were no lice lurking among it threads. Unless Pedro had slept on it. He stooped to pick it up and saw lying a few feet from it, his cross and his Bible. Of course, the ruffians had no need for those. Makepeace laughed sadly and shook his head as he unfurled the blanket. There was a worn place in the middle. By pulling it apart with his hands, he made a hole just big enough for his head. He slipped it on like a poncho and hung the cross around his neck.

The blanket was a little short. If he pulled it low enough to cover his thighs, it left his backside hanging out. If he covered his backside, his pubes were exposed.

For the better part of an hour, Makepeace hunkered beside the fire, depressed as Job, sleep evading his tired body. As his head finally nodded forward, he heard the rumble of a coach coming from the west, galloping horses drumming the ground. It had to be at least a coach and six!

181

His heart beat as fast as the falling hooves. No point in getting excited, he told himself. No carriage would stop for him. Not unless he did something foolhardy. Quickly stirring the fire and tossing on leaves to brighten the scene, he lay across the middle of the road.

There was no way the coach could go around him unless it rolled through the fire. The driver wouldn't likely take that course. It would scarify the horses and send them tumbling down the hill, out of control.

For a moment, they came so fast, Makepeace was sure they would rush over him, crushing his brains in the dirt. End for him— pray quickly! Holy Mother of God, watch over me in my hour of death! Blessed Jesus, take me into your arms and carry me into heaven.

Then, just as he hoped, the driver pulled the reins tight. "Halt, halt, you friggin' galloppaloos! Halloo! Stop you demons from hell!"

The horses' hooves came to a rest just inches short of Makepeace's skull.

"Hello!" the driver bellowed, tilting his head to the side of the coach to address the passengers inside. "Halloo, in there, me merry passengers! There's a man lying in the road. Appears to be dead. I'm putting the postilion down to see about him."

In the full moonlight, Makepeace watched a fat woman wearing a highly decorated headdress lean out the window. Little bells tinkled when she bobbed her head. "Go on with it, driver! We're late to Baltimore now."

The driver did not bother to lean over the side of the carriage this time. "Just have a little patience, madam. As soon as we move the body out of the road, we'll be on our way."

Already down, the footman cautiously approached Makepeace. As he drew closer, he called back, "I ain't got no candle, but he looks dead to me."

Makepeace groaned and sat upright. The footman jumped back and hollered as if he'd been struck by the driver's whip. "God have mercy!"

"God have mercy!" Makepeace echoed.

"What goes there?" the coachman cried. "Are you all right, footie?"

"Sweet Jesus, the man's alive!"

The little bells tinkled again as the high headdress leaned out the window. "Coachman, we'll have to give the poor soul a ride."

The footman gave back a good holler. "The poor soul is sitting in the road nekkid as the day he was born."

Makepeace stood up, the mule blanket swinging about this pubes. Feeling giddy in the head, he put his hand to the footie's shoulder to steady himself.

The high headdress leaned further out the coach window. If there were other passengers in the coach, she evidently had taken it on herself to speak for all. "Did that fart-catcher say naked? Pass on by! It's a trick to get a free ride."

"He's sick!" the footman shouted. "Mebbe about dead."

Makepeace wobbled and clutched at the footman, letting the poncho seek its own milieu. Maybe he was worse-off than he thought.

The high headdress's voice went up an octave, verging on hysteria. "Driver, do you not hear me?" The little bells tinkled merrily. "My uncle is the Lord Mayor of Baltimore Town and he's waiting to meet this coach. He may very well arrest you for being late."

"Damn it, Madam, I can't get this contrivance by. They has trees on one side of this damned road and a friggin' fire on the other! You want to shy the horses?"

"You can't ask persons of my station to ride with a naked nobody!"

From the opposite side of the coach, the door opened. Makepeace observed a man of unusual dignity step from the interior. Although his hair was not embellished with powder, he was dressed like a person of quality. He wore a frockcoat and black or navy breeches—in the moonlight, Makepeace couldn't tell the exact color—with large silver buckles at the knees. Draped across the man's cream colored waistcoat, a gold watch chain glistened. The man's black boots also glistened, stylish, new and unmistakably fine Spanish leather.

The courtly man walked over to Makepeace, stopped, and looked calmly at him. After a moment, he spoke. "Sirrah, I see you wear a cross and carry a Bible. I fancied you were a prophet, looking as you do, as if you have just stepped out of the Old Testament. I see now that you are much younger."

Makepeace pulled the poncho down to cover his privates.

"Mercy, please, I beg ye. I've been robbed of me mule and me cassock. The scabby scoundrels even took me rosary."

The high headdress's voice reached a new crescendo. "Robbed! You hear that, driver? There are robbers on this road!"

"Patience, good woman," the courtly man said. He turned again to Makepeace. "Can you walk of your own accord?"

The high headdress butted in again, not about to give up. "If that man is put in this coach, I shall get out. I shall walk to Baltimore before I ride with a naked man."

"He ain't getting in the coach unless he pays his pound." The driver's tone indicated he was certain that would solve the matter. "Nobody ain't riding for free."

The gentleman spoke. "My friends, I am Jonathan Seney, a lawyer and an officer of the Court. You may well be aware, it is against the law to leave this poor injured man in the road to fend for himself."

"We can't let the lawyers determine our future." The high headdress shook her tiny bells in emphasis. "Ignore the damned lawyer."

"Madam, the law is the law. It matters not who the lawyer is," Jonathan said.

"The law is the law," the woman mimicked. "Driver, strike those horses!"

"I beg your pardon, Madam. And driver, I suggest that you hold the horses. This man is in need. If we ignore him and he dies, we might well be held to account for his death. The law considers that the same as murder."

"We're going to get robbed and killed ourselves," the woman cried. "Let me tell you, my husband is good friends with Lord Baltimore. If we're killed, he'll hold you accountable for our murder!"

"Madam, yer not going to be killed. Yer under the protection of God," Makepeace declared. He clutched his Bible in his left hand and pulled down the front of the poncho with the other. He took a few steps forward, surprised at the renewal of his strength. "Have ye no faith in God?"

Jonathan Seney removed his frockcoat and held it open for Makepeace to put his arms through. Makepeace looked at the fancy silk lining and demurred.

"I can't be wearing yer articles."

"Nonsense," Jonathan said. "You have to cover yourself if you are going to ride in polite company. My waistcoat will keep me suitably warm."

Makepeace slipped his arms through the hole in Nelly's blanket, widened it, and let it slip to his waist so that it hung like a petticoat. Then he put an arm into a sleeve of the frock-coat while Jonathan held it, transferring his Bible to the opposite hand as he slipped into the other sleeve. The frockcoat covered his knees, front and back. When he buttoned it up, he was quite modestly attired, and warm.

The high headdress tried one more time. "Driver, leave both those men here to forage for themselves. That will leave us in the clear."

"Madam, if any harm befalls us, you may presume we will have cause to sue not only the Pennsylvania Coach Company, but the driver and the passenger who inveigled him into abandoning us."

"You can't sue me. You don't even know my name! How do we know you're a real lawyer?"

"You may come to my office on Cornhill street tomorrow and see my certificate from the Inns of Court in London. Thereby, you will know I can sue anyone I've a mind to. Furthermore, when served with a writ, the Pennsylvania Coach company will supply your name as well as that of the driver. You may be absolutely sure that we will see you in court."

Suddenly, the woman reversed her attitude, wailing in a much softer voice. "Oh, la, la, I don't want to be hauled into court! Oh la la, Mr. *Just-ass* will take everything I own and divide it up amongst the lot of you."

"Let them get in, driver," said another voice from within the coach. "We ought to be on our way."

"I've got to have me pound," the coachman said.

Makepeace became aggravated with the driver. "Would ye charge a Man of the Cloth for a ride?"

"Ain't giving nobody no favors, not Jesus Christ his-self. What faith might you be?"

"The religion of St. Peter. Catholic."

"I knew it. A friggin' papist! It'll be a pound and a shilling for you."

"Hear, hear," said Jonathan. "Have a care and mind your manners, coachman. I will pay his fare: a pound and two shillings, if you please. Give the padre rest . . . unless your doctoring skills are better than your manners."

XXVI

He that lives upon hope will die fasting.
Benjamin Franklin
Poor Richard's Almanac

The sheriff guffawed at Makepeace and refused to hang him.

"The county ain't got no executioner and I ain't about to do the dirty deed myself. Nobody would ever vote for me again. There ain't no Christian on the Eastern seaboard who would vote for me if I hanged a priest."

"God has laid a heavy burden on me," Makepeace said. "He wants me to pay me debt. It would be a sin on yer part to deny me destiny."

"If I put you in jail, I have to feed you. Our budget is just about spent up. Don't expect any giblet pie. Why can't you let well enough alone? Everybody is already forgot about you, not to mention the embarrassment you brought me. I wish you'd just go away."

"I apologize for the problems I've caused ye," Makepeace said, "But ye can't deny God's will, yer honor. He wants me to do me duty according to the law."

"You'll have to wait for us to hire an executioner. No one around here wants the job. I wrote a letter to a man in Saulsbury, but it'll take him a week to get here."

Makepeace discovered the atmosphere of the basement jail showed no improvement. The population of crawling things had greatly increased and although they marched like armies across the dirt floor, no dead bodies were left in their wake.

Makepeace was placed in the same cell in which he had left Friar Redmond soused with White Coin liquor. The other cell was occupied by a slave named Esakka.

187

As soon as the slave learned Makepeace was a priest, he spit on the earthen floor and cursed. "God has no use for me. Don't give me any of your white man's religion. God is white. He has no use for any black person."

"Yer bitterness is not to be discounted if ye have been mistreated because yer an African and a slave," said Makepeace. "I well understand how troublesome it must be for a person of yer skin color. What might ye be in jail for?"

Makepeace was startled to learn that Esakka was the slave who had been arrested for killing the girl Pedro had told him about. Esakka then related his year with the Gypsies and how Queen Esther's son had betrayed him to the bounty hunters.

It crossed Makepeace's mind that he had the power to help Esakka. He debated whether he would be believed if he offered to be a witness for the defense. It would certainly postpone the date of his own hanging. Now that it was before him, no matter how he felt about straightening out his life, he was none too eager to start his journey to the Promised Land, not when the first steps meant a climb up the wood stairs to the oak filly.

Jonathan was surprised to find Makepeace incarcerated with Esakka. There had been little conversation with the lawyer after he entered the coach the night they met on the road outside Mt. Airy. Makepeace had said that he was headed to see the High Sheriff of Queen Anne County.

Supposing Makepeace intended to do business of some sort with the lawman, Jonathan had refrained from inquiring further.

Most of the trip, Jonathan had silently reminisced over the pleasures of his trip to Philadelphia. Most graciously, Ben Franklin had put him up for two days and promised to write an article about him for his newspaper. Jonathan had then gone to Mount Vernon to see George Washington. Not having written ahead, he obtained only a polite audience with George's mother. She little heard what he had to say and mostly complained about George's stinginess and the manner in which he treated her.

After picking up Makepeace, for the remainder of the ride they continued in silence, except for the snoring fat woman who wore the high headdress.

Makepeace had shaved that morning. Jonathan was impressed by his clean-cut profile in contrast to the bearded apparition he had found on the highway. If Makepeace had not been wearing his own fancy frock-coat, he might not have recognized him.

"I trust you will not think it impertinent of me to inquire, do you have a lawyer?"

"Thank ye for asking, I've already been sentenced," said Makepeace. "I'm just waiting for me sentence to be carried out."

"How does it happen that a Man of the Cloth sits in jail already condemned?"

"A long story, yer Honor. I doubt ye want to hear it."

"Allow me, sir, hearing stories is my business. You will recall that I'm a lawyer and a member of the Court. If an injustice has been done, I want to hear about it. Esakka will be my first defendant in a case to be tried in the Colonies, but I did internship in the Inns of Court in London and have some confidence in my ability to see that those who are accused are treated justly and fairly."

"I don't think ye can do anything for me," Makepeace said. "God wants me to hang. It's part of me redemption."

"Perhaps God is only trying your faith," Jonathan said. "I have no wish to subject you or myself to unnecessary legal frivolity, but I will study the records of the Court and see if there is any way we can appeal your sentence."

"Yer kindness is appreciated," Makepeace said. "But I hold forth no hope that ye will work any miracles on me behalf."

XXVII

...it is not death,
but dying which is terrible.
Henry Fielding
Amelia

Jonathan spent several hours poring over the records of Makepeace's trial. No evidence existed that the trial was not conducted to the letter of the Law. The single error that existed on the judge's part did not bear the basis of an appeal. There was no point in embarrassing Judge Payne. It would not benefit Makepeace that he could see. And with Esakka's trial coming up, Jonathan did not want to make an enemy of the judge.

Makepeace had told Jonathan the story of Josie's death as Juan Pedro had related it to him. His testimony was important to Esakka's defense and Jonathan planned to use it. They had to be impressed by Makepeace returning to put his head in the noose. He would imply that it was done for no other reason than to prove Esakka innocent. He was certain the jury would find Esakka blameless.

In spite of Hortense Adams rendering a hysterical denunciation of Esakka as the guilty party, while her husband applauded from the spectator's rows, the jury did just as Jonathan predicted.

Makepeace wondered if God had not taken Friar Redmond from the scene in order to save Esakka. If Mrs. Adams had had the fake priest present to back her up, the outcome for Esakka might have been altogether different.

***

It was a lovely day for a hanging.

190

Unable to sate its appetite on the dawn mists, the sun busily devoured the tall white clouds that frosted the sky.

Glancing at the bountiful heavens, his arms bound to his chest by chains, Makepeace was disappointed that the Almighty had not seen fit to show His disapproval with a calculated amount of lightning and thunder, not to mention a goodly quantity of hail and pounding rain.

Gallows Field looked like a county fair with booths erected everywhere. The celebratory air was appalling. Hawkers offered food and beverages as well as souvenirs of the event. Clowns and jugglers proposed to carry out a bit of slapstick or buffoonery for a few pence. A roving artist solicited customers for silhouetted cutouts. Cockfights were scheduled at midday, but by then, Makepeace figured he would be shaking hands with God.

The hanging had been written up in The Gazette. Jonathan had shown the newspaper to Makepeace, telling him his story had a great deal of human interest. Hadn't he come back for his own hanging in order to save another—and a slave at that? Jonathan further predicted that there would be a large crowd at the hanging.

And while Makepeace felt a modicum of good will about going out in high feather, he dwelt on ways he could escape the gallows. None seemed plausible. He was in the pickle and deserved to be so, but hadn't he turned over a new leaf? Wasn't he in line for a little mercy? And not just mercy, a miracle.

Makepeace insisted that he was entitled to depart his mortal coil wearing a black cassock. When he demonstrated for the pastor of Saint Joseph the vast knowledge of Catholicism he had accumulated at the mission, the rector loaned him a gown to replace the one stolen by Sooty Sam and Juan Pedro. The rector did insist that Makepeace be put into a shroud before his interment and the cassock washed and returned to the church.

Makepeace still had faith in the cassock's magic. At least he had faith in the one that he had taken from Redmond. He wasn't too sure about this new one.

The sheriff had added an accessory to Makepeace's gown, a heavy set of chains that bound his wrists.

Several priests had shown up for the festivities. One introduced himself to Makepeace as Reverend Bennett Allen. He was a strange character with a roving eye for young women. Makepeace wondered if Allen were there to bless him or just for the frivolity.

A woman carried a nosegay of asters and goldenrod to the platform and handed them to Reverend Allen with the request that he give them to the condemned priest.

"He'll be dead before they are," Allen said in a plainspoken manner. He handed the bouquet to Makepeace with the sobriquet, "Life can be truly short. Shorter for some than for others, but God has his reasons. Bless His Holy Name!"

"Ye remind me of another priest I once knew," Makepeace said. "He was always telling people God had his reasons but then a strange thing happened. God evidently thought it was reasonable for a bear to eat him."

Allen looked visibly shaken by Makepeace's admonition. He reached into his cassock and brought out a small flask.

Makepeace's attitude toward the priest immediately warmed.

"This morning is a little balmy for October. Have ye got any brandy on ye?"

"None to spare." Allen returned the flask to its hiding place without sampling it. "Lord Baltimore has given me two churches to pastor, but neither one has a wine cellar."

"Well, bless his lordship," Makepeace said.

"Truth is, I forgot to fill my flask," Allen volunteered. "Or maybe I drank it. I can't remember. Do you know who that lovely little Mulatto woman is?"

Makepeace's eye lighted on Esakka's wife, certain she was the one the Reverend made reference to. "Don't know as I've ever seen her before," he lied. She had come once to the jail in the company of Jonathan. Esakka had seemed rather cold toward her and she had spent most of the afternoon visiting with him.

"Never mind," Allen said. "I do believe though, I should see if her soul is prepared to join the heavenly minions."

Allen left the platform and moved toward Ktura.

Makepeace noticed that Esakka was trailing his pregnant wife. Of course there was no way he could step off the platform and warn him about the lecherous priest. He finally caught Esakka's eye, and mouthed Ktura's name.

Comprehending Makepeace's message, Esakka moved closer

to Ktura to see what Allen's interest could be in his wife. Allen was starting off with the religious stuff, but Esakka was fairly certain his interest in Ktura was not in her soul.

"Has Jesus saved you, my dear? Do you have a husband? Or might you be in need of some assistance for little Hans in the kelder?"

Ktura attempted to rise to her feet. Big with child, she huffed and puffed, but gathered in each man's eye as she moved sensuously along.

A strolling huckster pushed himself between Esakka and the Reverend, providing a obstacle so that Ktura could not see her husband. The huckster carried a large yellow hat turned upside-down, with a sparrow in it. The bird's wings were clipped and it chirped in dismay, fluttering its shoddy stubs, longing to soar into the open sky.

At the Reverend's expression of interest, a grin broke across the huckster's scrawny face, revealing an ugly mouth of bad teeth. "Play mumble the sparrow—two farthings. Bite the bird's head off and win ten farthings."

"Before he pecks my lips off?" Reverend Allen shook his finger at the huckster. "We're not a bunch of country bumpkins, you chuckle-headed chuff. There are prettier lips I would rather have bite at me."

Allen extended a hand to help Ktura up, patting her behind as he did so. Ktura looked at the priest with a puzzled expression.

Esakka was piqued by jealousy as he watched Allen rub Ktura's belly, but he was determined not to interfere and only watched.

Allen grinned slyly at Ktura. "Will you be needing some financial help for—uh—little Jack-in-the-cellar?"

Ktura's eyes widened and she looked thunderstruck. "Jacob? Did you say little Jacob-in-the-cellar?"

"What might be this Jacob's other name?" Allen asked.

This priest was amazingly perceptive, Esakka thought.

Ktura's lip dipped into a pout. "Mouse."

Allen rubbed Ktura's belly. "And is Jacob Mouse the father of this child?"

"How did you know about Mouse?" Ktura asked.

Allen grinned. "God has given me insight into many things. Are you married to Mouse?"

193

"Of course I ain't married to Mouse." Ktura's face twisted into a petulance. "Don't nobody know where Mouse is."

"So you are in need of assistance," the Reverend purred. "A little money perhaps to buy the infant some swaddling?"

"I have a husband," Ktura declared.

Esakka was too stunned by these revelations to approve of Ktura's spate of honesty. Mouse was the father of her baby? And all the time, he thought it was Carlo. He wasn't surprised though, as he remembered Ktura's penchant for young boys. But one thing was certain, he had no more use for the woman. Mr. Seney could put her up for sale as far as he was concerned. In fact, he might suggest it.

"Well, be that as it may—"

"I've had a number of husbands," Ktura said.

A skeptical look rippled Allen's face. He evidently did not think Ktura referred to legal husbands.

"I'm sure we can come to a satisfactory arrangement, mademoiselle," Allen said. "An afternoon of fun and—"

"If it's any of your business," Ktura went on, "my husbands were young and handsome. The first was a Arabian prince with four wives and a hundred horses."

"My, my, hasn't God given you a merry tongue! I'll bet you could entertain me with stories all night long, after we—uh—get through—uh—doing the wicked deed."

"Wicked deed?" Ktura muttered. "Indeed, a wicked deed with an old man like you! Who wants to do the wicked deed with an old man?"

Allen moved his hand toward Ktura's waist, then shifted it upward, letting his fingers rest under her bosom. "Perhaps a few shillings would change your mind, lovely girl?"

Ktura stepped forward as if she didn't mind the touching. The Reverend's hand moved to cup her breast. Ktura lifted her foot and brought her wooden clog down on his toes with energy.

The Reverend grabbed his foot and hopped about, whimpering with pain. "You are a tease. I do love a woman with spirit."

He turned to smile at Ktura, but confronted Esakka.

"I'm her husband," Esakka said with a pride that was completely false. "What do you want with my woman?"

Before Allen could answer, a roar came from the spectators

nearest the platform. Esakka turned to look. Makepeace stood on the scaffold, evidently ready to say his final words.

Allen leveled a scornful glimpse at Esakka. "You ought to keep your wife in line." He turned and limped toward the wood scragging post.

Esakka followed the priest, intrigued with the strange sight of one priest giving absolution to another, both dressed in their black cassocks. He moved closer to the platform to hear what was being said.

"How did you get in this mess?" Reverend Allen asked Makepeace. He didn't wait for an answer, turning to the sheriff to ask, "If you're of a generous mind, I have a few words to say."

"If you got any homilies, we'll listen to 'em." The sheriff busily chewed his snuff and let a wad fly loose into the crowd below. "But there'll be no basket passing."

Makepeace gave the priest the benefit of an evil eye. "I don't suppose ye want to trade places?"

A hangman rode into the crowd, the black hood over his face, fully aware that his profession did not elicit admiration from his fellow citizens. He was a frightening spectacle.

The sheriff had let everyone know that he had borrowed the hangman from Tuckahoe County at double the usual fee.

Though anonymous, the hangman was an honored guest. The crowd settled down at his arrival. The main event of the day was near at hand. Esakka moved closer to the platform.

"Let's get on with it," the sheriff said.

Esakka realized he, too, could be waiting up there to be hanged, had he not been rescued by Makepeace's testimony.

Makepeace raised his face toward heaven and wished a chariot of fire would come down to whisk him into the clouds as the Lord had done for Ezekiel. But he turned his mind to more mundane things and spoke to the crowd.

"I know most of ye are here for the enjoyment of seeing a sinner pay for his sins. I trust ye can learn from my example. I ask the Gracious God, in me hour of tribulation, to keep me mind and body in harmony with His own. Grant me the strength to hold up me fainting spirit."

There came a loud "Amen!" from the spectators immediately in front of the gallows.

One man yelled, "Get on with the hanging. Send the wicked papist on his way to Hell!"

Makepeace raised his arms high in the air, his chains clanking across his chest. "Let His Grace overlook the cries of me heart and forgive me of them sins that haunt me soul."

A number of loud amens came from the crowd.

"With as much forgiveness as I can muster, I ask Ye to pardon me persecutors and those who deprive me of life, albeit in justice for me wicked ways. Amen."

On Makepeace's left stood Jonathan Seney. On his right was the Reverend Allen. The Reverend was still complaining about the heat. He leaned toward the audience. "Can someone bring me a drink of cool sweet wine? I am a-dry and can not speak with eloquence when my throat is parched."

As far as Makepeace was concerned, the Reverend Allen could die of drought, but then the priest drew a second flask from his person. Opening it, he wet his fingers and flicked a piddling amount of holy water in Makepeace's direction. Then Allen licked his fingers.

Makepeace stepped onto the three-legged stool and the executioner fastened the noose around his neck.

"Wait there, Mr. Hangman," the sheriff ordered. "You forgot to put the hood over the man's head."

The hangman muttered something through his visor.

"What did you say?" the sheriff boomed.

The hangman lifted his head and raised his voice. "I didn't bring no damned hood for the condemned. You're supposed to furnish that."

"I don't need the hood," Makepeace said calmly. "I'd rather not have it. I want to go out of here seeing my way clear."

Much whispering took place between the sheriff and the mayor, who had joined the hangman on the platform, along with Jonathan Seney. Makepeace would not even let himself entertain a hope.

"We can't hang a man without a hood," the sheriff declared. "It ain't civilized."

"I didn't bring no hood for him and that's all there is to it," the hangman said. "If you want to wait until I go back home and get my spare, I can do that. You'll have to pay me extra, though."

Makepeace wondered if this were the miracle he expected. It was a little bizarre, and he didn't think it would halt the hanging, but it was the only hope he had and he decided to cling to it.

"Well, I never heard I was supposed to furnish the man's hood," the sheriff said. "Maybe we can just hang you instead. Or better yet, you can put your hood over the crook's head. Let everyone see what your ugly face looks like."

A snort came from inside the executioner's hood. "You can do the hanging yourself, Mister Sheriff. I ain't taking off me hood and you ain't got no right to remove it. You do that and you never will get another executioner to do your dirty work."

The sheriff's face turned white. He looked to the mayor, then to Jonathan, then decreed, "Hang him without a hood. Get on with it."

Reverend Allen turned to Makepeace. "I'm an Anglican. Will it disturb your Catholic soul to hear the rites from my church?"

"Do yer best," Makepeace said.

Flinging another smidgen of holy water at Makepeace, Allen emptied the flask into his mouth and muttered, "*Anno anno Domini, ampersand et cetera.*"

"Is that all?" Makepeace asked, clearly disappointed that he was being ushered into the afterworld on such short shrift. "I might as well do me own."

"*Domino, domino, et cetera ampersand, et cetera, et cetera, hocus pocus!*" Allen proclaimed. He then sat down on the edge of the scaffold and looked over the swarm of people before him.

Giving Allen a frown, an elderly priest from Saint Joseph's stepped forward. When he had the attention of the crowd, he concluded Makepeace's rites of passage into the Kingdom in the customary manner.

The executioner kicked the stool from under Makepeace's feet and stood back as if to make a bow. Evidently, he thought better of it. Several people in the audience clapped and then cheered as Makepeace's body dropped with a thuh-gunk.

The executioner turned and started down the steps. The crowd parted as if he were a leper while he made his way through, heading for his blackened horse. Jumping on the animal, the hangman gave it the spurs and disappeared like a ghost in the glare of daylight.

Makepeace hung there, spinning slowly in the keen morning air, his arms and legs grappling unseen foes. His countenance was a pitiful sight. There was nothing handsome about his sculptured visage. The blood congealed behind its former prettiness. His face turned dark, purpling and swelling in God's fair sunshine. His eyes bulged. His tongue flopped. Saliva foamed on his rakish lips and drooled down his chin.

Suddenly, the rope broke. Makepeace collapsed on the platform. The rope dangled by a single thread. Immediately, the children's wailing ceased. The crowd fell silent.

"If it does not displease your authority, finish cutting him down," Jonathan said to the sheriff. "He was an honorable man and does not deserve to be carrion for birds of prey."

"Pour some honey on him and let the bees and vultures have him," an old man hollered.

"Shut up, you old fart," the sheriff ordered. He turned to Jonathan with a strange look on his face. The lawman's lips moved, but whatever he was about to say, he evidently thought better of it. He reached forth and sliced the remaining strand of rope with a hunting knife he pulled from the scabbard at his belt.

Reverend Allen joined Jonathan and the sheriff. They took the body and lay it on the ground in front of the platform.

At that point, the muscles in Makepeace's arms and legs jerked.

"They all do that." The sheriff wiped snuff-stained saliva from his mouth. "It ain't nothing but the dead man's dance."

Makepeace's body twitched and shook again.

The sheriff chuckled. "Oh, he's a real dancer."

Makepeace's hand jerked, his chains rattled. From his wrists and his arms, the links fell back to the ground.

Esakka, still keeping an eye on Ktura, watched her move toward Makepeace's prone body, her carriage proud and beautiful. Esakka trudged several feet behind her.

"Who's the woman?" asked a spectator.

"What's she up to?" asked another.

Ktura carried a small bucket. As soon as the fickle crowd became aware of her, Esakka thought they seemed willing to give her their sympathy, urging her along with whatever mission she might have.

Ktura splashed the water in her bucket onto Makepeace's face. Makepeace coughed and spluttered. His tongue came out and slowly licked the water around his lips.

"My God, he ain't dead!" the sheriff cried.

"It's a miracle!" Reverend Allen intoned.

Esakka moved in closer, along with the curious crowd.

Makepeace blinked his eyes and coughed again.

The sheriff choked on his snuff, grimacing as the sour substance traveled down his throat. "Holy Jack Pudding has got to be hanged again, dammit. What can we do? Mr. Executioner has already gone home."

Makepeace sat up, albeit weakly. When he did so, the remainder of his chains fell from his body. The crowd applauded.

Faintly, Makepeace felt a smile creep across his lips. His mind was boggled. Had he passed to the great beyond? Was it all over and was he waiting to be ushered into the Holy Presence of God? No— too many familiar faces stood about. None of them looked like angels. He knew the magic cassock had dealt him another miracle.

He weakly waved his hand for more water. There was enough left in Ktura's bucket to satisfy him. After he drank it, someone came forward with a flask and he downed a good swallow of brandy. Its burning descent into his gut assured him he was alive.

"Bailiff, transport this man back to the platform," ordered the sheriff.

"You be defying God if you hang him again!" an old man cried.

"It is truly a miracle from the Hand of God," Reverend Allen declared.

The crowd took up the chant. "Miracle! Miracle!"

"If I must die, I must die." Makepeace shook his head groggily and struggled to his feet. "I came back here on me own. It's me lot to die."

Except for Jarvis Adams and his wife, Makepeace could feel the crowd's sympathy was now with him.

The Adamses pushed forward, Jarvis resolute, his fat face like an overripe tomato. "I came for a hanging and I want to see a hanging. This varlet broke into my house in the middle of the night and robbed me blind."

Mrs. Adams was hysterical. "I don't want to think about him walking our streets again. You let that Negrah off that killed my Josie. I want this scoundrel hanged."

"Madam, you have seen him hanged," Jonathan said.

"My wife wants to see him hanged until he's dead," Jarvis said. "If it takes three or four hangings, it's only befitting. Claiming to get religion is a lot of cock-a-whoop."

"Hurry up and kill the crook," Mrs. Adams shouted. "It's hot and I'm developing the vapors. I don't feel like waiting all day to see him dangling from the yard arm."

Makepeace held up his hands in resignation.

"The man has been hanged once," Jonathan said. "Must he be hanged again?"

The sheriff stepped forward. "The judge said he's got to be hanged until he's dead and that's what I'm going to do. Let's get him back up here and get it over with."

"Ain't you got no mercy?" Ktura asked.

Esakka stood behind Ktura, extremely embarrassed, but Makepeace noticed he did not try to silence her. After a moment, he watched Esakka walk over to one of the booths selling souvenirs, and look them over somewhat intently.

"It ain't my job to hand out mercy," the sheriff stated. "You can let God have mercy on the crook. What was you saying, Mister Seney?"

"Sheriff, perhaps we should have a conference," Jonathan said.

"Let the crook speak for himself," an old woman said. "If he can preach a sermon, he ought to go free. See if he's really got the religion. Let's hear him preach a sermon!"

The crowd took up the chant.

"Yeah, let the scoundrel preach a sermon!" Reverend Allen chimed in.

Ktura moved with her water bucket to a shady spot near a persimmon bush. Esakka followed her, watching as she placed her bucket on the ground and sat down. From inside her skirts, she pulled out a short dirk and began to clean her fingernails.

Esakka scrutinized the knife. "Holy Gog and Magog, woman, what is this?" He reached down and pulled a short thread of hemp rope from around the hilt of the blade. He realized Ktura must have worked on the hanging rope, probably earlier in the day before anyone had shown up for the festivities.

"Is this what I think it is?"

Ktura looked at him defiantly. "Mind your own business."

As the resurrected Makepeace raised his arms, quiet soaked Gallows Field like a spring rain.

"I seen the Lord," Makepeace cried. "I seen Him in all His Glory."

A murmur ran through the crowd. Esakka moved back toward the platform, deciding to leave Ktura to her own devices.

"Like Saint Paul, I was cast off me mule," Makepeace continued. "The blessed Word came to me. Spread the good news to those that be trapped in their wicked ways, Jesus said to me. I have only one sermon and this be it: Even as I seen Jesus, ye can see Him.

"Ye ask why I stand on this platform in front of the gallows. Friends, I am here because Jesus wanted me here. I went west to get a new life, but Jesus stopped me. He threw me down from me mule and appeared in a cloud of light. He said, Go back. Make yer atonement. I didn't know why Jesus told me to do that, but when I reached Queen Anne, I discovered a man ready to hang for a murder he didn't do. My testimony saved him from this very gallows.

"I walked in the paths of the wicked, but He forgave me. Now I done me duty. I will pay the price for me sins, knowing God's Grace will allow me to enter the heavenly gates. Put the rope back around me neck, sheriff. It's what Ma predicted would happen to me. Get on with it."

"That man's a prophet," Allen shouted. "You can't hang a man of God."

The crowd echoed Allen's sentiment. "No! No! No! Let the preacher live!"

The people moved closer to the gallows platform, their voices growing louder and louder. Strong hands shook the wood structure as if they intended to destroy it. Reverend Allen fell to the floor. Thinking he had been struck by God, he lay there writhing in his sins and crying for mercy.

"Let the drunk preacher hang in his place," Ktura yelled.

The sheriff held his hands outward, a queasy look on his face. "I ain't got the authority to release the prisoner. But I ain't the executioner, either. Now what did you want to say, Mister Seney?"

Jonathan stepped forward. "Sheriff, I have studied the transcript of Mr. Makepeace's trial. It appears that when the honorable Judge Payne sentenced Makepeace, he was sentenced only to be hanged. The phrase until dead was omitted from the sentencing. Mister Makepeace has been hanged and the law has been complied with. You will no doubt want to confer with the Judge, but in the meantime, I suggest you dispense with the hanging activities. Otherwise you may find yourself in a courtroom accused of having gone too far. Perhaps even of having committed murder!"

The sheriff gulped and blinked, snuff drooling out the corner of his mouth. After he worked up a good spit and let it fly, he announced that the day's hanging activities were over.

The crowd cheered.

Makepeace was escorted back to the county jail.

XXVIII

Fly, fly betimes, for fear you give
Occasion to your fate.
Sir George Etherege
The Man of Mode

𝔄 miracle from Heaven had been bestowed on Makepeace. He would have liked one more conversation with Esakka about his loss of faith, but Judge Payne ordered him to leave Queen Anne County without delay.

When Makepeace mentioned that he needed to return the cassock to the rector, Judge Payne laughed. "He won't expect a crook to bring back his booty. You'll be in more trouble for traveling naked than for not returning something that was loaned to you. And it would be wise if you departed the Commonwealth for some other place."

Makepeace decided he would head West again. He would return to the mission in western Maryland, perhaps travel on to St. Louis and assist Jeremiah with saving the Indians.

Heavy rain fell from the heavens, punctuated by thunder and lightning, as if God were cleansing Gallows Field of what had happened earlier that day.

A little late for that, Makepeace advised the Almighty.

As soon as the storm lessened, a full moon appeared. Makepeace glanced warily at it, certain that it importuned trouble. As he left Anneville, striding down the road in the direction of the Kent Ferry, he thought someone had picked up his trail and was following him, but his efforts to waylay the person came to naught.

Near Glen Bournie, on the south side of Baltimore Town, Makepeace decided to camp by the side of the road. He brushed aside several twigs from his chosen place and laid his head on a tree

203

root.

As he settled in, he heard the crunch of dry leaves and twigs snapping. Someone was in the forest with him.

The stench came first, followed by the coppery smell of blood combined with the musty smell of rotting feathers. A moment later the apparition appeared before him. Makepeace could not help blinking his eyes.

Disenchanted with traveling alone, but leery of the man who approached him, Makepeace nevertheless rose and greeted him politely. "How ye doing, stranger?"

"My name's MacDuff Lawson, but I already met you. I couldn't never forget a Man of the Cloth."

"I remember ye, too."

Even in the moonlight, Makepeace could see that the vacant look in MacDuff's eyes had deepened, the pupils like two black pebbles. Each time Makepeace tried to look in his eyes, MacDuff turned and looked off to the side.

As before, a raven's head was tied in the loosely braided hair that dangled over the back of MacDuff's neck. He seemed to have absorbed the fowl's characteristics. His movements were less akin to that of a man than to the fluttering of a wounded bird. And then Makepeace realized MacDuff wore his cloak of dark feathers.

"I remember ye well," Makepeace said. "Ye carried me up the river bank last year."

Makepeace reminded himself that he was one of God's chosen. Did he not trust his Lord to protect him? Perhaps he could influence the slovenly traveler toward a better path.

"Ye look like yer living in the sunshine," Makepeace continued.

"Found a 'bandoned camp in the forest near Logstown. Don't know what happened to the traders who set it up, Father. Waited for them two days but they never returned. Went off and left their canoe and all their furs."

Makepeace looked at the man's hands. MacDuff's long dark fingernails curled like talons. For some reason, Makepeace envisioned them dripping with blood.

"Ye ought to a took the furs into Logstown and sold them."

MacDuff sat down on an adjacent log and drew his feathers about him. "Got me fifty guineas." He bared his black, broken teeth in a grin. "Where might ye be going?"

"Saint Louis. My friend is serving in the missions there."

"I'm headed for Queen Anne County," said MacDuff. "On a mission of me own."

"Just came from there." Makepeace swallowed a sigh of relief. Their paths were only crossing. If he kept moving north, he would be rid of the renegade.

"We might as well camp together," MacDuff said. "Build us a fire, spend the night on our hunkers. Iffen you want."

"I intended to get to Baltimore by tonight. I've got a long way to go and no mule to ride this time."

MacDuff seemed prepared for Makepeace's diffidence. "I'm wanting to ask you some questions, padre. Things been bothering me of late. You have a mind to be helping me, I'd appreciate it."

"What can I say?" Makepeace sat on the ground beside MacDuff. He had nothing the rogue could steal. Perhaps the man was truly searching for guidance. "But I have to warn ye, I ain't much on theology. The Lord called me to be of service to mankind, not count angels on the head of a pin."

"So be it." MacDuff cocked his head and listened to the forest. After a moment, he let out a shrill whistle, as if communicating with another bird. When he received no answer, he turned to Makepeace. "I'll get some wood together."

Makepeace watched MacDuff flit about. With his feathery cloak, he looked precisely like a huge bird selecting material for its nest. Nor could he keep his eyes off the creature's hands, fascinated by their claw-like nature.

After splitting the wood with an ax he took from his gunny, MacDuff arranged the debris in a stack, then pulled out a flint and worked on it until the fire sparked. Soon he had a comfortable blaze at hand.

Returning to his gunny, MacDuff pulled out several moldy ears of corn. He laid them among the coals, shuffling them until the damp husks sizzled. Smoke mingled with MacDuff's body odor, creating a peculiar stench like the burning of pin feathers on an undressed bird.

"I'm paying you back for that meal you gave me last year," MacDuff said. "Sorry I ain't got no fish."

After they ate, MacDuff parked himself close to Makepeace. He kept his ax by his side, clutching it as he spoke in a seemingly forthright manner.

"I'm still wondering if I did the right thing, taking those furs. Maybe I should have left them there for someone else to find."

Makepeace wanted to shift away from MacDuff, to see if he could elude the dreadful smell emanating from the feathery cloak. But he had not the cheek to be so rude. He wondered what wicked deed MacDuff had done, little believing he had come into possession of the furs without some violence.

"What did you do with your guineas?"

MacDuff bowed his head, obviously embarrassed. "I went to Girty's town."

"Perhaps ye need to do a little penance." Makepeace hesitated, remembering what Juan Pedro had done when given his penance.

"Figured losing my gold was penance enough," MacDuff said.

Makepeace nodded. He knew the man would not carry out any penance. "Perhaps the Lord will be happy with that."

"I got me another problem," MacDuff went on. "You might say it's a worser one. You see, padre, there's this bird lives inside my chest."

Makepeace looked at MacDuff. Again the man refused to meet his eyes. "Ye must be part Indian. Are ye a bird-dreamer?"

"I feel it here." MacDuff put his left hand on the middle of his chest. "It knocks against my ribs when it spreads its wings. It even swells up and pounds inside my head. Makes me do things."

"Are they worthy things or are ye beholden to a devil?"

"I ain't done nothing God didn't tell me to do. He talks to me through this bird. I think it's what you call a cockatrice."

Makepeace knew of the fabled bird. Its eyes were said to have the power of death. Nothing he had learned from the mission abbot had prepared him to help one gripped by such a monster. Exorcism, perhaps, but he was untaught in the mysteries of that ritual.

"Look in me eyes," MacDuff said.

He grasped Makepeace's forearm and pulled him toward himself. The birdman trembled so much that shivers ran from his body into Makepeace's, his eyes holding captive those of Makepeace.

"You can see ever' evil thing I ever done." MacDuff's voice

went back into his throat and his words came out like the slow rumble of thunder. "You can see the trader I killed for them furs. Look close, you hear? Look close. Maybe you can see what God's telling me to do . . . "

MacDuff's ax quivered in his talon-fingered hand. As he started to raise it, a muscular arm shot from behind him, clamping its fingers like dog's teeth around his forearm. The ax dropped from his grasp.

MacDuff grunted and looked surprised. Makepeace took advantage of the moment to strike MacDuff across the chin, sending him lurching backward. He landed on his shoulders in a pile of dry leaves.

The owner of the hand stepped forward.

Surprised, Makepeace stared at the slave Esakka.

"You saved my life," Esakka said. "Now, I have repaid the favor."

"Ye sure are a welcome sight," said Makepeace.

MacDuff scrunched on his haunches, balancing himself with his hand on the ground, a runner eager to sprint. He pulled his braided hair around to his throat and clutched the dead raven like an amulet.

Dead leaves crunched beneath MacDuff's shuffling feet. "I'll kill you both. Don't think I won't find you again. And when I do, I'll kill you. I don't care if one of you's a Man of God." A bird in the forest canopy mocked his harsh, scratchy voice, but he continued his screechy trill. "The other of you's just a slave. Ain't no penalty for killing black men."

"We can take him." Esakka picked up the ax and hefted it, ready to sling it like a tomahawk at MacDuff's head. "Shall I do it? Let me kill the bloody blackguard."

MacDuff burbled and choked on a wail, the mockingbird echoing his pitiful attempts at speech.

Makepeace looked at the sorry rogue. In his bird feathers, MacDuff seemed more pitiful than dangerous. Now that the moment had passed, he couldn't believe the man had tried to kill him. But wasn't forgiveness what his Lord preached? He consulted Esakka, "Ye don't think we should leave him to God?"

"By the good Lord, padre, he tried to kill you! No reason at all except he hungers for blood. If there's one verse in the Bible I believe, it's an eye for an eye and a tooth for a tooth. Let's take care of him now. Save ourselves the trouble if he comes sneaking back."

Careful not to stumble over the snaking tree roots, MacDuff inched away from the two men. "I didn't mean no harm. It's that bird what lives inside me. Makes me do things I don't want to do. I wouldn't kill a Man of God."

"As if you didn't already try." Esakka spat at MacDuff's feet and exchanged looks with Makepeace. "But I can see, padre, you can't find it in your Catholic heart to order the man's execution."

"Blessed are the peacemakers," Makepeace said.

Like a stricken bird, MacDuff slipped further back into the trees. He glanced despairingly toward his gunny, but made no effort to retrieve it.

Makepeace was torn between granting MacDuff a reprieve or signaling his death. Hadn't he been near the same threshold just a few hours ago? What if he had not had his reprieve? Could he deny that to another?

"Let him go."

Esakka's impatience bespoke itself and he spat again at MacDuff. "So be gone with you, fool."

The renegade fluttered off like a bleeding chicken that has just been parted from its neck. Esakka eased himself onto a dead tree limb and shook his head.

"Thinks he's a raven, but he's just a loon."

"Ye never said a truer word."

"I don't want to sleep here. He knows where we are. We'll need to keep an eye on our backside."

"We'd better keep moving," Makepeace agreed. "What are ye doing out here tonight?"

"I've been with you ever since you left Kent," Esakka said. "Wherever you're going, padre, I'm going. Like in the Bible, you be my Naomi and I'll be your Ruth. Wherever thou goest, I will go with you."

"What about your child?"

"My child? I have no child," Esakka said. "I heard Ktura tell that drunken priest that Mouse was its father. I don't owe her anything."

"Ye can go with me, but as far as I'm concerned, yer a free man. If ye belong to anybody, ye belong to God."

"If I claim I'm a free man, someone will take me in for bounty. Someday, I'll save up enough money to pay Mister Seney for my freedom, but right now, I'm only a runaway. Just let me be your servant."

"So be it. There's an inn at Dorrs' corner where I performed a wedding last year. The innkeeper has a good heart. We can stay there tonight."

Acknowledgments

A novel is crafted with the assistance of many people and I wish to extend my thanks to my teachers, B. K. Reeves, and Chris Rogers, and to the members of my critique group who listened to the many writes and rewrites of this story: Bill Stevenson, Stacey Keith, Rebecca Nolen, Vanessa Leggett, John Hathorn, LaVerne Cobb, Michelle Devlin, Lynne Gregg, Karen Jennings, Joelie Key-Tissot, Evie Appel, Kay Finch, Mavis Rabourn, and Barbara Ray. My apologies to anyone I may have omitted.